FATAL
SECRETS

Also by William Noel:
Broken River, Shattered Sky

To order, **call 1-800-765-6955.**
Visit us at www.reviewandherald.com for information
on other Review and Herald® products.

WILLIAM NOEL

FATAL SECRETS

REVIEW AND HERALD® PUBLISHING ASSOCIATION
HAGERSTOWN, MD 21740

The author assumes full responsibility for the accuracy of all facts and
quotations as cited in this book.

Unless otherwise noted, Bible references in this book are from the *Holy Bible, New
International Version.* Copyright © 1973, 1978, 1984, International Bible Society. Used by
permission of Zondervan Bible Publishers.

This book was
Edited by Kalie Kelch
Designed by square1studio/Ron J. Pride
Photo/Illustration by Photos.com/Ron J. Pride
Electronic makeup by Shirley M. Bolivar
Typeset: 11/13 Bembo

PRINTED IN U.S.A.

09 08 07 06 05   5 4 3 2 1

R&H Cataloging Service
Noel, William Fred, 1955-   .
    Fatal secrets

    I. Title.

                813.54

ISBN 0-8280-1888-X

For my son, Nathan, and my daughter, Breanna.
So many times, as you have been growing up,
you have reflected God's love to me
in ways that have refreshed my faith during times of trial.
May you always live and grow in that love.

CHAPTER ONE

"Mommy! Could you hurry up? I'm really hungry," 8-year-old Jennifer complained through the closed door of her parents' bedroom in their hotel suite. She looked at her father, who was struggling with the bow tie of his tuxedo in front of a mirror in the living room. "What's taking her so long, anyway?" Jennifer asked.

Mark shrugged. "How should I know? Whatever it is, she doesn't want me in there . . . Want me to tie your bow?"

Jennifer turned around so her father could tie the wide satin strips on the back of her long royal-blue velvet dress. It took three tries to get a knot that looked neat. "Tight enough?" he asked.

She turned around and craned her neck to examine her back in the same mirror her father had been using. "That'll do," she answered. The bow wasn't exactly straight, but it was a lot better than if she had tied it.

A broad smile spread across Mark's face as he surveyed his daughter. This was the child who two years ago had been so ill with leukemia that they had feared she would die. The combination of good medical care—including a brand-new medication—and a lot of prayer had saved her. The weeks she'd spent in the hospital and the side effects of all her chemotherapy treatments seemed like a distant nightmare, vividly remembered but gladly forgotten.

Jennifer looked so pretty tonight! Her brown hair had almost been to her waist before the chemotherapy treatments caused her to lose it. She had temporarily replaced her brown locks with a striking blond wig. Now her hair was back, just passing her shoulders, layered and curled by her mother.

7

"You know, we need to get new family pictures done, and when we do, I'd like you to wear that dress," Mark said with a warm smile.

Jennifer giggled and twirled, watching her skirt spread to its full width. "Really? Daddy, do you think I'm pretty?"

"You bet I do! And when you're grown-up, I bet you'll be every bit as pretty as your mother," Mark declared. He turned and knocked on the bedroom door. "Hope! If you don't come out here soon, I'm going to order room service and cancel our dinner reservations!"

"I'll be out in a minute," her muffled reply came through the door.

"That's what she said 20 minutes ago," he muttered, plopping down on the couch. He found the TV remote control and began flipping through channels.

"Hey, I want to watch that!" Jennifer protested as he flipped past something on Animal Planet about dogs with jobs. He flipped it back.

Three minutes later Hope looked herself up and down in the bedroom mirror and resisted the temptation to give her hair another squirt of hair spray. She'd done all that she could, and her stomach was starting to rumble. The dress fit a bit more snugly than the last time she'd worn it a dozen years before, but the zipper had slid up with barely a moment's hesitation. After glancing at her hair still another time, she picked up the beaded purse that matched her floor-length dress and turned toward the door.

"I'm ready," she said seductively as she opened the door and stepped out on her stiletto sandals. Seeing Mark's jaw go slack as he took in the sight confirmed her success in achieving surprise for this special evening.

"Wow! Mommy, you look pretty!" Jennifer exclaimed with equal surprise.

"Thank you, sweetie," she answered, her eyes still fixed on her husband. "Remember the last time I wore this dress?" She twirled around on her toes so he could take in the full sight. The top of her dress sparkled in a thousand places, while above the floor-length satin skirt displayed little flowers printed on a georgette overlay. A scattering of body glitter reflected off her bare arms down to the watch mounted on an engraved bracelet on her left wrist. The only differences between tonight and the first time she'd worn this outfit were the additions of a wedding band on Hope's left ring finger and the purse in her hand.

"Oh, I remember," he answered warmly as the sweetness of the memory mixed with the moment. "I definitely remember."

Jennifer turned her palms upward and shrugged her shoulders. "OK, Mom. I give up. Where were you the last time you wore that dress?"

"Your daddy knows. Let's see if he remembers."

"The finals of the Miss Tennessee Pageant." Mark turned to Jennifer. "That was the night we met. I was one of the escorts in penguin suits—a tuxedo like I'm wearing now—for the formal-wear competition. I had the fortune of being your mother's escort when she was on stage . . . and then escorting her to the party after she won."

"You were Miss Tennessee?" Jennifer was amazed. "How come I never saw your crown?"

"You know that wooden box up on the top shelf of the bookcase in the living room? Just to the right of the TV?" Hope asked.

Jennifer thought for a moment before nodding.

"It's in that box. If you want, I'll show it to you when we get home." She looked back at Mark. "You ready to go celebrate our tenth wedding anniversary?"

"It would be nice if I knew where we were going. I mean, if you insist that I wear a penguin suit, then it must be someplace really nice," Mark said as they went out the door.

"Trust me, it is," Hope answered with a teasing smile. "Oh, by the way, Brandon Campbell and his wife are joining us."

A look of disappointment crossed Mark's face.

"There's some sort of company business we need to discuss that he said he would talk about only over dinner with all of us, and it's on the company expense account. You don't mind, do you?"

"Well, I guess. I mean, we're all dressed up, and I'm sure not paying some sky-high price to eat at some hoity-toity New York restaurant that you see featured on the Travel Channel. At least not if it's going on my credit card," Mark declared as he closed the suite door behind them.

"Actually, Brandon invited us about two weeks ago, and it just happened to coincide with our anniversary. Do you mind if we mix a little business with pleasure?"

"Brandon? You mean the guy who anchors the *MBS Evening News?* We're going to dinner with Brandon Campbell?" Jennifer squealed. "Can I get his autograph?"

Hope smiled at her daughter as the elevator door opened. "I don't think he'd mind that a bit. I hear they have a son about your age who's coming along. I expect you to be on your best behavior with him, OK?"

"Yes, Mom," Jennifer said with a mix of resignation and frustration.

Five minutes later their taxi deposited them in Rockefeller Center, where they saw an awning displaying the simple legend "Rainbow

Room." "I think I've heard of that name before," Mark said. "Is it nice?"

"Only the toughest reservation in town," Hope cooed, snuggling close on her husband's arm as they approached the uniformed door attendant. "Lancaster," she said melodiously. "We're meeting the Campbells. Party of six."

The attendant opened a leather-bound notebook and studied it for a moment. "Yes, ma'am," he replied. "Welcome to the Rainbow Room. We hope you enjoy your evening with us." He opened the door to admit them into a foyer of shining marble, polished brass, original artwork, and large floral displays. Two elevators framed by polished marble walls formed the far side of the room.

"I can hear somebody's credit card screaming already," Mark whispered to his wife as they crossed the room and entered one of the elevators.

The elevator stopped at the sixty-fifth floor and admitted the trio to a picture of opulence lit by crystal chandeliers and candles atop silver candle stands. Expensive draperies framed large windows that gave a dramatic view of the setting and darkening sky as it surrendered the day to the million lights of midtown Manhattan. A tuxedoed waiter greeted them. "Lancaster, I presume? Your guests are already seated. Follow me, please," he commanded as he turned to lead them toward their table.

The Campbells rose to greet them as they approached. Brandon introduced them to his gorgeous wife, Annette, and their son, Tyler. Hope introduced Mark and Jennifer, and they took their seats around the table.

"Would you care for a bottle of wine as you begin?" a tuxedoed waiter asked as he distributed their menus. "We have a large selection of the finest wines from around the world."

"Uh, do you have anything nonalcoholic? For her?" Mark asked, pointing toward Jennifer.

"And for him," Brandon echoed with an eye on his son.

"Ah! Sparkling cider for the youngsters. We have a number of selections for you to choose from. They're at the bottom of the wine list."

Jennifer was first to find the page. She scanned the list and whistled. "Mom! Dad! Do you see these prices? The cheapest sparkling cider is $22 a bottle! Why can't you just let me have a glass of whatever it is you're drinking?"

"Ah, but those are the finest sparkling ciders in the world, and you're dining in one of the finest restaurants in the world!" the waiter answered with a note of haughtiness. "You'll also note that we don't serve burgers or tacos here."

Jennifer blushed, and so did her parents. "You can probably tell this isn't our usual type of dining establishment," Mark offered in explanation.

"Ours either," Brandon answered. "Annette and I are just a couple of farm kids from Kansas here in the big city, so, like you, we're generally more comfortable at the local steak house. But tonight's a special night, so we're celebrating, right? Even better, we're doing it on the company's tab."

The wine steward returned with a bottle of sparkling cider and a bottle of wine that Brandon had selected. Once glasses were filled, Brandon raised his glass to offer a toast. "To friendships, both personal and professional, and to future success," he proclaimed. "Oh, and to many more years of happy marriage for both you and us."

Soon menu selections were decided, delivered, and being enjoyed. Conversation revolved mostly around how each couple had met and how Brandon and Hope had each gotten into television news reporting. Brandon shared stories of how Hope had performed during their network's coverage of the disaster on the Mississippi River. Hope told of how nervous she had been working with Brandon the first time.

Before dessert was served, Brandon took Annette to the dance floor for a few tunes from the 14-piece orchestra playing on the stage. Mark and Hope watched as Tyler, trying hard to be a young gentleman, invited Jennifer to follow. "No sense in us being the only people not getting our toes stepped on," Mark said as he stood and extended a hand to assist Hope from her chair. Twenty minutes later all were back at the table.

"The evening's getting late, and we need to head home before long," Brandon announced. "Feel free to stay as long as you like. But before we go, I wanted to tell you why I invited you here and why the company's paying for this evening. You see, I don't like the idea of crashing anniversary celebrations."

Mark and Hope glanced at each other. "Trust me, this is a lot higher-class celebration than we would have planned on our own," she smiled. "Plus, we've enjoyed having this time to get acquainted with Annette and Tyler." She smiled in their direction.

"Thank you. I've enjoyed it too," Annette answered. Tyler tried to stifle a yawn but couldn't; soon Jennifer was doing the same.

"Looks like I need to make this short," Brandon said as he reached inside his jacket and extracted two envelopes. One was a business-sized envelope of obviously expensive stationery. The other was an almost square envelope of engraved paper, apparently an invitation or announcement. He handed the second one to Hope first.

"What is it, Mommy?" Jennifer asked with sudden interest.

Hope slid a nail under the seal to open it, extracted the card inside, and began reading aloud. "The Radio-Television News Directors Association cordially invites you to attend their annual Edward R. Murrow Awards Dinner. Friday evening, October 14, at 7:00 p.m., International Banquet Room, Waldorf-Astoria Hotel, New York City."

"The Murrow Awards? Brandon, this is . . . unbelievable! I knew I'd been nominated. But . . . why?"

Brandon grinned widely. "Well, if you remember, we nominated you for a Murrow Award because of your reporting from Israel last year. Best international spot news reporting." He pushed the longer envelope across the table toward Hope.

She felt a tremble in her hand as she reached to take it. No delicacy now. She ripped it open. The letterhead announced that it was from the Radio-Television News Directors Association, Edward R. Murrow Awards Judging Committee. It was addressed to her. "Congratulations! The members of the judging committee are pleased to announce that you are the first-place winner in the Spot News Coverage category for the Television Large-Market Division." Hope squealed loudly, and Mark leaned over to give her a congratulatory hug and kiss. She resumed reading. "We are looking forward to having you attend our annual awards banquet on Friday, October 14, where you will be presented with your award." She choked on the words and had to stop reading.

"I trust you'll be able to attend? All of you?" Brandon inquired. "All expenses paid by MBS."

"You bet!" Mark and Hope nodded as they answered together.

"We're really proud of you and the work you've been doing. You've earned the honor," Brandon declared as he rose from his chair to depart. His family rose with him. "With your permission we will now bid you good night and leave you to celebrate as late as you like."

"A Murrow Award. Honey, that's terrific!" Mark exclaimed as the Campbells disappeared.

"I can't believe it. I just can't believe it," Hope repeated as her eyes again reviewed the invitation and letter in her trembling hands.

Jennifer wrapped her arms around her mother's neck and gave her a big squeeze. "I don't know what a Murrow Award is, but I think you deserve it," she declared, then yawned widely.

Hope looked at her watch. "It's almost 10:00. We've been having such a good time that I didn't realize how late it was getting. We've got to get Jennifer to bed."

"This place has an even better view than our hotel," Jennifer observed as they turned away from the windows. "You know what Tyler did when we were dancing?"

"What?" Mark asked, his paternal protectiveness becoming aroused.

"He asked me for my e-mail address and phone number. Said he wanted to keep in touch with me. You know, be a pen pal or something like that."

"Well, did you give it to him?" Mark asked.

"No. I mean, he's a really nice boy and all, but I'm too busy to write and stuff."

~

Thirty minutes later Mark carried a sleeping Jennifer into their hotel suite. "Shall we put her pajamas on her?" he whispered.

Hope shook her head. "She's OK. Just take off her shoes and tuck her in bed." Hope pulled down the covers, then slid the blanket and sheet over Jennifer as Mark brushed stray hairs off her face. Stepping back, they moved close together and for several moments stood gazing at their daughter as she lay in exhausted sleep, her face bathed by the glow from the city that never sleeps.

"I love you," he whispered to his wife with a softness matching the glow in the room.

"I love you, too," she answered tenderly. "Hard to believe it's been 10 years."

"I'm so lucky to have you."

Hope nestled her body close to his, then turned her face upward for a passionate kiss. "Our bedroom's over there," she whispered as Mark left a trail of kisses down her neck. "Why don't you come over and see me?"

"H'mmm. Sounds like an offer I can't refuse."

CHAPTER TWO

Saturday morning found the family heading for tourist sites. Jennifer fairly flew up the stairs to the top level of the ferry *Lady Liberty II,* where it was moored next to Manhattan's Battery Park. She found a vantage point near the bow where she could take in the full view every moment of the 20-minute trip to the Statue of Liberty. As they approached the island, Mark snapped several pictures of Hope and Jennifer with the statue in the background. Then they took turns: Mark and Jennifer, Mark and Hope, and then all three together with another tourist behind the digital camera. The boat passed the statue and began its turn toward the pier on the south side of the island.

"You look like you've got something on your mind," Mark said to his wife as they again looked over the rail.

"Oh, what gives you that impression?"

"You're being quiet, as though you're off in your own little world. What's up?" he pressed.

Hope stared off into the distance. "Well, I'm weighing a career move," she said.

"What kind of career move?" he asked as he slid an arm around her waist and pulled her close. "Got an offer from CNN or CBS?"

"Well, as a matter of fact, yes. Well, not offers. Not yet, anyway. Inquiries. You know, vice presidents calling and asking if they can talk to me over lunch. Things like that. CNN, CBS, and FOX all called me on Thursday, and the vice president for news over at ABC called me yesterday morning. And you know, now that I've had a chance to think about it, Brandon's invitation to dinner last night was no accident either."

"Why do you say that?" Mark asked.

"They must have an inside track on the Murrow Awards. I mean, they must have all known that I was a winner before it was announced. That letter Brandon gave me last night from the News Directors Association was dated today. How did they know what it said, or what the invitation said, if they didn't have inside information?"

Mark tried to identify what Hope was staring at in the distance. Maybe it was something on one of the marine piers on the New Jersey side of the Hudson River or a seagull floating on the breeze. It definitely wasn't the Statue of Liberty. "Does this mean we're moving to New York?" he asked.

"Don't know. Maybe Atlanta, if it's with CNN. New York. Los Angeles. It could be just about anywhere," Hope answered. "I mean, they've got bureaus all over the world. So, how'd you like to live in Moscow or Beijing or Rio de Janeiro?" She smiled teasingly.

Mark smiled at the thought of living in an exotic city. "Well, you're at the top of your game. I can find computer programming work just about anywhere, so I think it's only fair that Jennifer and I go wherever your work takes you."

Hope wrapped an arm around her husband and stretched up to give him a kiss. "Thanks for being so supportive. I guess you're right. I could probably negotiate some six-figure salary and in a couple years maybe even seven figures. Who knows, maybe even have my own morning show. 'American Daybreak With Hope Lancaster,'" she imitated an announcer's voice.

"Sounds good to me," Mark declared. "So why do I get the feeling that you're having second thoughts?"

Hope watched a seagull riding the breeze over the ferry as she composed her thoughts. "I'm a wife and a mother first. But lately it seems I've gotten that turned around, and I've been a reporter first and a wife and mother second. I mean, I just can't keep running off to who-knows-where and leaving you behind for days and weeks at a time. A few days aren't all that bad, but times like that long stint in Israel last year? Now, that was really hard! On me, on all of us. I don't want to have to keep going through that again and again. You and Jennifer are more important to me than any job."

The boat shifted under their feet as the captain reversed the engines to slow the ferry's approach to the Liberty Island pier. Other passengers began packing the lower deck in anticipation of getting off. "I'm glad to hear you say that, because we've missed you. Having Jennifer in the hospital and you away at the same time was really hard." He pulled his wife closer.

"I've already had a talk with the vice president of the news division at MBS," Hope said.

"About this?"

She nodded. "That's who I was talking with this morning when you were still asleep. He's made me an offer that I'm seriously considering," Hope said hesitantly. She studied Mark's face for a reaction.

Mark felt his heart skip a beat as he waited for Hope to continue.

"MBS owns and operates channel 3 back in Memphis. They've offered me the position of lead anchor with the understanding that they can call on me for special assignments from time to time. The biggest thing is that there will be no overnight travel."

"That sounds wonderful!" Mark exclaimed. "Are you going to take it?"

Hope's attention was momentarily diverted as a deck handler tossed a heavy line around a bollard on the dock and ran toward the stern to catch another line. The boat pulled gently against the pier, and the Lancasters joined the movement of tourists toward the boarding ramp. "I don't know," she finally answered.

"What's there to decide? I mean, you enjoy news reporting, and you want to be home. Sounds like the best of both worlds," Mark offered.

"But I'm just not sure about it. Back home I'll be at the top of the career ladder with nowhere higher to go. And if I let this pass, then I might not get another chance at my dream job. I'm thinking, *Yeah, I can try again in a few years when Jennifer's older.* But when that time comes, I'll just be older, and these jobs only go to the young and pretty, with perfect smiles and wrinkle-free faces."

"Hey! Can you two pay attention and talk later?" Jennifer called out excitedly from a few paces ahead.

The Statue of Liberty towered ever closer as they alternately skipped and sprinted across the plaza toward the old fort forming the statue's base. "I can't believe we're here! Whoopee!" Jennifer ran farther ahead. "Last one to the door's a rotten egg!" Mark and Hope ran to keep up. "I won!" Jennifer celebrated.

"OK. You won. But now you've got to pose for a picture," Mark declared. He stepped back as mother and daughter posed. It took them a half hour to work their way through the museum in the base of the statue and find their way to the tight spiral staircase leading up to the crown. Their legs felt rubbery with fatigue by the time they scaled the more than 300 steps to the top. But the experience was worth it, even if there was a limited view through the small windows in Lady Liberty's forehead. They gazed out at the landscape before spiraling back down the stairs.

En route back to the ferry, they turned several times to look up again at Lady Liberty's back. "Isn't this exciting?" Hope asked Jennifer.

Jennifer grinned broadly as she skipped along cheerily. "Now I feel like I'm a real American," she declared. "I can't wait to tell the kids at school where I went this summer!"

Back aboard the ferry, the family again found their position near the bow on the upper deck, where they watched the skyscrapers of Manhattan growing larger.

"How much time do you have to decide?" Mark inquired.

"The job at channel 3 starts two weeks from Monday. I still feel somewhat torn between taking my career to the next level and being at home more. I can't stop thinking about it. The network job offer is very tempting, but then again I keep thinking about how important my time is with you and Jennifer. I mean, Jennifer's growing up so fast, and I don't want to miss out on mother-daughter stuff because I'm off on assignments across the globe." Hope stopped and stared at Mark. "I guess that's my answer. I want to be here, with you and Jennifer. Regardless of how tempting the network job offers might be, I'm going to accept the offer at channel 3."

Mark studied his wife's eyes and found in them the familiar resolve declaring that she had truly made up her mind and could not be convinced otherwise. "It'll be good to have you home," he said softly.

"I'm looking forward to it," Hope said with new confidence as she reached an arm around her husband's waist and gave him a squeeze.

～

Lunch for the Lancasters was a genuine New York City treat: footlong hot dogs topped with sauerkraut, chips, and canned sodas from a Nathan's Famous vendor cart in Battery Park just yards from where they got off the ferry from Liberty Island. They found a shaded park bench and sat down to dine. Pigeons soon gathered around them, looking for handouts. Jennifer obliged them with pinches off her bun.

"What's a Murrow Award—I mean, who's this Murrow guy, anyway?" Jennifer wanted to know.

"A long time ago, before there was such a thing as television, Edward R. Murrow was a respected radio news reporter. Then, when TV was invented, he began doing news on TV. I guess you could say he was the first network

TV news anchor," Hope answered. "He set the example of integrity that the rest of us have tried to follow. That's why the award is named for him."

"Is it a big award like an Oscar?"

"Well, I guess you could say that. I mean, it's one of the highest awards that a TV or radio news reporter can be given. I guess you could call it the 'Oscar' of the broadcast news industry," Hope answered.

"So, I guess that means you're a great reporter," Jennifer said, smiling.

Hope laughed. "I like to think I'm a good reporter. I mean, I work hard and try to do my best all the time. Obviously some other people think I'm doing a good job."

Jennifer stuffed the final piece of her hot dog in her mouth and began looking around at the skyline towering above them. She stared at the skyscrapers a few minutes' walk away.

"What are you looking at?" Mark inquired.

"I was just looking at all the skyscrapers. They sure are tall." Jennifer continued to stare at the buildings, obviously deep in thought. "Daddy, didn't you say the World Trade Center used to have the tallest buildings in New York? Were they even taller than those buildings over there?" Jennifer asked.

"Yes, they were even taller than those buildings," Hope answered for Mark, whose mouth was full. "You know, if you want, we can go have a look at ground zero."

"But I heard they took down the public viewing platform because the new construction had started," Mark countered.

"They did, but the public doesn't have these." Hope reached into her purse and pulled out her media credentials: laminated photo ID cards that included a New York City Police Department press pass. She hung the lanyard around her neck so the cards dangled against her chest. "It's amazing where you can go with these, and I know just the place where we can get a really good view of ground zero," she declared as she stood up. "You ready to go?"

"Yeah! Let's go!" Jennifer squealed.

"First, let's hail a cab, 'cause it's a long walk from here," Hope commanded as she led the way to a nearby street. Stepping right to the edge of the traffic lane, she raised her arm and whistled. A cabbie a short distance away responded; the trio dove in, and she instructed the driver exactly where she wanted to go. Several minutes and $9.25 later the cabbie deposited them at the front door of an elegant office building.

"Why are we stopping here? I thought we were going to ground zero," Jennifer whined.

"Just wait and see," Hope answered as they entered the lobby. She showed her press ID to the security guard, who waved them to an elevator. Moments later they stepped off on the fifty-fourth floor and into a plain-looking hallway. The muffled sounds of large equipment could be heard through the walls.

"Sounds like we're on the air-conditioning floor," Mark observed.

"That's right," Hope answered.

"So why are we here?" Jennifer wondered aloud.

"You'll see in just a moment," Hope said as she led them around a corner and pushed open a door into the summer sun. They were on the building's roof. Hope walked straight to the four-foot-high wall and planted her hands on the top.

"You wanted to see ground zero. Well, here's a bird's-eye view," she declared with a smile and a wave of her arm over the wall's edge. The sheer size of the void below contrasted starkly with the altitude of the surrounding buildings. A train station filled several levels in the southwest corner, and a subway station was visible along the eastern wall. Large construction cranes stood at various points around the site as the reconstruction work was becoming more organized.

"Wow!" Mark exclaimed, his words almost stolen by the breeze.

"Those people and cars down there—they look so tiny," Jennifer exclaimed as she peered over the edge against her father's restraint.

For several minutes they stood in silence as Mark snapped pictures.

"Mom, isn't this the place your cousin Lisa died?" Jennifer asked.

Remembering her cousin, who in many ways had been almost a sister to her, was like a knife in Hope's heart. She swallowed hard and fought to keep from crying. "Yes, this is the place," she answered, her voice choking. "Right there."

"Where is she now?" Jennifer asked.

"In heaven with Jesus," Hope declared.

"If cousin Lisa's in heaven with Jesus, does that mean that the bad men who hijacked the planes are in hell?"

Mark felt an unfamiliar anger rising inside him as he surveyed the sight. "They thought that what they did would guarantee them a place in heaven, but I don't believe it. I hope they're burning in hell and that they burn there forever," Mark said angrily.

"I hope so too," Hope added with coldness in her voice.

CHAPTER THREE

Why customers would pay top dollar for pizza if the dough had been tossed into the air and twirled around had always been a mystery to Amir Al-Hamzi. At the same time, what was no mystery to him was how good a living tossing and spinning pizza dough provided him.

Seven years ago he'd arrived at Los Angeles International Airport, an immigrant from Egypt with less than $200 in his pocket, no job, and no home. Before arriving, he'd networked over the Internet with members of the Egyptian immigrant community. So after exchanging some of the Egyptian pounds in his wallet for U.S. dollars, he'd found a pay phone and dialed a number he'd been given. An hour later someone in a car had pulled up to the curb and called his name. Hearing his name in Arabic had been music to his ears in an unfamiliar world filled with English.

Over the next few days the friend had helped him find a small apartment and a job working nights as a janitor. Somehow, one year later he'd found the money to lease this retail location among the T-shirt shops, arcades, and other amusement-oriented businesses lining Speedway Boulevard on California's famous Venice Beach.

A pizzeria was a natural business for such a location. He'd named it "Al's Pizza." Besides being part of his Arabic name, "Al" was such a distinctly American name. Just one year ago he'd become a naturalized citizen of the United States of America.

Not that Amir had abandoned his old allegiances. Indeed, during that first year in the U.S. he'd begun attending a mosque where the imam's sermons railed against the evils of the land in which they were living, calling the faithful of Islam to obey God's will by rising up, cleansing the land of those sins, and forcing the infidels to convert to the true faith. Friends he had made among the true believers had lent him the money to start his business.

Another old allegiance from which Amir never wavered was to his family. Each week after tallying the books from his business, he took a city bus for a half-hour ride to a Pakistani-owned grocery store in a neighborhood of Los Angeles dominated by immigrants from the Middle East and Southern Asia. Once inside, he traded pleasantries with the owner, who then invited him into the back office. There they sipped tea and enjoyed hearing each other speak in Arabic as they arranged for money to be transferred to Amir's parents in Egypt.

Amir knew from the messages he received from his parents that only about half the money he sent actually made it to them. Yet he didn't complain because of how he felt about where the remainder was going. One subtraction was a fee paid to the members of the Hawala network, who transferred the funds across borders without the official banking records that would make the money traceable. A second subtraction was a payment to his investors. The last—and largest—was "for the benefit of Islamic mission and humanitarian projects." Though it was never stated aloud by anyone, Amir knew that not all of those projects were peaceful. The American invasion of Iraq and unwavering support for the Zionist state of Israel angered him and made him all the more willing to support pro-Islamic activities.

As Amir sipped his tea, the grocery store owner dialed a phone number and began speaking in Pashtun, the language of much of his native Pakistan and the adjoining southern portion of Afghanistan. The conversation lasted several minutes. "I have been asked to convey a special message to you," the store owner said in Arabic after hanging up. "Because of your faithful support of the cause of Islam in this land, you will soon be given a chance to serve in a great way."

"How will I know when and in what way I will be called on to serve?" Amir asked.

The store owner waved his hand dismissively. "It is not for you to know the time or the way. That will be as God wishes it to be. Be patient, because the time will not be long."

∽

The hallways of Featherweight Software in Memphis were as familiar to Mark Lancaster as those of his own home. Perhaps more so, considering that he'd spent most of his waking hours there, sometimes six or even seven days a week, for almost nine years.

The company had been known as Mitchell Software Developers, a small group that wrote custom software for a variety of customers in the computer industry. Mark was among the first programmers hired by founder Gene Mitchell. That was in the heyday of the digital revolution, when everyone willingly exchanged shares of company stock for the lure of higher salaries, hoping that one day the company would be sold for a premium price and those shares would be worth a fortune. Their dream was realized unexpectedly when Gene Mitchell met and fell in love with Lisa Ferrar, the CEO of Featherweight Software. Gene got a wife and a fortune out of the deal. Lisa got a husband and Mitchell Software Developers, which became the Memphis branch of Featherweight Software.

The deal turned Mark's shares into enough money to pay off the mortgage on the house, buy new vehicles, and add a five-figure sum of money to the retirement savings account he shared with Hope.

Then came the earthquake that temporarily rerouted part of the Mississippi River and threw the country into an economic tailspin. When people began having to choose between buying food or software, it wasn't long before Featherweight management was forced to announce the first layoffs in the company's history. Within weeks Mark found himself without a job for the first time since he had been in high school.

But now he was back, eagerly awaiting his first assignment. As he strolled through the front door, the first thing Mark noticed was the lack of a security guard or receptionist at the front desk. Second was the eerie quietness. Entire rooms that had once been filled with creative people, many of whom had reported to him or his subordinates, were dark and quiet. Instead of hearing conversation and the clicking of keyboards, he now heard only the soft rumbling and hiss of air moving through ductwork hidden above the suspended ceilings.

"We're setting up over in B wing," Art Whitfield, Mark's new supervisor, announced after welcoming him back, even though the two had never met before. Art had been brought in from Featherweight's corporate offices in Palo Alto, California, to organize this project. The leather soles of their shoes clicked against the tile floor, echoing off the bare walls to their right and then being absorbed by the fabric-covered cubicle walls on their left. Mark touched the top of one wall and swept up a layer of dust. Finally they stepped into a large room where perhaps a dozen cubicles were arranged around the perimeter of the room. A large conference table filled the center of the space.

Art pointed Mark toward an unoccupied cubicle. "Make yourself at home. If you need anything, the supply cabinet's over there." He pointed to a closet across the room.

"So much for getting my office back," Mark complained under his breath as he looked around his new work space.

"For what it's worth, I know the feeling," Art replied. "But as this project grows and we bring on new people, we'll be the core team." He waved his hand toward the larger room they had just passed through. "In another month or so that room will be filled with people who'll be working for us. Now, grab a legal pad, and let's get you oriented on the project."

Mark began searching the supply cabinet standing against one wall. For a moment he stopped and just stared at the contents. It looked as if someone had closed the door only moments before, though he knew it had really been months. The thought sent a shiver up his spine. Finding a pack of legal pads, he tore open the cellophane wrapper and extracted one. Yes, it felt good to be back at work, he admitted to himself. Yet it felt strange because things were so different. It was both exciting and frightening at the same time.

≈

Captain Sonja Cabrini carefully studied the functional parts of the Boeing 757 airliner as she did her preflight walk-around inspection. To the casual observer inside the Diamond Airways terminal at Los Angeles International Airport it looked like a disorganized stroll as she went this way and that. However, for her it was routine and a calculated inspection. At each wheel well she bent over, craning her neck to inspect the hydraulic lines running along the walls, making sure there weren't any leaks. She also inspected the electric cables for damage. The midmorning brightness on this late-summer day reflected blindingly off the concrete and made the inside of the wheel well so dark that she needed a flashlight to see. There were no obvious hydraulic leaks or other damage. It was time to move on and inspect the wings, including the massive single engines hanging there.

At the tail she met a mechanic descending in the bucket of a snorkel truck. He had been doing something near the top of the vertical stabilizer 40-some feet above the ground. "How's it looking?" Sonja asked. "Think it'll get us to Dallas?" The mechanic, whose ears were covered with large blue hearing protectors because of passing jet engines, answered with a smile and a double thumbs-up.

Five minutes later Sonja was climbing the ladder on the outside of the Jetway and entering the plane's cabin. Peering aft toward the forward galley, she saw the caterer moving his last rack of prepared meals into place under the watchful eye of a flight attendant. "We about ready to go, Susan?" she asked.

"Right on time," Susan answered. "We'll be ready to start boarding in just another minute or two."

Sonja made her way to the front of the plane, where she found the door to the cockpit ajar and her copilot, First Officer Alan Markland, sitting in the right-hand seat and working down a systems checklist. "You ready to go home?" she asked as she closed and secured the terrorist-proof door. Now they were cut off from the rest of the plane, and the passengers could begin boarding.

"Only thing we're missing is the passengers," he declared.

Sonja grabbed an overhead handhold, stretched her left leg over the pilot's seat, and eased herself onto the cushion. Reaching down, she felt for the switch that would move her seat forward to where she had the best view of the instrument panel and out the windows while still letting her short legs reach the rudder pedals. "Back in the saddle one more time," she proclaimed.

Sonja did a visual check of her radio headset before inserting the custom-fitted earpiece, clipping the microphone onto the side of her sunglasses, and plugging the end into the radio jack on the wall to her left. Then she turned her attention to completing the systems checklist.

A motion to the left of the plane caught her eye. Reflexively, Sonja looked that way and saw the Jetway starting to move back from the plane. At the same time she felt the small change in pressure on her ears, telling her that the cabin door had been closed, locked, and sealed. A moment later they felt a slight bump as the arm on the pushback tug was attached somewhere underneath them. "You cleared for pushback yet?" a voice in their earpieces asked. It was the ground crew member who was connected by headphones plugged into a panel under the nose.

Alan squeezed the push-to-talk switch on his control yoke. "LA Ground, Diamond 1284 is ready for pushback."

"Diamond 1284, LA Ground. Cleared for pushback. Advise when ready to taxi. You'll be in line for departure on runway zero-six right."

"Did they say zero-six right?" Sonja asked, then answered her own question as she glanced down at a display in the center console giving them the current airport weather data. The start-up of summertime Santa Ana winds meant low visibilities from desert dust filling the air, and taking off toward the east instead of the west.

Alan told the ground crew member to do his thing, and a moment later the giant aircraft was moving backward from the terminal, then being turned into a traffic lane where it would be detached from the tug and left to go its way. His eyes scanned northward toward the Hollywood hills. They were lost in the haze. "An hour from now we'll be lucky if we can see the far end of the runway."

"Starting number one," Sonja announced. She reached onto the center control panel and lifted a small lever directly behind the left throttle. The lights dimmed slightly as the huge electric starter in the engine under the left wing began drawing a heavy amount of current from the auxiliary power unit in the tail. A barely audible whine matched the rising needles on the engine speed and oil pressure gauges. Then the fire in the engine lit, and the needles leaped higher, followed by numbers rising into the green zone on the engine's temperature gauge.

Alan reached up and flipped a pair of switches on an overhead panel. "Feeding fuel from the center main tank," he declared.

"Roger. Number one is up and stable. Starting number two," Sonja announced. The second start lever was lifted, and the gauges for the right-side engine responded. For almost a minute the pilots just sat in silence, studying the various gauges.

"Both engines are stable. We're ready to go," Alan said. "Want me to call it in?"

"Go ahead," Sonja allowed.

"Diamond 1284 is ready for taxi," he radioed.

"Diamond 1284 is cleared for taxi to runway zero-six right. You're number seven in line," the ground controller directed crisply.

Alan acknowledged the clearance, and Sonja pressed her toes against the rudder pedals to release the brake lock. The plane immediately began rolling forward. It moved slowly at first, so she pushed the throttles forward just a half inch. The plane responded by moving fast enough that she pulled them back almost as quickly.

The path to the runway took several turns: a left past the end of the Diamond Airways terminal and past two more terminals; a right; and finally a left onto the main taxiway beside their expected runway. From there it was a straight run past maintenance hangers and the Coast Guard air station. They were within sight of the ocean when they stopped to await their turn on the runway.

The air traffic controllers were choreographing a tightly sequenced ballet. Every 60 to 90 seconds a plane either landed or took off on this pair of runways on the north side of the airport. On different radio frequencies another set of controllers was doing the same thing with the pair of runways on the airport's south side.

One by one the airliners took their turns. A Boeing 747 was on final approach for runway six right. A 200-foot-wide strip of grass separated the taxiway and the runway. Still, it looked as though the giant plane was headed right toward the waiting planes until the last few seconds, when it flashed past and settled onto the runway. Its wheels puffed a cloud of smoke as they gripped the concrete.

"Reminds me a little of playing chicken," Alan muttered over the intercom.

Sonja smiled at the thought and then heard the tower controller's crisp voice directing them to "taxi to position and hold."

"Diamond 1284," she answered as she lifted her toes off the brakes and pushed the throttles forward just a bit to get the 757 moving. She swung the nose around the corner in a wide sweep that ended with the nosewheel exactly on the runway center line.

"Diamond 1284, cleared for takeoff," the tower controller announced.

"Diamond 1284 is rolling," Sonja replied as she let off the brakes and slid the throttles all the way forward. The thrust pushed everyone aboard back in their seats as they rocketed forward. "Here we go." They were off the ground and their landing gear was coming up before the plane was over the departure end of the runway.

~

There was something in Mark's behavior that triggered a degree of concern in Hope. He just wasn't as talkative as usual, not saying much about how his day had gone. She wanted to inquire directly what was on his mind, but she waited until a more discrete moment when Jennifer was taking her bath.

"I'll tell you later," he responded.

"Is it good or bad?" she pressed.

"I'll tell you later" was all he would say. That pushed her level of concern higher. It was only after the family had had worship together and Jennifer was tucked into bed that he began to describe his day.

"I'm trying to be thankful to have this job, but I'm not sure I'm going to like it," Mark said.

"What's wrong?" Hope asked as she sat down next to him on the couch and took his hands in hers.

"Oh, it's everything." He pulled his hands away so he could gesture. "I mean, I'm working in a cubicle out in B wing instead of having my old office. It's like . . . I've been . . . well . . . demoted. Plus, I'm going to have to travel. I mean, it'll be a month or so before I have to go anywhere, and that'll just be in the U.S. But after we get this system tested and installed at the factory out in California, we'll be installing and customizing it at customers' plants all over the world."

"What's wrong with that?" Hope asked.

"You know what a homebody I am and how I hate traveling."

"You're a first-class homebody, for sure," Hope observed as she moved closer to her husband. "Just hope we won't be on the road at the same time."

"Guess you'll get to teach me a few tricks about how to pack."

Hope smiled. "Maybe I could teach you a thing or two."

"What happens if we both have to travel at the same time? Could Jennifer stay with your mother?"

Hope shook her head. "I'll turn down an assignment before I'll let that happen. I mean, at least one of us has to be here with her, and I've traveled so much that I want to be the one."

Chapter Four

FBI Special Agent Walter Keller looked as though he might lose his breakfast at any moment. "Pass me the Dramamine, will you?" he croaked as he clung to the ladder leading to the boat's upper deck.

Agent Jimmy Henderson eyed his partner with a look of superiority that only an old sea dog can give a landlubber. "Man, these swells are only two or three feet. What're you gonna do when they're six or seven?" he called back as he passed the box of medication. "Hey, if you gotta puke, at least get your head over the side first."

Keller groaned. "I'm afraid that if I put my head over the side I might fall in."

"Don't give me any ideas, partner." Henderson's grin got a little bigger. "Mess my deck, and I'll make you wish you'd fallen in."

Keller took a swig from his bottle of soda to wash down the pill, trying to accomplish the whole effort without making himself any dizzier. "You know, I thought surveillance would only make me sick from boredom."

Henderson glanced at his fishing pole, which sat with its handle in a pipe mounted in the boat's side rail. Putting his binoculars to his eyes, he scanned the nearby boats. He paused to watch the occupants of another boat pull in a large fish. "Too bad we don't have any bait on our lines," he complained. "A fish like that, and we could cook dinner for the whole office."

"You can have my portion," Keller groaned.

"Hey, partner! The way I cook fish, even you'd enjoy it. I mean, I grill it over mesquite until it's just so, and I use this special sauce that my mother taught me how to make. M-m-m. I can taste it now. Nothing like it!"

"Just remember, we're here to land a different kind of fish. That is, if this guy's really up to something illegal—and if I survive," Keller groaned before plopping onto a padded seat.

"Don't worry. If you die, I'll have a new partner before your funeral's over," Henderson kidded.

Keller twisted over the side and began heaving.

"Should I call headquarters and tell them I need a replacement now?" Henderson asked.

In his weakened and nauseated state Keller slid toward the deck. "What's our Egyptian friend doing?" he asked weakly.

Henderson looked at the video surveillance monitor. The picture was from a camera mounted high atop the radar mast and aimed toward a boat more than a half mile away. The gyro-stabilized aiming system borrowed from pilotless Air Force drones kept the camera aimed precisely at the target vessel at all times. The picture was so steady that you could barely tell that the boat on which it was mounted was rolling gently on the swells. All the operator had to do was use a joystick to move the X to the center of the picture on the target, then press a button to lock it on target. The electronics did the rest.

"Why don't you just call the office and tell 'em we're coming in? I mean, he always heads back to the marina about the same time 'cause he's gotta go back to making pizzas," Keller complained. "You know, I think I need a career change. I need to start making pizzas. I mean, I'm out here getting seasick, and he's trolling around on a 35-foot boat that he paid for in cash with profits from his pizzeria."

Henderson looked across the water toward Amir Al-Hamzi's boat for a moment, then turned back to the monitor. "Looks like he just landed a pretty good-sized fish. I can picture him now back at his apartment grilling an inch-thick steak layered in bread crumbs and my special sauce," Henderson said.

"There you go again talking about food," Keller groaned.

$\sim$

"Hurry up, Jennifer!" Mark yelled up the stairs. "You only have a few minutes to eat your breakfast before we have to leave for the day-care center."

"I'll be down in a minute," she called back.

"What's gotten into her?" Mark asked. "Ever since her hair grew back she's been spending extra time fixing it when most girls her age just brush and go."

"Don't be so hard on her. She's gone through a lot this past year," Hope said softly as she dropped a breakfast pastry into the toaster and pushed the lever down.

Jennifer bounded down the stairs. "Thanks, Mom," she said as she reached for the milk to pour over her cereal.

"Why aren't you eating, hon?" Mark asked.

"I had a toaster pastry a minute ago, and I don't feel like eating anything more this morning," Hope answered. Suddenly a strange expression came over her face before she bolted from her seat and across the living room to the bathroom. In moments she had lost what little breakfast she had eaten.

Mark was right behind her. "What's wrong, sweetie? Are you OK?" he asked with great concern. He wet a washcloth with cool water, wrung it out, and gave it to her to wipe her face when she stood up.

"I don't know what hit me. It just came over me all at once," she said weakly.

"You look pale, dear." Mark helped her to the living room couch. He put his hand on her forehead, and a moment later declared that she didn't have a fever.

"Mommy, I want you to go to the doctor today." Jennifer imitated her mother with hands on her hips.

"That sounds like a good idea, but right now you both better get busy eating, or you'll be leaving here hungry," Hope encouraged.

"I'm moving, Mom!" Jennifer called out as she headed back to the dining room. She gulped down more of her breakfast before dashing up the stairs to brush her teeth.

Mark glanced at the clock before swallowing the last of his orange juice. "You're right. I'd better get moving, or I'll be late for work. You sure you're going to be OK?"

"I'll be fine," Hope answered a bit shakily. "I think I'll try to see the doctor today."

"You *sure* you're going to be OK?" Mark asked again.

"I'll be OK. Just let me sit here for a few minutes and get my strength back," Hope said as she settled back on the couch. "I don't want you to be late for work. Do you still have time to drop Jennifer off at the day-care center?"

Mark eyed Hope with concern as he nodded and prepared to leave. "Are you sure I don't need to stay home and take you to the doctor?" he asked again.

Hope smiled a twisted smile. "They've been running ads all week on channel 3 about me coming back today, so it'd be really ironic if I didn't show up for my first day back at work."

"C'mon, Jennifer! It's time to go!" Mark called as he headed for the garage. He gave Hope another look that questioned her plans.

She waved him on. "I'm feeling better already," she said just to get him heading out the door. Something inside told her she'd be OK. But right now the last thing she wanted was food. Just the smell from the remains of breakfast made her stomach feel as though it was doing flips. Gradually the feeling faded, and she decided to go to work instead of seeing the doctor.

~

Returning to channel 3 was a homecoming of sorts for Hope. After all, it was the station she'd started at as a cub reporter right out of journalism school, working her way up through the ranks to anchor before being called to the network. With only a few changes the faces were the same she'd left one year before to go cover the disaster on the Mississippi River and a war in the Middle East.

There were warm hugs and energetic handshakes all around, until gruff-mannered news director Bob Knoller grunted a "Welcome back" and handed her a printed outline of the stories being worked on for the 5:00 and 6:00 p.m. newscasts. "Write your intros and transitions, and get them over to the teleprompter file by 4:00 p.m.," he ordered. "Oh, and some guy from MBS New York called. Peter somebody or other wants you to call him. Something about the first of your 'occasional' assignments." Just as quickly as he had appeared, Bob turned on his heels toward his office. Suddenly he turned around. "By the way, you've got a 1:00 p.m. appointment over at TressMax. That down style's gotta go. Get something that makes you look like an anchor."

"I love you too, Bob," Hope muttered sarcastically to his back as he disappeared into his office.

Hope had to try three times before getting Peter Leventhal on the phone. "Hey, Peter! What's up?" she greeted him cheerfully. "Dare I ask where you are?"

Peter laughed. "Believe it or not, I'm at home."

"Home? As much as you travel, I thought your home was a motel room or a seat on a foreign airline!" Hope laughed.

"Sure seems that way, doesn't it? Hey, what I want from you is low pressure. What can you tell me about a man named Robert Merrill Ingersoll?"

Hope thought for a moment. "H'mmm. Let's see what we have on him." She turned to the computer terminal on her desk and went to the station's news archive search program. She typed in "Ingersoll, Robert" in the name search option. "You know, that's one of those names that sounds familiar but I can't say why," she said as she waited for the search results to appear. The screen changed, and a list of stories came up. "Let's see. We've got, oh, a dozen or more stories about him in the station archives. Looks like we've got a few more than that about a company called RMI."

"That's his company. Robert Merrill Ingersoll Industries."

"What's the story angle?" Hope inquired.

"This is all on deep background right now. Our sources are telling us that RMI is under investigation by the Securities and Exchange Commission for accounting fraud. You know the drill: inflating their income numbers to keep the stock price up, that sort of thing," Peter said. "I want you to build a stock video report about the man and his company. Oh, and e-mail me whatever copy you find on him, OK?"

"Will do," Hope confirmed.

"By the way, how's Mark adapting to having you home?"

"Quite well, actually. He's been called back from the layoff, so he's getting used to a new job with a lower salary. Plus, he's adjusting to working in a cubicle instead of a window office. As you can guess, he's not real happy. It's just not the same place."

"How are things going for you at the station?" Peter wanted to know.

"Well, so far, so good. I mean, this is my first day back from vacation. Bob Knoller's his usual grumpy self, but it's nice being back with all my old friends. Kind of like slipping my feet into an old pair of shoes that I haven't worn for a while."

"Well, we're going to try to leave you there. At least for a while," Peter said. "But you never know what tomorrow will bring in our business."

"So I've learned," Hope laughed. "So I've learned."

∼

Getting information about Robert Merrill Ingersoll was both easy and difficult. The easy parts were reviewing channel 3's file reports about him and going through the online archives of the Memphis *Herald-Tribune*. There were pictures of him and his trophy wife at major social events where they helped raise money for local charities. In one story he was announcing the creation of 120 new jobs at a specialty manufacturing plant the company was building. Off and on between her anchoring tasks, Hope spent the better part of two days gathering information. She visited the RMI Web site and printed every page. After reviewing them, she formulated a list of general questions she would like to ask in an interview—assuming she could get one with Robert Ingersoll himself. Last, she contacted RMI's public relations department to request an interview and ask what further information they could provide.

"Mr. Ingersoll is too busy for media interviews right now," the public relations director politely but firmly declared. He did promise to send her a video about company activities and to try to get answers to written questions.

"What we know is that Robert Ingersoll started out in the family's transportation business running tugboats and barges on the Mississippi River. After he took over, he expanded it into port operations and long-haul truck transport," Hope described to Peter. "Over the past few years RMI Industries has diversified into manufacturing electronics and doing some things for the military that are shrouded in secrecy."

"What's his lifestyle like?" Peter asked.

"He's definitely a high-society type. All the hoity-toity parties and such. Big donor to worthy community causes and the like," Hope answered.

"Where does he live? What kind of house does he live in?"

"That I don't know."

"Well, find out," Peter ordered. "How much is he worth? Where does he go to church? What does he do for fun? If this story pans out, we may need to know where to stake out to get a comment from him. You know, coming out of the country club, or whatever."

"I'll see what I can do," Hope promised before hanging up.

A visit to the Shelby County tax assessor's office revealed that Robert Ingersoll owned a 200-plus-acre tract of land in the country northeast of Memphis on which he had a house and several other buildings.

Hope turned to the Internet and followed links to satellite photos of the area. Sure enough, the area including the Ingersoll home was available at one-half-meter resolution, meaning that each pixel in the digital image corresponded to a piece of ground 18 inches square. That would give at least some idea of how big a house he lived in and what it looked like. Hope could see that a car was parked in the driveway and tell what color it was, but not what make or model.

The size of the Ingersolls' horseshoe-shaped home was impressive even from orbit. The swimming pool behind it and the buildings that could pass for guesthouses right behind the pool and at two nearby sites were no surprise. What caught Hope's attention was a long black strip running across the western part of the estate. A runway? Yes! There were large numbers painted on each end indicating a compass orientation like those on an airport runway. A taxiway extended off to the east at the south end toward a building she judged to be an aircraft hangar. A shape that looked like a medium-sized twin-engine corporate aircraft sat in front of the building.

"That's a great way to get around," Hope said to herself as she clicked the "print" icon in the toolbar of her Web browser.

Out of curiosity Hope moved the map locator box over the city of Memphis and to the south side, where she judged their home was located. Then she began zooming in until she could identify streets. After a few more adjustments, she had located their neighborhood, and that picture, too, was coming off the printer. Then she called Peter.

"Find out what you can about that airplane. Once you have the ID number, we can contact the FAA and get the record of his flight plans. That way we can get an idea of where he is and how much time he's spending where," Peter instructed.

Getting the aircraft ID number was easier said than done. A drive past the Ingersoll estate revealed what the aerial photo did not: the airstrip and everything else was out of view from the road, behind rows of trees and acres of pasture.

Knowing that such an airplane must require periodic maintenance, Hope began researching the companies that serviced corporate aircraft at nearby airports. It didn't take long to learn that the plane in question was a Beech King Air, a midlevel corporate plane with an expensive, customized interior. The plane was large and fast enough to get to each of RMI's plants within a 1,200-mile radius without refueling. However, going across the country would be faster on a commercial airline.

Hope awoke early the next morning and decided to review her growing file on Robert Ingersoll and RMI. She had just spread the papers out on the dining room table when she heard Mark's alarm clock begin beeping upstairs. She was still stacking papers and stuffing them into the folder when he came down for his preshower cup of coffee.

"Whatcha lookin' at?" he inquired sleepily.

"Oh, a story I'm doing background on about a local industrialist."

"Who?"

"Robert Merrill Ingersoll. Ever heard of him?" she asked.

Mark poured himself a cup from the automatic coffeemaker and began stirring in cream and sugar. "Now that I think about it, isn't he someone we know at church? Remember a few years ago when your dad was leading that fund-raising effort to build the new church? Wasn't Ingersoll that 'mystery donor' who told your dad to go ahead and order all the steel, concrete blocks, and bricks and send him the bill?"

Hope thought for a moment. "You might be right. I'd have to ask Mom about it. All I remember is that Dad was pretty tight-lipped about the identity of the donor. What makes you think it was him?"

"Who else in the church has that kind of money?" Mark answered before taking another sip from his steaming mug. "I'll see you in a few minutes," he said as he turned to head upstairs.

The morning bouts of nausea were becoming a daily routine, and when she felt the first wave come over her, Hope knew her breakfast would be limited to nibbles on a few soda crackers. Maybe she should heed Mark's pleas and make an appointment with Dr. Beaumont. But that would come later. Right now she had to get breakfast on the table for a husband and daughter who would be flying out the door in the next hour.

A half hour after Mark and Jennifer departed, Hope called Dr. Beaumont's office and got an appointment that would allow her to get to work on schedule. The timing could not have been better. She tossed the RMI file onto the right front seat so that she could look at it in the waiting room, and then turned her vehicle into traffic. "It's just a matter of time until I find the ID number on that plane," she reminded herself as she mentally reviewed the file. In her days as a cub reporter she'd honed her news-hunting skills. Now she could ask tough questions with the best of her compatriots and competitors. Over the years she had compiled a long list of "scoops" to prove her skills.

One traffic light stood between Hope and the doctor's office. She waited in the left-turn lane for a break in the oncoming traffic. The light turned yellow as she waited. Several oncoming cars slowed to a stop, so she eased her foot off the brake pedal and onto the gas in order to move into the opening. But the driver in the outside lane decided to run the light. Hope slammed on the brakes, barely avoiding a collision. The contents of the folder on the passenger seat went flying. "You idiot!" she yelled angrily at the other driver as she glanced down at the contents of the folder scattered across the floorboard.

Hope let the papers rest until she was parked. "I guess I should be thankful that I didn't get into an accident," she admonished herself as she scooped up the papers and tried to push them back into the folder without creasing or wrinkling any of the sheets. Suddenly something in one of the pictures caught her eye. Robert Ingersoll was announcing an expansion of his company's nearby factory, and he was standing in front of an airplane. The plane's tail number was clearly visible in the background. "There it is! Right in plain sight! Why didn't I see that before?" she exclaimed.

Hopefully my appointment won't take too long, she thought as she signed in at the receptionist's desk. *I need to get to the station and file a Freedom of Information Act request with the FAA.*

CHAPTER FIVE

W hat's got you grinning so big today?" coanchor Andrew Timm asked as he and Hope walked onto the set for the 5:00 p.m. newscast. They laid their copy on the desk, swiveled into their respective chairs, and reached for their clip-on microphones.

Hope ignored the question as she threaded the microphone cable over her shoulder and then pulled on her suit jacket so that the wire would be hidden.

Andrew pulled his jacket closed and looked down to be sure his microphone was connected. He slid closer to the desk and pushed his intercom earphone into his ear. "Come on; you're ignoring me. So when are you going to let me in on your little secret?"

"Oh, it's a very little secret," Hope teased. "And it's all mine." She buttoned up her jacket and pulled herself up to the desk. After picking up her printed copy, she began doing a read-through of her introduction so that the sound technician could set the level on her microphone. "Good evening, and welcome to *Channel 3 News* at 5:00. I'm Hope Lancaster."

"And I'm Andrew Timm," her partner picked up the script automatically. His eyes were fixed on the teleprompter, where an unseen operator in the control room was keeping up. "Citizens in the unincorporated areas around Memphis are protesting a plan to raise their property taxes. County leaders say they need the money to provide essential services, such as better roads, new schools, and improved fire protection. But citizens argue it's just big government trying to get bigger. Kelly Wong reports." He paused for a beat. "Sound, do you have a level on me, or should I keep reading?"

A voice came back through their earphones telling them that all was ready and two minutes remained until they would be on the air.

Hope did a short read of her first story introduction, then reached under the desk for the water bottle that was supposed to be waiting for her on a shelf beside her knee. The shelf was empty. "Where's my water?" she asked without taking her eye off the camera. No answer came from the darkness beyond the cameras, and no one moved from behind them to answer her question. "Would somebody mind telling me where my water bottle is?" she repeated, this time a little louder and with a detectable note of irritation. When no answer came, she stood and reached to disconnect her microphone. "I guess I'll just have to get some water myself," she complained.

"Stay there, Hope!" the director called over the studio speaker. His voice sounded as if it had come from heaven the way it boomed from speakers hidden in the rafters high above the suspended lights. "We've got a bottle coming. It'll take a minute, though."

Andrew looked at her as she eased back onto her stool. "How is it that you can get mad and still be smiling so big? What's your secret?"

"I told you it was just a tiny secret, and that's all I'm telling you," she declared.

"Oh, it's one of *those* secrets," Andrew teased. "Shall we schedule your maternity leave?"

"Oh, you're good, Andrew. Really, really good, you know that? You're just lucky I don't have my water bottle yet."

"Fifteen seconds!" This time the director's voice came not from above but through their earphones. "Quiet on the set."

Both anchors straightened up in their seats and fixed their eyes on their respective automated cameras. Somewhere off in the darkness they could hear the studio door being closed carefully and the quiet squish-squish of athletic shoes crossing the epoxy-coated concrete floor as someone approached the news set. Hope could hear someone to her right and felt a bump against her leg as the person reached under the desk to place something on the shelf beside her knee. The introduction to the evening newscast began playing just as the messenger withdrew. Then came the director's countdown in their ears: "Three . . . two . . . one . . ."

"Good evening, and welcome to *Channel 3 News* at 5:00. I'm Hope Lancaster."

"And I'm Andrew Timm . . ."

Within three minutes they had been through two stories and were into the broadcast's first look at the weather forecast. Then came the first commercial break. Their eyes remained fixed on the cameras for at least two seconds after the red "on air" light went dark and the yellow "standby" light illuminated.

Hope reached under the desk for the water bottle. Instead of her accustomed 16-ounce bottle, it was a much shorter four-ounce bottle. She held it up. "OK, who's the wise guy who gave me a miniature? Would someone kindly get me a bigger bottle?" she requested before twisting off the cap and downing the entire bottle in a few swallows.

"Oh, we can get you a bigger one if you want," the director's voice came from a speaker somewhere above the lights, "but we thought we'd better start you off with a baby-sized one."

"Baby-sized? All right, guys! What's going on here?"

"Well, you did say you had a tiny secret that you weren't telling us about, so we guessed it had something to do with a baby," the voice declared from above.

Hope shook her head. "You know, that's the problem with wearing a microphone," she said.

"And being on TV," her coanchor added.

"Stand by. We're coming back from commercial in 10," the director commanded, and attention suddenly was refocused back on the cameras.

≈

"You're in an upbeat mood tonight," Mark observed as the family gathered around the dinner table. "Something special happen at work?"

"Oh, it's just been a good day. A *very* good day," she answered as their hands extended to form a prayer circle.

Mark offered a prayer of thanks over the meal. "So tell us about your good day. What happened that has made you so giddy?" he asked.

Hope smiled inwardly as she hungrily chewed her first forkful of sweet potato.

"Mom, are you feeling better? Did you get sick again this morning?" Jennifer asked with a mouthful of food.

"Dear, how many times do we have to tell you not to talk with food in your mouth?" Hope admonished. "And no, my morning sickness hasn't gone away. But Dr. Beaumont is hopeful it'll last only a few more weeks."

Mark's fork froze in midair halfway to his mouth, a surprised look on his face. "A few more weeks . . . ? You're not . . . ? Are you?"

Hope grinned widely and nodded.

Mark sprang excitedly from his chair to embrace his wife and kiss her passionately. "Oh, honey! This is wonderful news. I just can't believe it!"

"What's going on?" Jennifer protested. "What's all the excitement about?"

"I think what your mom's trying to say . . ." Mark began.

". . . is that I'm pregnant," Hope finished his sentence.

"You're pregnant? You mean, you're going to have a baby?" Jennifer squealed with delight before springing from her chair and throwing her arms around her mother. "I'm so excited. You mean I'm going to have a baby brother?"

"Well, it's too early to know . . ." Mark started to answer.

Jennifer sprang from her chair and began dancing around the room. "I'm gonna have a baby brother! I'm gonna have a baby brother!"

The parents smiled and enjoyed the sight for a moment.

"It *is* a boy, isn't it?" Jennifer asked from the archway leading to the living room.

"We don't know yet. It will still be another three months before Dr. Beaumont can do an ultrasound and tell us if it's a boy . . . or if it's a girl," Hope stated.

"Well, what do you want? A boy? Or a girl?" Jennifer pressed.

"The baby's sex has already been decided. We just have to wait and find out," Mark answered.

"Well, I think it's a boy," Jennifer declared.

"How about sitting back down and finishing your supper," Hope commanded.

Throughout the rest of the meal the threesome chatted excitedly about the baby, discussing which room the nursery would be located in and how the relatives would react to their special news. They finished eating and cleared the table together. Then Jennifer headed off to the living room to watch a little TV before getting ready for bed.

"So, how far along are you?" Mark asked as he helped Hope load the dishwasher.

"Six weeks."

Mark put another plate in the rack. "Six weeks. H'mmm. That'd put your conception date about . . . ." He paused to calculate, and glanced across the room at a calendar. "That weekend in New York."

Hope smiled as she relished the memory. "Let's see. Corner suite on the thirty-fifth floor with a great view of the city lights. Dinner in a fancy restaurant."

"The announcement of your Murrow Award," Mark added.

Hope giggled.

Mark leaned over and gave her a long, tender kiss. "Now go call your mother," he said. "I'm sure you are dying to share our good news."

Hope made a beeline for the phone and punched in her mom's number. Susan Morris answered on the second ring. They exchanged familiar pleasantries.

"I have some wonderful news," Hope declared excitedly.

"You're pregnant," Susan answered.

Hope couldn't believe her ears. "How did you know?"

"Oh, call it an educated guess. The tone of your voice. Maternal intuition," Susan responded. "I'm happy for you. When are you due?"

"February 4."

"H'mmm . . ."

"OK, Mom. When's your guess?"

"February 2. That lines up exactly with your weekend in New York."

Hope ran the calculation in her head. "That's pretty close."

"Are you guys coming over this weekend for first Sunday? I'd really like it if you could," Susan appealed.

"Well, now that I'm not traveling anymore, I don't have any reason not to," Hope answered. "Sure. We'll be there. Right after church."

～

"How did your mom figure it out?" Mark wondered aloud as Hope slid into bed and pulled up the covers.

"That's a good question," she answered. "You know what puzzles me?"

"What?"

"Her confidence. She was so definite about the date. How could she be so confident?"

Mark reached over and turned off the bedside reading lamp, then snuggled up to his wife. "M-m-m. You feel good."

"So do you," she said softly as they slid even closer together.

"I love you, Mommy," Mark said between kisses and caresses.

"I love you, too, Daddy," she whispered.

Mark slid down under the covers, placed one hand on Hope's abdomen, and moved his head close. "Hello in there. This is your daddy. I can't wait until you're born and I get to hold you."

~

"Do you realize this is the first time we've been able to get together—all of us—for a first Sunday dinner since right after your dad died?" Susan Morris commented to her daughters and daughter-in-law as they finished getting the meal on the table. She looked at Hope. "First Carla had the baby and he started having ear infections. Then David had to start traveling for his work. Then you had to be away on some stories. I think Allison and Jeff are the only ones who've made it every month."

"Amazing how busy we've all become," Carla answered from the dining room, where she was placing a pitcher of fruit punch on the table. "Looks like we're set. Do you want me to call the guys?"

Susan surveyed the place settings, all the food, and the two high chairs. "Don't we need a booster seat for Daniel?"

"How did I miss that!" Carla laughed. "Three kids, and you'd think I'd remember to bring in the booster seat," she proclaimed as she found her purse on a corner of the kitchen counter, extracted the car keys, and headed outside to retrieve the seat.

Susan smiled and turned to Hope. "You know, when you kids were little, both you and David were potty-trained before Allison was born. I can't imagine how she keeps her sanity with three so close together in age and all of them in diapers."

"Well, Mom, I think it's like you used to say: God gives mothers an extra measure of grace and tolerance," Hope replied. "Listen to us! Here we are about to eat Sunday dinner, and we're talking about poopy diapers! I'm glad the guys are in the living room, because this is something only mothers can talk about without gagging."

Minutes later the family was gathering around the table. From her position at the head of the table Susan directed people to specific chairs. It was the place from which her late husband had presided over previous first Sunday dinners—a family meal on the first Sunday of every month. Hope wanted to say something, to tell her mother to move over, that she was taking Daddy's chair. But no, her father had been dead for seven months now. However, it still seemed odd as she reached out to hold hands for the blessing that it was her mother's hand she grasped, not her father's. Susan asked David to pronounce the blessing over the meal, which he did with a voice that reminded Hope even more of her father. Right now she missed him so deeply. She fought a tear as her brother prayed.

"What's wrong, dear?" Susan asked softly as they sat down.

Hope let out a long breath as she composed herself. "I was just missing Daddy. David sounds so much like him."

Susan smiled sympathetically and reached for the first serving dish being handed her direction.

"How can you be so happy? I mean, it's first Sunday. He hasn't been dead a year and . . . *and you're sitting in his chair?*" Hope accused, her voice starting to break on the last words.

"Dear, I know this is where he used to sit, but it's not his chair anymore. Life moves on. Plus, he's closer than you think," Susan answered as she took a biscuit and passed the bowl along. Her eyes darted from the bowl to somewhere past Hope as if they were focused on someone beyond those seated at the table. Hope instinctively looked over her shoulder to see if someone was standing behind her. All she saw was the wallpaper and the large painting of a nature scene that had been hanging in that position for years.

"What do you mean?" Hope asked as she took the next serving dish from Mark. "You miss Daddy, don't you, Mom?"

"Oh, I miss him. But I'm not sad anymore." Susan smiled serenely. Once again she looked past Hope and smiled as she accepted the next serving dish.

Again Hope looked around, but saw only the wall and picture.

"But . . . how could that be? How can you feel that way?" David asked from across the table.

"I'll have to tell you sometime. Just not now," Susan answered as she eyed a just-emptied serving dish. "Did I fix enough chicken for everyone?" Her eyes surveyed everyone's affirmatives before she returned to the chair between Hope and Mark, that serene smile returning to her face.

Hope's eyes darted to the other faces around the table. David and Carla were paying attention to their second child, who was seated in a high chair behind them. Allison was digging her fork into the green bean casserole while Jeff was distracted by a nephew's noisemaking. Was her imagination deceiving her? Was there a strange breeze in the room? Not unless the air-conditioning had just come on. There was a coolness, a motion, in the air right behind her. But the nearest vent was in the floor at the far end of the room. *It's possible. After all, I am pregnant and more sensitive to things.*

"What was going on in there?" Hope and Mark asked each other at the same time as they walked to the car.

Mark pulled his door closed and reached for his seat belt. "I'm not sure, but it was strange," he said with emphasis on the word "strange." He started the engine and shifted into reverse.

Hope held up her hand for him to stop and pointed toward the back seat, where Jennifer was still buckling up. "You know, I think it was good planning on your part that you bought an SUV with a built-in child safety seat mounting and monitoring system," she said, changing the topic. The parents kept the conversation light until they got home. When Jennifer asked permission to go play with a friend next door, both parents immediately approved.

"What happened at Mom's house?" Hope asked again the instant Jennifer jumped out of the car and raced across the front yard to the neighbor's house.

Mark shivered. "I don't know, but it made the hairs on the back of my neck stand up. I mean, it was like somebody walked behind me—only nobody was there."

"I had exactly the same feeling. Whatever it was, it was real. I wasn't imagining it," Hope declared. "Question is, how am I going to ask Mom about it? I mean, we don't even know what's going on."

Mark delayed answering as they walked into the house. Hope put a dish of leftovers in the refrigerator before joining him on the couch.

"I can't explain it, but . . . I know what I felt, and it was real. But I'm not sure what it was that I felt," Mark stated.

"Here we go, starting to sound like the Supreme Court defining pornography: we can't tell you what it is, but we know it when we see it—or feel it." Hope's attempt to be funny failed. They sat in silence for several breaths.

"I'm concerned," she finally admitted.

"Me too. Now, if I only knew what I was getting concerned about." Mark scrunched his face to the right and almost closed his right eye in the odd expression he sometimes used when puzzling over something. "Well, the only thing certain is that we're not getting any answers by sitting here looking at each other and saying 'I don't know what's going on.'"

"OK, let's start at the beginning and focus on what we do know," Hope said. "I know that I got upset because Mom was sitting in Daddy's place, and I'm not used to him not being there for first Sunday dinners." She began choking on her words. "Then she had this really peaceful look on her face, and she looked right past me. I know she looked past me because her eyes were focused on something behind us."

"What do you think she was looking at?" Mark wondered.

"I have no idea. That's what's so strange," Hope said. "The other thing that bothers me is that it seems as though she's worked through her grief awfully fast. She's not talking about crying or being sad anymore. I mean, she was sad at first, but then it was as if somebody had given her a happy pill. She's gotten involved in a seniors group, and she's going places and doing things, and she's turned into this independent woman that she never was before."

"But she has a good retirement income, and except for keeping up the house and playing with her grandkids, what else does she have to do? Give the woman a break, Hope! Her husband's dead, and her children are grown. Let her live her life and have some fun doing new things. Don't go holding that against her."

"OK. You're right." Hope got up from the couch. "But that doesn't explain that, well, creepy feeling you and I both got a couple hours ago when we started to eat lunch. I think I need to call Mom and ask her what's going on."

Mark fixed her with a look that stopped her in her tracks. "And what if she says that nothing happened, that it was all in our imaginations? What are you going to say then?"

Hope studied her husband's expression for a moment. "You're right." She made her way back to the sofa and sat down next to him. "But something strange happened. Something really, really odd. I'll wait a while, but I'm definitely going to ask her about it. It's just a matter of when."

CHAPTER SIX

The first rays of dawn brightened the eastern sky as Amir Al-Hamzi walked from his Venice Beach apartment toward the Gates of Heaven Mosque for the first prayer service of the day. The cool, salt-tinted morning air reached deeply into his lungs and invigorated his pace. Truly, this energizing must be the reason Allah commanded the faithful to prayers at this hour! It focused the mind on spiritual issues at the start of the day. *That is good. Very good,* he thought.

Arriving at the mosque, Amir went through the rituals of taking off his shoes and washing his face and hands before stepping onto the thick carpets lining the main worship hall. Being Friday, the Muslim day of worship, far more of the faithful were in attendance than could be found on other days. *"Allahu Akbar"* ("God is great"), they greeted each other, even if it was the first time they had met.

Many faces in the crowd were familiar from attending these morning gatherings. He scanned the faces and from time to time greeted someone he knew. Perhaps it was a regular customer at the pizzeria or an employee from the Pakistani grocery where Amir went to send money to his parents. Yet the face he sought was the one he was least likely to recognize, because the man spoke to him only during prayers, when all faces were looking toward Mecca. How the man was able to slip onto the prayer mat next to him and then slip away unrecognized amazed him. Would there be a new message today? New instructions? He would have to wait and see.

Amir joined a line of the faithful on the men's side of the mosque and joined in the prayers. This morning he listened to the sermon by the imam,

who exhorted the faithful to continue supporting efforts aimed at convert-
ing the world to the true path. After final prayers Amir rose from his place
on the thick carpet and made his way to the entrance, where he stepped
into his shoes and back into the sunlight.

Perhaps his instructions would come next Friday. After all, wasn't all
of life *inshallah*—as God wills?

～

Walter Keller leaned against a tree across the street from the mosque.
"Sphinx is moving your direction," he reported over the radio to his partner, who sat in a car a block down the street. "Sphinx" was a reference to
Amir Al-Hamzi's Egyptian origins and the radio code name they'd given
him.

"Roger that," Jimmy Henderson answered. "He's not making you
seasick, is he?"

"Not yet," Keller answered as he maintained visual contact from across
the street.

～

The humidity of the steamy July morning hit Mark as he walked down
the driveway and retrieved the Sunday newspaper. It was one of those days
when, unless you wanted to be bathed in sweat standing still, the only
place to be was inside enjoying the air-conditioning. Back inside, Hope
was still wearing a bathrobe, wondering aloud which sundress to wear to
church while she still had the figure to fit into them. Jennifer was bouncing around, already dressed and ready to go. In just a little more than an
hour all three and one fourth of them, as Mark had become fond of describing his family, would be picture-perfect and on their way to church.

"Congratulations, Dad," a friend greeted Mark inside the church door,
vigorously pumping his hand. "We were beginning to think Jennifer was
going to be an only child."

"I was too," Mark agreed.

Hope saw Jennifer off to her Sunday school class before going to her
women-only study group. Mark chatted with friends before finding the
path toward his men's class. After attending their respective classes, Mark
and Hope met in the church foyer before entering the sanctuary.

"Let's sit over here." Hope guided Mark toward a pew on the right
side near the front of the large sanctuary. Heading there was habit for her.
After all, it was where she had sat each Sunday with her mother, brother,

and sister while growing up. Of course, those were the days when their father was still alive and pastor of the Second Avenue Baptist Church. This Sunday it was just the two of them, because Jennifer was with friends at children's church over in the youth building, and other faces, some familiar and some new, filled the rest of the pew. Soon the pastor and elders filed onto the platform. The minister of music stepped to the podium and invited the congregation to open their hymnals and sing along or follow the words on the large video screens above the choir loft. As they sang the first hymn, Hope glanced around the sanctuary, searching for her mother. Susan was nowhere to be found. But Hope did spot her brother, David, with his wife, Carla.

Hope scanned the faces on the platform. One of them looked oddly familiar, as though she knew who it was but couldn't recall the name. She elbowed Mark and hissed a question in his ear.

Mark looked at his bulletin and pointed to a name in the worship order. Robert Ingersoll! He would be leading the congregation in prayer.

Hope stared at Ingersoll for a moment. Yes, this was the man! Just then she began feeling the first pangs of conflict over the RMI story. On the one hand, she was a reporter doing her job. It didn't matter who the person at the center of her story was. If he'd done something wrong, it was wrong. Who he was didn't matter. On the other hand, this was a church member, and members were supposed to be the spiritual body of Christ. So reporting about him could seem like an act of disloyalty, even betrayal. More than that, he was an elder in her church, a man respected for his spiritual leadership. How could such a respected, spiritual man permit something so illegal as his company was suspected of doing? *Perhaps I should call Peter and ask him to assign someone else to the story,* she thought. Then the competitive side of her argued that she really didn't know Ingersoll. *The church connection might even give me access to inside information that could give me an advantage when the story breaks.*

"What'd you think of the sermon?" Mark asked on their way to the youth building to collect their daughter.

"Uh, what did you say?"

"The sermon. What did you think about the point he made about the need for Christians to be active in social issues? You know, things like protesting abortion and kids being given condoms at school."

"Forgive me, dear, but I wasn't paying much attention," Hope replied.

"I can tell. What's on your mind?" Mark asked.

Hope shook her head. "Something to do with work. I don't want to talk about it right now."

"It's that Ingersoll guy, the one who was on the platform, wasn't it?"

Hope smiled. "You know me too well. You seen Jennifer yet?" A moment later their daughter came down the hall laughing and chatting with friends. "Have you seen Grandma this morning?" Hope asked.

"She was one of our teachers. You know, she was in this skit in which she had to play a teenager, and she was so funny." Jennifer giggled as she imitated something from the skit.

~

That evening Hope sat down on the couch with the latest issue of *National Geographic* and turned a few pages before staring off into space.

"Something on your mind?" Mark asked gently.

She nodded. "I'm concerned about Mom."

"Me too. But once again, I'm not sure what I'm concerned about," Mark said.

"Well, what do we know?" Hope asked as she focused on a point in the distance. "For starters, I'm missing Daddy right now."

Mark reached over and gently caressed the top of her bare foot. "What got you started feeling this way?" he asked softly.

Hope inhaled raggedly. "Oh, I was just thinking about last Sunday at dinner. You know, seeing Mom sitting in Daddy's place. That hit me really hard and reminded me that he really is gone." She began choking on her words. "Then there was that thing we both observed. You know, when she was looking past us."

Mark smiled and gave her foot a squeeze. "I guess it's natural to feel the way you do. If it were my mother, I'd be concerned too."

"I just wish I knew what was going on," Hope said thoughtfully.

"Me too."

They shared a tender gaze before going back to their separate readings.

~

Diamond Airways Flight 1284 floated down the glide slope as steadily as if it were glued to the invisible radio beam used to guide planes onto the runway in times of poor visibility. The multicolored Boeing 757 settled gently onto the runway with little more than a bump and no hint of a bounce, something rare even among the most skilled pilots. The thrust reversers did their job, and in moments the plane was turning off the runway and heading for its assigned gate at the Dallas-Fort Worth International Airport.

"Not bad. Not bad at all," Copilot Alan Markland observed as they cleared the runway.

"I don't like it, but I have to admit that I'm impressed," Captain Sonja Cabrini responded. "How many years have we had the capability of letting the computer land the plane and we haven't trusted it enough to do it?"

"How many years have we been unwilling to sacrifice our pride and admit that the computers can do the job as well as we can?" Alan answered. "I've used it lots of times when I've been really tired. They actually encourage us to use it to improve safety."

Sonja was silent as they lined up on the gate and moved slowly forward until the ground crew member crossed his orange signal batons, the sign for them to stop. She pressed and locked the brakes. "Shutting down one and two," she announced as she flipped the engine-shutdown levers located below and behind the throttles. The engine gauges in the center of the control console began spooling downward as the fires in the turbines went out.

Alan reached here and there, checking settings and flipping switches as he did his part of the shutdown routine. "You hear the story about the engineers designing the Triple Seven's control systems?" he asked. "Triple Seven" was a reference to the Boeing 777, an airliner considerably bigger than the 757 but also powered by only two engines.

"What's that?" Sonja asked as she pulled out her logbook to record the completed flight.

"Well, the engineers decided there would be three generations of computerized flight control systems. First there's today, when we have a pilot and a copilot and we're helped by the computer. In the next generation the copilot is replaced by a dog. The pilot's job is to make announcements to the passengers while the computer flies the plane, and be ready to take over in case the computer fails. The dog's job is to bark now and then to keep the pilot awake. In the third generation the pilot's job is to monitor the computer while it does everything, and make announcements. The dog's job is to bark ferociously if the pilot ever attempts to touch the controls."

Sonja laughed as she completed her logbook entry. "You want to do the walk-around while they refuel the plane?"

Alan unfastened his harness, slid his seat back, and lifted himself into an erect posture. He unlocked the cockpit door and looked back through the passenger compartment, where a uniformed cleaning crew was already at work. "Sure. It'll give me a chance to loosen up and get ready for the next landing."

"And while you're out, why don't you go to the gift shop and buy yourself a dog collar?" Sonja suggested with a teasing smile.

CHAPTER SEVEN

E verybody ready to travel?" Art Whitfield asked as he looked at the six other faces seated around the table. He opened the large manila envelopes in front of him and began reading off the names written on the smaller envelopes inside.

"Terri Pelosi." He slid an envelope down the table toward her.

"Mark Lancaster." This one got tossed the short distance across the middle of the table, plopping in front of its addressee.

"James Wilson."

"Carl Booth."

"Audrey Phillips."

"Shane Roth."

"We leave Monday morning at 10:25 on Diamond Airways Flight 886 to Dallas-Fort Worth, then on to Los Angeles. You'll need to be at the airport by 9:00 a.m. to have enough time to clear security. We'll be back on Friday. These are your travel schedules, tickets, and rental car and motel reservations."

The faces around the table registered only slight surprise. After all, this was the trip they'd been told to expect, yet they had not known exactly when it would happen.

"DDS is expecting us for a plant tour and meetings starting at 8:00 a.m. Pacific time on Tuesday and running through Wednesday, possibly into Thursday. If we don't work on Thursday, I guess we can all go and enjoy Disneyland, or something fun out there," Art said. "Well, that's all I have for today. Go get back to work, and start packing for the trip."

~

"You don't sound very excited," Hope observed as she slipped into bed beside Mark and slid close enough to kiss and cuddle. "Traveling isn't so bad. You'll be home before you know it. And coming home is the best part— trust me," she said with a wink. She propped herself up on her pillow and placed both hands on her abdomen. "Want to say hello to Little Bit?"

"So it's 'Little Bit' this week, is it?" Mark leaned closer. "Remember all the little pet names we went through with Jennifer before we started picking real names? Let's see, there was Wyatt Earp for all the morning sickness you had. Then there was Flipper when she started moving around and tickling your insides."

Hope giggled as Mark tickled her abdomen. "And Squirt when she started sitting on my bladder and making me go to the bathroom all the time."

"Looking at you now, I wouldn't believe you're pregnant," he said. "You look . . . beautiful."

Hope swatted Mark's shoulder. "What are you trying to say? That I don't look beautiful when I'm further along in my pregnancies, when I'm huge? Huh?"

Mark knew he was trapped. "You always look beautiful. You . . . uh . . . just don't look pregnant right now."

She let out a frustrated sigh. "I'm at the stage when I've got the morning sickness, but nobody believes I'm pregnant without a urine test. Next comes the stage when people I haven't seen in a year come up and say things like 'Been putting on a few pounds lately?' I mean, right now I can't win for losing!"

"Then comes the third trimester, when you can't wait for it to be over," Mark added.

After several more minutes of cuddling, Hope plumped down on her second pillow, settled back, and picked up her Bible to begin reading. From inside the front cover she extracted a small booklet, checked the listing for that day, and thumbed to the book of Psalms.

"Whatcha reading tonight?" Mark asked as he began scanning the latest *National Geographic*.

"Last five psalms."

"Sounds like a lot," he observed.

"Well, it's not as big as when my assignment included Psalm 119. That one's 176 verses long." Silence filled the room as each set about their reading and Hope closed her eyes for a short prayer. *Lord, show me something I really need to know,* she prayed silently.

Mark was into a *National Geographic* article about forest life in a remote spot on the globe when he felt his wife move and inhale sharply, as if surprised. "You OK?" he asked, pulling his eyes off the picture.

"I'm OK."

"Well, something got your attention. What was it?"

Hope paused a moment before answering. "Well, I asked God to show me something that I needed to know, and I think He just answered my prayer. Only I don't know what to make of it. I mean, it's like He's telling me these verses are important. It's just, well, I don't know why."

"Well, what do they say?" Mark turned a page in his magazine and glanced in her direction.

"Listen to this. Psalm 146, verses 3 and 4: 'Put not your trust in princes, nor in the son of man, in whom there is no help. His breath goeth forth, he returneth to his earth; in that very day his thoughts perish.' Why would those verses be so important?"

Mark thought for a moment before his eyes wandered back to a colorful photo layout. "I have no idea."

"Guess I'll have to wait and see," Hope replied as she went back to her reading.

For the crew of the U.S. Navy P-3 Orion sea surveillance aircraft, it was just another boring mission—up to 12 hours filled with nothing but monitoring their surveillance systems and trying to keep from getting airsick when they flew through storms instead of around them. Commercial airliners would route around these squalls, but the Navy ordered them to check underneath in case an enemy vessel or submarine was hiding there. Not that there were any "enemy" vessels. It had been at least a dozen years since a Russian submarine had patrolled the American West Coast. Still, National Command Authority, namely the president and the joint chiefs of staff, justified these missions as a means of preventing terrorism. If they monitored the approach of ships to the West Coast of the United States, perhaps they could prevent one of them from dropping off terrorists undetected.

Three hours had passed since Sweeper 5 had lifted off from Point Mugu Naval Air Station near Ventura, California. The first leg of their course had taken them on a northwesterly zigzag path 300 miles out to sea, checking the identity of ships approaching ports from points across the

Pacific Ocean. Some commercial vessels were identified by their radar signatures, and by the fact that they had been keeping a steady speed and course since the last time they were checked. Most small vessels were dismissed as pleasure craft, fishing vessels, or the service boats tending the offshore oil rigs found in certain areas along the coast.

The list of ships in this part of the Pacific Ocean was long. Large fans of ships stacked high with cargo containers were headed for ports around San Francisco Bay, Los Angeles, and San Diego. Huge supertankers from such places as Valdez, Alaska, made their way slowly toward refineries in Santa Barbara and Huntington Beach. Electronics and textiles of all kinds came from Korea, Japan, and Malaysia. Smaller freighters from Central America delivered shiploads of bananas, concrete for construction, and phosphates for fertilizers.

Petty Officer Kevin DiPlacio grabbed the back of his seat to keep the turbulence from sending him head over heels. When the plane tipped the opposite direction, he moved around the seat and planted himself in it. In a practiced motion he pulled the shoulder harness over his flight suit and fastened the ends into the buckle that held his lap belt and center strap together. After pulling the straps tight, he reached down and tugged on a control handle that moved his seat closer to the large radar screen and smaller computer console he was responsible for monitoring.

Across the aisle crew member Ramon Santoro watched DiPlacio's return to his duty station. "You know, on the space station they have leg restraints to hold you down while you do your business," he said.

"Yeah, but they're not getting bounced around like we are," DiPlacio answered as the plane took another dip and jump. "I think I'll wait a while for lunch." He switched his radar from surface surveillance mode into weather mode and waited until it made a full sweep of the sky. "Looks like we're headed for some smoother weather here in a few minutes, so I won't have to wait long after all."

Santoro laughed. "You mean you forgot our orders? We're not supposed to fly in the clear air."

"No, the reason we fly in clouds is so you can't take a nap," DiPlacio shot back.

Santoro operated the powerful optical tracking system mounted in a glass bubble on the bottom side of the plane. Borrowed from an F–14 fighter, it could take close-up pictures of a ship 50 miles away and make it look as if it were docked at the next pier. Such photos could be immediately transmitted via satellite to commanders ashore.

Two other crew members, left without much work, were the weapons systems and sonar operators, each with work stations toward the back of the plane. The weapons systems officer, or "whizzo," made sure the trio of Harpoon anti-ship missiles under each wing and the anti-submarine torpedoes in the launching bay in the plane's belly were functional while still being kept in "safe" mode. With all the ships in the area classified as "friendly," the probability of him having to launch any weapons was remote.

The sonar operator had only slightly more work to do because he also operated the magnetic anomaly detector, or MAD. The MAD, which looked like Pinnochio's nose sticking out from behind the tail, was good at finding submarines, but in these waters they all wore the Stars and Stripes and were headed to or from patrol zones in distant places.

Sweeper 5's route would continue as far north as the California-Oregon border before turning back south. Approaching the Mexican border, they would stay over international waters while flying as far south as Cabo San Lucas at the southern tip of the Baja Peninsula.

Right now they were precisely 97 miles due west of the city of Monterey, California, and still heading northwest. With the turbulence easing, DiPlacio decided that maybe it was time to pull a dinner tray from the refrigerator rack and slide it into the microwave oven. The thought made his stomach rumble as he reached for the release lever on his seat harness. Just then he felt the plane bank to the right. A glance at his radar screen showed that they were again headed for some rough weather. Should he take a chance and try eating before they got there? Or should he wait? His stomach rumbled again, and he headed for the galley located just behind the cockpit.

Approaching the cockpit, DiPlacio decided to take a look through the forward windows and exchange a few words with the pilots. "What's up?" he asked as he leaned through the open cockpit door.

"Command just gave us a new target to check out. Bearing 245, range about 140 miles. They want us to see if we can get some pictures for them," the pilot answered.

DiPlacio did some quick calculations. At their speed that would give him exactly 22 minutes to cook and eat his lunch. It'd be a little rushed, but he could do it. On the same token, maybe he'd better eat a little faster because their new heading and speed would put them right under another squall line.

His timing was almost perfect. DiPlacio was just putting the last spoonful of pudding into his mouth when the plane lurched and jumped. He stuffed the trash into a tethered receptacle beside the galley and made his way back to his radar station, arriving just as the pilots pushed the nose over into a rapid descent.

"Nice landing," Santoro observed as DiPlacio plopped onto his seat and struggled to stay in it through the next bumps until he could get his harness fastened. Minutes later they broke through the clouds into the 500-foot gap between sea and clouds. Surprisingly, there was no rain. In seconds he had the target ship identified on his radar screen.

"Photo, your target is at 2:00, range seven miles," DiPlacio reported to his crew member, who began toggling a joystick and watching the images on the screen in front of him. It took several seconds to find the ship. Pressing a button on the top of the joystick locked the imaging system onto the target and held it there as steadily as if it had been mounted on a tripod on dry land. Though the entire sequence was being recorded on videotape, from time to time he squeezed a trigger on the joystick to capture a freeze-frame.

The plane orbited the ship once before ascending again into the murk. DiPlacio leaned over to see what images had been captured. A moment later they were joined by the copilot, who grabbed handholds tightly to stay upright. "What've we got here?" the copilot asked.

It took the photo operator a couple minutes of searching the maritime database to find a match for the ship's profile. "Looks like a tramp freighter that came out of a shipyard in Jakarta, Indonesia, sometime between 1978 and 1990," Santoro declared. "Design's a lot like the old Liberty ships from World War II." He enlarged a picture of the ship's stern and zoomed in on the painted name. Several of the letters were obscured by rust. Next he scanned a list of ship names listed in an international registry until he found a match. Typing the name on a computer keyboard brought up a photo that had been taken through the periscope of a submarine on patrol several years before.

"Bingo!" the photo operator exclaimed. "The *Sumatra Prince*. Home port of Jakarta, Indonesia."

"Notice anything odd about that ship?" the copilot asked.

"Well, it's 325 feet, which is a bit shorter than most transpacific ships," Santoro answered.

The copilot pointed at the cranes. "It's a general cargo carrier. Instead of loading it with containers, they lift pallets and nets with the onboard cranes. We mostly see ships like that on runs up and down the coast in Latin America, not on transpacific runs."

"Looks like it's riding a bit high in the water, too," DiPlacio added.

"Well, look at this, will you?" the photo operator exclaimed. All heads turned toward his computer screen. "The database says it can go only 2,500 miles without refueling. Indonesia's what? Five thousand miles away?"

"At least," the copilot answered.

"It doesn't have the range for a transpacific run, but there are no reports of its having stopped anywhere en route for fuel," Santoro replied.

"Maybe that's why it's riding so high in the water. Maybe they filled their cargo holds with fuel to make the trip," the copilot speculated.

"So, what do you figure they're carrying?" Santoro wondered aloud before resuming reading the information on his computer screen. "They're not registered in the customs database as heading for any port in the United States, so maybe they're headed to Mexico or Central America."

"That doesn't make sense. That'd put them, oh, at least 500 miles off course. Nobody's got a navigator that dumb," the copilot observed. He looked at DiPlacio. "Keep a close track on him while we're still in radar range. Get a bearing and speed on 'em, and report it to command. They may have some intel on the *Sumatra Prince* that we don't have."

"Aye, aye, sir," DiPlacio responded as he fastened himself back in his seat. "Designate the *Sumatra Prince* as Target Alpha." A few keystrokes later the *Sumatra Prince* was an emblem on the radar screen as they moved away to survey other targets. As for the ship's heading and speed, the computer monitoring the radar system would compute those items and uplink the data over the satellite.

"You and the missus got any plans for your days off?" Santoro asked.

"Well, Friday we're going grocery shopping. Or should I say diaper shopping?" DiPlacio answered. "It's amazing how many diapers one kid can go through in a week. I mean, diapers are the largest single item in our grocery cart. Hey, we gotta get you married so you can discover the wonders and expenses of parenting."

"No way, man. I'm having too much fun being single," Santoro grinned.

⁓

The message that was slipped to Amir Al-Hamzi at the Gates of Heaven Mosque during the Friday morning prayer service was clear and cryptic at the same time. It was a set of GPS coordinates and instructions to bring food for himself and two others for two days. The rendezvous time would be between 10:00 p.m. Sunday night and 3:00 a.m. Monday morning. He was simply directed to "go there and wait."

Saturday afternoon he took the assistant manager aside and told him that he would be going away for two days. He was entrusting the pizzeria to this young man who somehow had never felt motivated to go to college but who had an intuitive sense for what customers enjoyed. "Do a good job, and you might be up for a raise," Amir instructed.

The clock seemed to move in slow motion all evening as Amir wondered what awaited him. It took effort to contain his growing anticipation and act normal. Walking home in the evening air usually calmed him, but tonight the summer Santa Ana winds were blowing off the desert. Instead of inhaling salt-tinged moist air deep into his lungs, he felt his sinuses being dried by a humidity measured in single digits and dust that reduced visibility to less than a mile.

He tried to sleep late Sunday morning, but was awake as the first rays of sunlight poked through the blinds on his bedroom window. He packed a change of clothes and some toiletries into a gym bag that he left by the front door. Then he went to buy groceries.

Leaving the supermarket, he flagged a cab and settled in for the ride home. Upon reaching his house, Amir told the driver to wait while he went inside to retrieve the gym bag he'd packed that morning.

For a moment he lingered in the doorway, wondering if he would ever see this little apartment again. It was comfortable. It was nothing fancy, but it was still home. The reason for his insecurity was that he had no idea why he was being sent more than 30 miles farther out to sea than he had ever taken his boat before. What could possibly be waiting for him out there?

For a man who lived simply and managed his business finances with great care, this boat was the one great extravagance in his life. Some 18 months before, he'd gone deep-sea fishing with a friend for the first time in his life and had enjoyed it so much that he had begun giving seaworthy pleasure boats a closer look. What he had found was a bewildering universe of toys and comforts, performance and style. The boat he had finally picked was the envy of his neighbors in the marina. At 35 feet in length, the *Top Hat's* hull hid twin diesel engines under the fishing deck in the stern. If pushed to full power, they could drive the boat across calm seas at more than 30 knots. A small live well for keeping live bait was built into the stern wall. Two larger live wells for keeping catch alive were built into the deck. Just forward of the open fishing deck was a sheltered weather deck from which he could steer. Down a short stairway on the left was a bathroom of barely adequate size that included a shower. To the right was a small galley with a folding table with two bench seats. Past them were six bunks and storage spaces.

Above was a sleek upper deck and a raised fair-weather bridge from which the boat could be steered. Towering over everything was a mast that held a pair of radio antennas and a stick-shaped rotating radar antenna.

Amir pushed the nagging thoughts from his mind and jogged back to the waiting cab. During his ride to the marina he again thought about his boat. But all anxiety disappeared as he thought about his boat, his pride and joy, being used for the glory of Allah!

It took two trips to deliver the grocery bags from the taxi to the boat. Looking at his watch, Amir realized he had plenty of time to make his destination. He forced himself to take his time stowing the groceries in the refrigerator and cupboards. Going to the main deck, he tuned the marine band radio to the frequency for the Coast Guard's continuous weather broadcast. Visibility was down to two miles, with haze and an offshore wind at 16 knots. Waves were running at two feet or less past Catalina Island. *Could make steering crosswind a bit tricky, but it'll be a good day,* he thought. *No, a great day. I'm on Allah's business.*

All it took was a touch of the "start" button before each diesel engine rumbled to life. They were felt as much as heard. Amir cast off the bow and stern mooring lines and positioned himself in the main deck cockpit. A glance around showed no one else in the channel between the boat slips, so he moved both throttles in reverse just long enough to get the boat moving. Once clear of the slip, he moved the left throttle into forward and the right into reverse to bring the boat hard around, then both into forward to ease away from the slips at no-wake speed. Several minutes later he pulled up to the fueling dock to top off his tanks. Minutes after that, he was idling past a marina populated by yachts so expensive that they made his boat look like a rowboat.

Even at this no-wake speed the throbbing of the diesel engines made Amir's heart beat faster. The marks on the buoys he passed told him he was nearing the mouth of the channel and about to enter the open ocean. Still, the haze made it hard to tell when he crossed that line. A glance at the radar screen showed when he was in the open water.

Normally these waters would be packed with pleasure craft. But today the combination of wind and haze was keeping most boaters at home. Perhaps that would also prevent undesired eyes from seeing whatever he was being sent to do in these coming hours.

Amir pulled from his pocket the note that he had been given at the mosque. He turned on the navigation computer and let it begin tracking the navigation satellites before entering the GPS coordinates for his destination. A moment later the picture on the screen changed to a map showing where he was headed, the best route there—which happened to be a straight line—and how long it would take him to reach his destination at his current speed. Assisted by the wind, he would arrive at his destination somewhere around dark.

Behave normally. Do nothing to attract attention to yourself, he told himself. Amir went to the fishing deck and opened one of the gear lockers along a side bulkhead. From it he extracted a pair of fishing poles and rigged them with large-fish lures. He mounted the poles in holders on either side of the boat so the lines would trail behind without tangling. Next he turned the boat so his stern was directly against the wind and moved the throttles to idle. That way he could use the wind to move his boat along fast enough to look as if he were fishing but too fast to catch anything unless he happened to snag it. The whole purpose was to look as if he were fishing while actually making his way to the rendezvous point. He pulled a cold soda from the refrigerator, seated himself in the fishing chair mounted on a pedestal in the center of the fishing deck, and tried to relax.

It seemed the sun would never set. From time to time Amir checked the navigation screen. The wind was moving him nearer the 12-mile line considered to be the official territorial border of the United States, yet he was still a considerable distance south of the rendezvous point. Both his current position and the rendezvous point were well within the 200-mile "protective and economic zone" the U.S. government enforced.

His stomach reminded him of how much time had elapsed since he had eaten lunch. Amir took a look at the radar screen and, seeing that no other boats were in close proximity, slipped below deck and popped a frozen dinner into the microwave oven. Seven minutes later he was dining on chicken with penne pasta and mixed vegetables as he watched the bobbing of the boat tip the juice in his bottle this way and that.

Darkness finally settled through the haze, and Amir reeled in his lines. With the exception of two boats servicing offshore oil rigs, no other boats were within five miles. He typed several commands into the navigation controller, and the boat turned northwestward toward the rendezvous point. The throttles moved forward without his touch, and the rumble of the engines increased enough to move a leisurely eight knots. He had only 34 miles to go and would make it in plenty of time.

Just before 10:00 p.m. he climbed the ladder again to check his position. He was within one mile of the target coordinates. As he reached the exact coordinates, the computer eased the throttles back to neutral and turned the boat into the wind.

Surrounded by darkness, unable to see any stars and rocked by the waves, Amir soon surrendered to his body's desire for sleep and stretched out on a bunk.

$\sim$

A voice reached through into Amir Al-Hamzi's subconscious and tried to rouse him from his slumber. It called once, then twice. What finally got his attention was realizing that the voice was calling to him in Arabic. The words included a key phrase, a question asking if he was loyal to Allah and willing to serve Him. Then a swath of light enveloped the boat and pierced the darkness of the cabin where he lay sleeping. Quickly he pulled himself awake and onto his feet. In a few steps he was on the afterdeck, blinking into the glare of a spotlight from somewhere above. From behind the light he could hear voices, mechanical sounds, and water splashing against something very close. He shouted back in Arabic that he was a loyal servant of Allah and that he was there because he was obeying orders. *Inshallah.*

The light shining in his eyes was switched off, and two others from either side of his boat came on, illuminating the area in a way that allowed him to see. The side of a rust-streaked freighter stood a few yards away and several stories above him. A docking ladder hanging over the side was lowered to a few feet above the water as a voice told him to back his boat under the ladder but to be careful that the vessels did not collide. The swells had risen to three feet, so it would be tricky. It was something he had never done before, so it took several minutes to bring his boat into position beside the freighter.

Two men waited at the bottom of the ladder. As the stern of Amir's boat slid under them, they took turns jumping onto the deck. Each landed hard, one bouncing off the fishing chair and landing on his side, the other catching the seat and landing on his feet.

Once on their feet, the men introduced themselves. One was Abdullah something-or-other. The second was Muhammad. Just Muhammad. Abdullah began signaling to someone up in the darkness, and a moment later a cargo net appeared above them. Muhammad grabbed the rope dangling from below it and guided the contents toward the deck, where duffel bags and long cylinders were quickly unloaded. Then the net disappeared upward into the darkness.

"Let's move away," Muhammad commanded in Arabic.

Amir was more than happy to widen the gap, and pushed the throttles forward.

"May Allah be praised!" the pair shouted to each other as they gained their sea legs.

Hearing the enthusiasm in their voices sent a shiver of excitement up and down Amir's spine. But what was their purpose for being here? He still had no idea. Whatever it was, they were all servants of Allah, so he would obey their instructions.

"Let's be on our way. We are many kilometers from where we need to be," Abdullah commanded.

Amir turned the bow to an easterly heading and advanced the throttles to speed them on their way.

"No, my friend," Muhammad cautioned. "Not so fast. You see, we must rest so we will be ready to carry out our task, and we must wait until the afternoon, when the weather is right."

"Then why are we here at this hour?" Amir asked.

"So the infidel's satellites and surveillance planes will have a hard time finding us. It is easier to hide under clouds and haze than an open and sunlit sky. Plus, we must not behave in any way that will draw attention. So go slowly," Muhammad cautioned. "Victory is the reward that comes to those who are patient."

CHAPTER EIGHT

Jennifer gave her father an extra-long hug. "I'm going to miss you, Daddy. I want you to come home early," she said at the airport curbside check-in station.

"I'm going to miss you, too. I promise I'll call tonight before your bedtime. OK?" Mark said before giving her another hug and kiss. "What are you going to do with the rest of your morning?"

"Well, Mommy's going to drop me off at the day-care center and go to work. Then Grandma's going to pick me up this afternoon since you won't be here, and I'll stay with her until Mom gets off work."

"I'll try to call you as soon as I get into the airport in LA," Mark promised as he embraced Hope. "I'm going to miss you."

"It feels strange. I mean, you leaving instead of me," Hope spoke softly into her husband's ear. "You sure you have everything?"

"Everything. Even my toothbrush." He smiled as they parted. They waved to each other; then Mark disappeared through the automatic double doors into the terminal with his suitcases in tow.

Hope eased her SUV into traffic and found her way toward the airport exit. Fifteen minutes later she was dropping Jennifer off at Growing Kids, the day-care center Jennifer attended one block away from her office. After a hug and a kiss, she turned her attention toward the workday ahead.

According to Peter Leventhal, today was the day the Securities and Exchange Commission would formally announce their investigation of RMI. Several days ago she'd taped a report that would give MBS viewers an overview of the story. Would anything new be revealed today that would require her to reedit the story? She would have to wait and see.

As was her routine upon arriving in the newsroom, Hope reviewed the story assignment board to try to get a feel for how busy the day would be. Next she reviewed e-mails and returned phone calls, sometimes simultaneously. Another reporter was working on a story about a double murder on the city's north side. It would be the lead story on the noon news. Probably at 6:00 p.m., too.

Her assignment arrived. A developer was using the city's eminent domain authority to force the sale of several lots in an older part of town that included a church attended by working-class people. The church members were protesting that the city was using its authority improperly and forcing them to give up their treasured house of worship. The developer argued that his plan to build an upscale shopping area would help the city achieve its objective of revitalizing a decaying area.

Hope worked the phones to make interview appointments. The first to go on camera would be the head of the city's community development department.

"Hey! Kyle!" she shouted across the newsroom to catch the ear of a photographer. "You're my shooter today. Can you be ready to go in 10 minutes?"

He nodded, and shouted something back that she couldn't quite understand. She sat back down and scribbled some questions in her notebook.

It was after they had parked outside the city hall that Hope thought about checking to see if anyone had left her a message on her cell phone. She reached into her purse, felt around among her essentials, and came up with the phone. Looking at it, she realized that it had been off since Saturday night. *That explains why it's been so quiet!* She pressed the power button and waited for it to log into her carrier's system. The envelope icon appeared in the upper corner of the screen, telling her she had messages waiting. She selected the "retrieve messages" command and used her shoulder to hold her phone against her ear while closing the car door and moving to carry Kyle's camera tripod.

There were three messages from her mother, each increasingly urgent and insisting that she call immediately.

"Hold on a minute, Kyle." She excused herself once they passed the security guard, and dialed her mother's number. "Hi, Mom. What's up?"

"Why haven't you been answering your phone?" The tone in her mother's voice startled her.

"What do you mean?"

"You haven't let Mark leave on his trip yet, have you?" she asked with a tone of great urgency. "I was trying to warn you."

"Warn me? About what?"

"Not to let Mark go on his trip. He's in danger. Great danger," Susan Morris nearly screamed. "I've been trying to warn you, but you haven't been answering your phone."

"Sorry; we turned off the ringer last night on our home phone and my cell phone because we didn't want to be disturbed. I guess I forgot to turn them back on," Hope answered defensively. "Mom! What's gotten into you? What are you talking about?" She felt a knot starting to grow in her stomach.

"You wouldn't believe me if I told you, but you've got to trust me. You've got to get in touch with him and tell him not to get on that plane to LA. His life depends on it!" The urgency in her mother's voice was bordering on panic, and the knot in Hope's stomach was starting to grow.

"Mom! Mom! You've got to calm down. What makes you think Mark's in danger?"

"You've just got to trust me on this one, OK?"

"No! I'm not going to just take your word for it unless you tell me why. I mean, did you have a dream or something?"

There was a moment of silence. "Not a dream. It was something else." Susan's voice was less hysterical but still very insistent.

"What else? You've got to tell me what else if you want me to believe you," Hope insisted. "Now, calm down and tell me how you got this information."

"Are you sitting down?"

"No. I'm nowhere near a seat, and I'm out on a story, so why don't you tell me quickly what's going on?" Hope demanded.

"It was your father who told me."

"What?" Hope fairly exploded with disbelief. "Mom! He's dead! How could he have told you?"

"Yes, dear; I know he's dead. But he's been coming back and visiting me, and last night he told me to warn you about Mark's flight to Los Angeles. If you want him to live, he must get off that plane! Your father told me something terrible is going to happen."

Hope felt her jaw hanging open, and for a moment she struggled both to know what to say and how to say it. "Uh . . . how long has this been going on?" she finally stammered.

"Oh, three months, I guess. Oh, Hope! He's told me the most wonderful things. Like your baby—he told me you were pregnant before you did. And it's a boy, and he will be born two days before the due date. Oh, and the things he's told me about heaven! I just can't wait to get there and be with him," Susan gushed.

"I can't believe my ears," Hope declared.

"Oh, and there's more. Remember the last time you were all at my house for first Sunday? He was standing right behind you and Mark."

A cold chill ran up and down Hope's spine as she remembered the moment when both she and Mark had whirled around to look and had found nothing behind them.

"Only I can see him," Susan continued. "Oh, it's such a wonderful gift God has given me! I'm not lonely anymore, and he gives me special messages from God that are so encouraging."

Hope struggled to close her open mouth. "So what exactly is the message about Mark?"

"That he's in great danger, and you've got to keep him from getting on that plane to Los Angeles."

Hope felt her stomach twisting into one giant stress knot. For a long moment she stared into space in stunned silence and wondered if she would be able to contact Mark.

"Something wrong?" Kyle asked.

The urgency of her mother's message was both compelling and unbelievable. She had no idea what to do or say. Before hanging up, she mumbled something to her mother about seeing what she could do.

"You OK?" Kyle pursued.

"I . . . I'm OK," she finally answered as she tried to shake off what she had just heard and get back on track to continue their story assignment.

They had taken only a few steps toward the elevator before her phone rang. It was Peter Leventhal with word that he needed her to rework her report for the 5:30 network news. The deadline was 3:00 p.m. Would she do it? She agreed.

Hope's next call was to her news director. She and Kyle would do the interview they were on, but another team would need to pick up the interview with the church spokesperson and finish the report.

What about Mark? Her mother had been so emphatic. It had infected her, and she now realized that her hands were shaking. She looked at her watch and reviewed Mark's flight schedule in her mind. By this hour he was somewhere in the skies approaching a stopover in Dallas. She might as well complete the interview she was on before calling his cell phone.

Hope had to force herself to concentrate. She felt mechanical and anything but attentive as she asked her questions and completed the interview.

Back at her desk she turned to the Internet for Mark's precise flight schedule. His flight was on schedule and had landed in Dallas 20 minutes before. She dialed his cell number and waited.

"We're sorry, but the cellular customer you have dialed is not answering . . ." the recorded voice told her. She hung up the phone.

An e-mail message from Peter detailed how he wanted her to change the RMI report. One section had to be cut. New information meant that another part of the report had to be rewritten. She would have to reedit the entire story. It would be at least two hours' worth of work that would barely make the deadline.

She tried Mark's number again. "We're sorry . . ." This time she slammed the receiver back onto its cradle and muttered a protest bordering on profanity.

After retrieving a set of data tapes from a rack, she claimed the next available edit bay and enclosed herself in the soundproof space. The quietness enabled her to make the changes Peter had requested and record her voice-overs to match, but it did nothing to calm her fear-filled spirit. When she finished, she looked at the clock. *Mark's flight is probably boarding by now.* She sent the report to New York over the high-speed data line.

Peter sounded disappointed. "Not your greatest work, but I'll have to live with it," he said. "Go take care of whatever it is that's bothering you."

~

Actually, Mark had never left his seat, because the flight that had started in Memphis had landed in Dallas and remained only briefly before continuing to Los Angeles. His cell phone was still tucked into a pocket in his computer carrying case.

~

"We're tight and ready for flight," the lead flight attendant reported over the telephone from the passenger cabin.

Captain Sonja Cabrini scanned the digital display panel in front of her and found the clock with the words "Time to Pushback" above the digits that were counting down. "We'll have pushback in about two minutes," she answered before hanging up. "How's the weather en route?" she asked her copilot without taking her eyes off the systems checklist she was reviewing.

"The weather map shows some thunderstorms building over west Texas and eastern New Mexico that we might have to route around.

After that it's clear until we get to southern California and start our descent. The Santa Ana winds are picking up, so we'll start getting some turbulence in that area," Alan Markland reported. "Visibility at LAX is expected to be down to about two miles or less, with no clouds but thick haze up to about 6,000 feet and clear above. Expect approach over Long Beach, then north and in over the water with sequencing onto runway zero-six left."

"Sounds like another beautiful afternoon under the smog in good ol' LA," Sonja smiled. "Got your gas mask ready?"

Sonja was waiting for Alan's response when her eye caught a motion outside the window as a ground crew member signaled that he was ready to begin their pushback. She answered with a thumbs-up, and the plane began to move backward.

"Starboard fuel pumps on," Alan reported.

"Roger on the fuel pumps. Starting number one," Sonja answered as she pulled the engine start lever.

"Diamond Flight 886, you are cleared for taxi," the ground controller replied before telling them they would be second in line for their runway.

"How did we get so lucky?" Alan asked. "I'm so used to being number six or eight here that I don't know what to do."

"Just don't start barking, OK?" Sonja answered with a playful smile in her copilot's direction.

"Only if you keep your hands off the controls," he shot back.

~

It seemed as if the knot in Hope's stomach would soon encompass her entire abdomen, and she struggled to keep from breaking down in tears. Conflict consumed her. On the one hand, she remembered something her father had taught her when she was a small child: that in spite of how much we may miss our deceased loved ones, they cannot return and talk to us, that any being portraying themselves as our deceased loved ones is, in fact, a demon sent to deceive us. How desperately she wanted to believe that thought! On the other hand, there was such urgency, such conviction, in her mother's call with a message attributed to the same man. If the first fact was true, then what was she to make of the warning? Did she have reason to fear for Mark's safety?

Get a grip, Hope chastised herself. *Satan is trying to scare you, and so far he's doing a pretty good job of it.*

She checked Mark's flight schedule on the Diamond Airways Web site. His flight was less than 45 minutes from landing in Los Angeles.

～

It was midmorning Los Angeles time before FBI agents Henderson and Keller realized that their quarry was not in his usual places. They discovered this when Keller went inside the pizzeria to order their lunch and did not see him. Eating while they drove, they fairly raced to the marina to see if Amir Al-Hamzi's boat was still moored. It wasn't. Worse still, no one was around who could remember seeing him leave.

"Relax. We know where he is," their supervisor told them. "He's out at sea."

"How do you know that?" Henderson wanted to know.

The supervisor chuckled. "You're not supposed to know this, but we installed a locator beacon on his boat a few weeks ago. Get on your boat, and we'll give you his GPS coordinates."

Keller had mixed emotions. He was excited to learn about the tracking beacon but groaned at the thought of going back to sea. "Mind if we stop by a store and get some Dramamine?"

"Let's get some food and drinks, too," Henderson suggested as they headed to a nearby convenience store.

Thirty minutes later they were loosening their ties and heading out to sea. Henderson guided the boat through the no-wake zone while Keller opened a Coke and downed his Dramamine. "It isn't the waves. It's your driving that's making me take this," he teased.

"My driving. Ha! You think I was bad last time; just wait till we get past the no-wake zone. I'll show you some driving!" Henderson shot back.

Keller studied the haze and limited visibility. "Looks like we're gonna need a healthy dose of luck to find that guy. It's like he's, well, disappeared—if he's out there. And if he's doing anything, how are we supposed to stop him? With these peashooters?" He patted the 9-millimeter semiautomatic on his hip.

Henderson smiled a wicked grin. "No. I'll just tie you to an outrigger, swing you over his boat, and let you puke on him."

Keller eyed his partner. "Know what? You're sick."

Henderson pushed the throttles, and the boat fairly leaped forward. He said something to his partner, but the wind whipped the words out of his mouth and over the stern, drowning them in the roar of the single diesel engine below their feet. He pointed toward the radar and video surveillance system, and Keller knew that it was time to get them activated. In this haze they would be the primary search tools.

Keller unfolded his cell phone and called the office. It was tricky, but he managed to copy the latest GPS coordinates for their target. Looking at the chart, he estimated that Amir's boat was about 16 or 17 miles away on a course headed their direction. But in this soupy haze they could pass within a few hundred yards and neither would see the other as anything more than a blip on a radar screen.

In minutes they would be out of cell phone range, and, except for the marine band radio that everyone could hear, they would be out of communication with the world. That could be a real problem, because all FBI radio communication was supposed to be on secure channels.

∼

Amir Al-Hamzi did not like the idea of being so far out to sea. The GPS display told him that land was over the horizon. But that was the problem: it was over the horizon and out of sight in the haze. In a few miles he would cross the invisible 12-mile territorial limit marking the border of the United States. True, the U.S. exercised a 200-mile "economic protection zone," but the legal limit for most laws ended at the 12-mile line.

"You have fishing gear?" Muhammad asked. "I hear there are many fish in these waters. I have often wanted to fish in the deep ocean."

"I thought you were here on a mission," Amir answered. "What is our mission, and when will we carry it out?"

"*Inshallah,*" Muhammad answered with a shrug. "The time for being a martyr will come soon enough. In the meantime, let's have a little fun."

Martyrdom was not something Amir had seriously considered, so the prospect made him shudder. His hand quivered as he pointed to the locker where the fishing rods and tackle were stored. In minutes both Muhammad and Abdullah had lines in the water using hooks baited with chunks of kosher hot dogs, about the only thing they could find aboard that resembled fish bait. Amir kept just enough power on to keep tension on the lines as they trolled for whatever would take the bait.

They did not have long to wait; within moments Abdullah had a bite. For the next half hour he fought the unseen creature to the surface, where Amir gaffed the 30-pound fish and brought it aboard.

"What a monster you have caught!" Muhammad exclaimed as the fish flipped and flopped and bled on the deck. "What kind of fish is it?"

All eyes turned to Amir. "I have no idea," he protested. "I'm not a

70

fisherman. I don't even want to touch the thing!" He opened a compartment cover in one of the side walls, brought out the end of a hose, and began washing the fish's blood into the sea.

All eyes watched as the creature's flopping reduced to twitching and then nothing. "We must catch more," Muhammad commanded. "This is our cover. If the authorities ask what we are doing, we are just out having fun. Once we have more fish we will go closer to shore."

Amir's gaze moved to the gear the men had brought aboard and left lying on the lower cabin deck. He didn't know what was in the bags and cylinders, but whatever the contents, they were heavy. He'd discovered this fact when he'd had to push them out of the way to use the bathroom. Finally he got up the courage to ask what was in the bags.

"You will see when the time comes," Abdullah replied. "In the meantime, let's keep fishing. I am enjoying it. This is the first time in my life I have been fishing."

CHAPTER NINE

The sun was near its zenith and there were several fish aboard before Muhammad declared that the time to move had come.

"How far do we have to go?" Amir inquired. "And what direction?"

Muhammad and Abdullah studied the GPS display and calculated their course and distance. "Take bearing one-one-four. I'll tell you when we've reached our target area, where Allah wishes us to strike a blow for Him," Muhammad ordered.

Amir studied the display and realized they were headed back to the area of Marina del Rey. Was he merely supposed to bring the men ashore to do something there? He would have to wait for further instruction, because these men were giving him no clues.

"Let's get going. But not too fast. We don't want to attract attention," Muhammad instructed. "Drive like everybody else does."

Amir pushed the throttles forward until the bow cut a modest wake and the rolling over the swells was about all his passengers could stand. He studied their faces and smiled broadly. Maybe this landlubber had gotten his sea legs after all!

∽

That message cannot be from God. It has to be from Satan, Hope tried comforting herself for the umpteenth time. "Lord," she prayed, "keep Mark safe on his trip. Keep Satan from carrying out his plan, whatever it is."

Despite her prayers, Hope found little strength in them. Focusing on her work for more than a few minutes at a time was virtually impossible.

Worse still, it seemed as if the hands of the clock were glued in place.

"Something bothering you?" The typically unsympathetic news director surprised her. Hope only nodded. "Anything I can do?" he inquired.

Hope nodded. "Have backup ready to go on the air in my place. I've already done my piece for the network, and I've written the intros for the stories that have come in. But right now I'm not sure what shape I'm going to be in come airtime."

He nodded, and disappeared around the corner. From the distance Hope heard him calling to someone to get a certain reporter on the phone and back in the studio by 4:00 p.m. Knowing she could leave if she had to helped her feel just a tiny bit better.

⁓

To prevent any possibility of a competitor overhearing or seeing their work, Art Whitfield had forbidden all members of the team from using their laptop computers to do any company business or from even discussing it while en route. So they passed the time reading novels or magazines purchased at an airport newsstand. Those who dared to turn on their notebook computers were doing such things as watching movies on DVD, composing e-mails, or playing games. It all added up to a severe case of boredom for Mark as he stared out over the left wing. He decided there were three things he didn't like about being in a window seat.

First was the narrowed foot space that resulted from being against the curved outside of the plane. If being packed in with nearly 200 other people wasn't enough, the curved wall made him feel claustrophobic.

Second was the inconvenience involved in passing drinks and snacks across two people or making them get out of their seats so he could get up to go use the bathroom. After his first trip he decided to prevent his seatmates the inconvenience for the rest of the flight.

Third was the limited view. He had to crane his neck to see much, but the wing and the altitude prevented him from seeing anything of interest on the ground.

The flight attendant came by offering headsets so passengers could hear the audio on the in-flight movie. The title didn't interest him, so Mark turned back to his book. But after a few paragraphs his eyes again began wandering to whatever could be seen around him. He studied the Airphone mounted in the back of the seat ahead and debated using his credit card to call Hope just to brag that he was using it. But the prospect of $6.95 for the first minute and $3 a minute after that deterred him.

Looking forward along the wall, he noted that the emergency exit over the wing was just two rows ahead.

"Hey, Pete. You have any plans for how to spend our evenings while we're in LA?" he asked the coworker seated next to him.

"Not really. My wife searched the Internet and came up with some ideas for places to eat and the like. But I figure I'll just ask the concierge at the hotel. They always know the best places."

~

For Keller and Henderson it was like trying to find the proverbial needle in the haystack, except that the needle was moving around in the haystack. They didn't want to discuss their situation openly on the marine band radio, but they were out of range of land-based cellular service.

Sphinx was out there somewhere. Henderson drew a line on the chart from Marina del Rey to Sphinx's last known location. Then he drew parallel lines at two miles on either side of that line and formed a box with the land on the east and the last location to the west.

"We can search that area using our radar," Keller observed. They set out on a zigzag course where they would move close enough to observe a target with the camera system before turning and zipping off in another direction. At the west end of their range they still had not seen Sphinx's boat.

Keller shook his cell phone in his hand. "I wish we were close enough to land to call the office," he shouted to the haze.

Henderson looked at the chart and turned the boat northward at full throttle. Ten minutes later he motioned for Keller to join him on the upper deck. "Try it now."

"Where are we?"

"Oh, about two miles off Malibu. Check your signal and see if you can call in now."

Puzzlement painted Keller's face.

Henderson waved at the haze. "Trust me. It's over there."

Keller looked at his phone, then dialed. "Where is Sphinx now?" he demanded. He wrote down the GPS coordinates he was given, turned to the chart, and punched a finger hard against a location several miles south and somewhat east of their location.

"He's inside our search box. How did we miss him?" he protested. A blip on the radar screen corresponded to the map location.

Henderson swung the boat around and pushed the throttles until the boat was flying over the swells.

~

"It's time for afternoon prayers," Muhammad announced without looking at his watch or the sky.

Amir looked at his watch. The first afternoon prayers were still an hour away. He started to open his mouth and correct his zealous friend, until he saw the hardened lines around Muhammad's face.

Lacking a blanket or rug, as would be proper, the trio elected simply to kneel on the deck and prostrate themselves in the general direction of Mecca. Abdullah began the prayer chant.

Amir opened his mouth to begin, then realized he did not know the chant Abdullah was leading. So with his face to the deck he listened and prayed silently.

"Have you not prayed the martyr's prayer?" Abdullah inquired.

The question sent a chill up and down Amir's spine. "I do not know it, so how can I pray it?"

"We know that our strike against the infidels will succeed *inshallah,* but we have no assurance we will live. Two hours from now we may be here— or we may be in heaven enjoying the presence of Allah and the pleasures of the 70 virgins He will give us as a reward for what we are about to do."

The trio again turned their faces toward the deck as Abdullah's and Muhammad's incantations continued. What should have been a time of receiving peace from Allah was only filling Amir with fear.

"What is our mission?" he asked timidly after they arose.

"Your mission is to drive us to where we can accomplish *our* mission," Muhammad answered. "I must warn you that should our mission be successful, you will never be able to return to your life in the land of the infidels."

The rumble of an airliner rolled through the haze from somewhere in the distance.

Abdullah glanced upward searching for the sound, then studied the navigation display and tapped a point on the screen two miles to their east. "Take us there. That is where we will strike."

Amir balanced himself against the tipping of the swells and studied the screen. It was as he scanned the area around their target location that he began to suspect their mission objective. The site was barely three miles from the west end of the runways at Los Angeles International Airport.

❧

"I think he's stopped," Keller shouted above the roar of the engines. The blip was still at least two miles away in the haze, nine minutes at their current speed but still too far for either their eyes or the video surveillance system to see anything. Henderson kept up their speed until they were about three fourths of a mile away and the form of Amir's boat could be seen in the distance. He brought the throttles to idle and waited for Keller's report from the main deck.

"It's his boat, and it looks like he's got company! I'm counting three people aboard, and one of them looks like Sphinx."

Keller called the office to confirm the coordinates of the locator beacon. They matched. "Now we wait. Hey! Pass me a Coke, will you? And what else have we got in there for munchies?"

❧

The men began unpacking their gear and spreading weapons out on the deck. Abdullah unwrapped a pair of AK-47 assault rifles and spent the next 20 minutes fieldstripping and cleaning them to be sure they were functional. He stowed them in an empty compartment underneath a padded seat facing the stern.

Seeing the rifles made Amir's heart beat faster. What made his eyes go wide were the missile launchers Muhammad extracted from the large shipping tubes. There were four missiles in all. Sitting in the galley area so he could not be seen from the outside, he attached two of them to firing control boxes, then hoisted each to his right shoulder and tested the electronics. The smile on his face telegraphed his pleasure.

Muhammad listened to the stream of approaching airliners as they appeared out of the haze for a few seconds, passed low overhead like ghosts, and then melted again into the dust. "It is time for our glorious quest!" he shouted. *"Allahu Akbar!"*

"Allahu Akbar!" Abdullah echoed and repeated as each man shook a fist to the sky.

Amir turned in the captain's chair and joined the chant. *"Allahu Akbar! Allahu Akbar! Allahu Akbar!"*

"Because this is your first mission, I will give you the privilege of the first shot." Muhammad pointed at the readied rockets.

"May Allah be praised," Abdullah shouted before picking up the first missile.

"What are those?" Amir asked.

Abdullah laughed loudly as he stepped between the fishing seats. "The infidels call it the Stinger. It is a surface-to-air missile. We are using the very weapons the Great Satan makes, and attacking him with them!"

Amir felt a mix of anger, surprise, and downright terror surge through his body like an electric shock as another jet roared overhead and Abdullah turned the launcher upward to follow it.

"Do not be afraid. Just stay up there." He pointed to the upper deck. "And once we have fired the missiles, we will need you to take us away and back to the ship on which we came," Muhammad instructed.

"But . . . but didn't you just pray the martyr's prayer?" Amir sputtered.

Muhammad eyed his driver with a cold stare. "I am willing to die if Allah wills it. But my wish is to live and to strike again many times in the future."

~

"Good afternoon, ladies and gentlemen. This is Captain Cabrini speaking," Sonja began her prelanding announcement. "We'll be landing in about seven minutes. The current temperature in Los Angeles is 97 degrees, with a high of 99 expected this afternoon. Our approach is taking us a few miles out over the ocean. That's because they're experiencing strong Santa Ana winds off the desert. There's not a cloud in the sky, but as you can see, it's a pea-soup haze because of all the dust in the air. Visibility is less than one mile, so this will definitely be an instrument approach. I'm turning on the seat belt sign and ask that each of you follow the instructions of our cabin crew as we prepare for landing."

Mark felt the plane banking toward the right and what he guessed was the north. The haze was still too thick to see anything on the ground. Or was it water below them now?

The flight attendants made their circuit of the cabin to make sure everyone had their seat belt fastened, their seat in the full upright position, and the tray table in front of them stowed.

~

"What're they doing?" Keller asked as he leaned over Henderson's shoulder to study the video screen.

"They ain't fishing, that's for sure," Henderson answered. Then he saw the first missile lifted onto a shoulder, and his mouth fell open. "They've got a missile!" he screamed. "A Stinger, an SA-7, or something like it. Call it in, man! We need some help out here!"

Keller hit the speed dial on his phone and began shouting at the receptionist who answered the phone at the FBI office. She put him on hold for what seemed an eternity before a supervisor answered. He began describing the scene at machine-gun speed. The supervisor asked him to slow down and speak more clearly. He tried, but it wasn't easy. It took two more tries before the message was communicated.

"Well, what do we do? Stand here and wait? I mean, we've got this big boat. Maybe we could ram them or something," Henderson suggested.

"The boss told us to sit tight and wait for help."

Henderson felt his jaw dropping toward the deck. "You mean, just stand here and watch them do whatever they're going to do? I thought we were supposed to be preventing terrorist acts, not watching 'em!"

Keller began punching buttons on his cell phone.

"Who ya calling?" Henderson questioned.

"You'll see. Hello! Is this 911? This is FBI Special Agent Walter Keller. I'm on a boat about two miles offshore from Los Angeles International Airport. Right now I'm watching a trio of potential terrorists—no, real terrorists—on a boat about a half mile away from me, and it looks as though they've got shoulder-fired missiles. We're right under the approach path to the airport, and we need as much help out here as possible."

"What'd they say?" Henderson asked after his partner had been silent for a moment.

"To hold on. They're sounding the alarm and trying to get us some help."

∾

Abdullah peered up through the haze to locate the next airliner as it approached. It was coming from the west. He swung the missile around to try to lock it onto a heat source as the plane appeared out of the haze. The column of lights in the sight raced upward, indicating a good heat source. His smile grew large, and he squeezed the trigger. The missile raced out of the tube with an earsplitting hiss and quickly reached a speed of more than twice the speed of sound. Yet in a few seconds it was obvious that the heat source it was chasing was not the plane but the sun behind it. The plane continued its approach unaffected as the missile tried to attack the sun, then exploded into a rain of shrapnel when it ran out of fuel. A moment later the scattered pieces peppered the water somewhere in the distance.

A curse arose from Abdullah's lips before the crack of the detonation reached their ears.

~

"They've fired a missile!" Keller shouted both to his partner and to the 911 operator. Their camera remained locked on the boat with the video recorder running while their eyes followed the missile toward its ultimate end.

"It missed! It missed!" Henderson shouted. "I can't believe it, but it missed."

~

Sonja Cabrini banked her plane hard to the right and lined up on the radio beacons that would guide them down to runway zero-six left. In seconds they passed over a beacon mounted on a buoy eight miles offshore, and she pulled the throttles back so their rate of descent would match the angle of the glide slope radio beacon. That beacon would guide them to a touchdown point atop the huge numbers painted on the end of a runway they would not see until seconds before touchdown.

"One hundred sixty knots. Slowing to 140," Alan Markland called as he read down the prelanding checklist.

"Diamond 886, Los Angeles Tower. You are cleared to land on runway zero-six left," the air traffic controller advised them.

"You going to fly it or ride it?" Alan asked. The question he was really asking was "Are you going to land the plane yourself or let the computer do it for you?"

"You think I'm just along for the ride, don't you?" Sonja smiled as she answered. "You know how it goes. I gotta get my minimum number of landings for the month."

"Lowering the landing gear," Alan announced. He reached forward and pulled down a lever. An instant later they could feel the wind buffeting the plane as the landing gear doors opened and the wheels began creating drag on the otherwise sleek airframe.

~

"Maybe we ought to try shooting the other direction," Muhammad suggested as he shouldered the second missile launcher and looked northwest. He had only moments to wait before the next plane was heard through the haze. A giant twin-engine airliner appeared out of the haze, and the readout on the infrared detector began registering a strong heat signature. The readout leaped to maximum just as the plane passed over the boat. Muhammad squeezed the trigger, and the missile screamed off in its supersonic pursuit of severely subsonic prey. They had less than 10 seconds to wait. The missile traced a gentle, unerring curve toward the back of the right engine.

～

"LAPD's alerting their anti-terror squad and their SWAT teams," Keller shouted. "But it'll be at least 10 minutes before the first helicopter gets here—and I bet it won't be armed!"

～

For the electromechanical brain in the missile, it was all a matter of following the brightest heat source it could sense. While its partner had chased the sun, this missile had focused on the heat source in the back end of the right engine.

A hundred times a second the electronic brain sent course corrections to the guidance fins on its tail, so the infrared dot barely moved away from the center of the sensor in the missile's nose. Then, when the heat sensor registered that it was in proximity of a temperature typically found at the back end of a jet engine, it sent an electrical impulse to a trigger, detonating the two kilograms of high explosive the missile carried.

Jet engines are at the same time amazingly durable and highly sensitive machines. Long intake blades at the front suck massive quantities of air into the front of the engine, pulling the plane forward while pushing the air into smaller compressor blades. A spray of fuel feeds a fire that continually forces itself toward the back of the engine, along the way spinning blades that keep the front blades turning. As these hot gasses leave the engine, they produce more thrust in the form of a tornado-like jet of white-hot air.

It was this blast of heat that the missile chased and in this wind that it detonated. Shrapnel ripped into the back of the engine and underside of the wing, ripping holes in the extended flaps and puncturing the wing fuel tanks. This released streams of jet fuel into the slipstream, where they immediately turned into fireballs. Other pieces ripped small holes in the fuselage.

All but one person in the back half of the plane felt the explosion as much as heard it. That one man, who had a window seat, died instantly as a piece of the missile ripped through the plane's thin skin and slammed into his head. He made no sound, but the wind whipping past the new opening created a roar and lowered the air pressure in the cabin.

Finding herself splattered with blood, the woman sitting next to him began screaming hysterically.

~

"They hit it! They've just hit an airliner!" Keller screamed into his phone.

"Partner, we're going in," Henderson shouted back. He rammed the throttles forward and brought the boat around onto a collision course with the terrorist boat. At the same time he reached to his waist for the 9-millimeter semiautomatic pistol residing there. A glance down at Keller showed him doing the same with his right hand while grabbing a railing with his left.

~

Sonja's first sign of anything wrong was a digitally recorded audio warning that began screaming "Fire in the right engine! Fire in the right engine!" Instinctively she reached to the top of the center console to press the fire suppression button. She ran into Alan's left hand, which had reached the button a split second ahead of hers.

The runway was in sight and they had plenty of altitude, so her first concern—making it to the runway—was satisfied. What she couldn't know was if the main landing gear was damaged and if they could land safely.

"Diamond 886 has fire in the right engine. Eight-eighty-six is Mayday," Alan fairly screamed into the radio.

"Roger, 886. Confirm Mayday," the tower controller responded mechanically.

A scan of the engine performance gauges on the center panel display showed that the right engine was slowing. "We've lost the right engine," Alan confirmed.

Sonja was so attuned to the plane that compensating for the loss of power on the right was instinctive. The left engine tried to turn the plane to the right, so she pressed the left rudder pedal a little harder to keep lined up with the runway. Still, she caught herself holding her breath as the wheels reached for and thumped hard against the concrete. She let herself breathe again as she realized that the wheels were rolling instead of dragging.

Now all she had to do was stop the plane. Normally that was done using thrust reversers, giant clamshells that diverted the thrust from the back of the engine around and forward to slow them. However, having only one engine was turning things from normal to dicey in a hurry.

Sonja pulled the thrust reverser for the left engine and pushed the throttle forward while standing on the right brake. The plane pulled hard to the left. She compensated by pulling the throttle back some. The plane swerved right. She pushed the throttle forward, and the weave repeated. Finally she just stood on both brakes as hard as she could while adjusting their course with the throttle. The far end of the runway was approaching fast. Still, somehow they were slowing.

Under normal circumstances they would have stopped and turned off the runway some 2,000 feet back. The giant upside-down 24 with an equal-sized R were just ahead when the plane finally stopped. They had used all but 500 feet of the more-than-mile-long runway.

~

Lonnie Moreno was the senior air traffic controller on duty in the control tower when he heard Diamond Airways Flight 886 declare emergency. He looked westward and lifted his binoculars to his eyes. It was easy to find the plane as it appeared out of the haze because the right engine was on fire and the wing trailed a thick stream of fire and smoke. "Shut down the north side of the field!" he shouted to the other controllers as he reached for the red phone that immediately connected him to the airport's fire station. "Aircraft on approach to zero-six left is on fire. Repeat. Aircraft on approach to zero-six left is on fire. We are shutting down all traffic on the north side of the airport."

The impact of Lonnie Moreno's order was quick. Like the ripples on a pond when a pebble is dropped in, it spread from Los Angeles International Airport to airports both across the United States and around the world. First, planes on approach to the north side of the airfield were diverted to nearby airports in Long Beach, Ontario, Orange County, North Hollywood, Santa Barbara, and San Diego. Flights approaching the south side of the airport were allowed to continue normally.

Then the phone at Moreno's work station rang. It was the 911 operator relaying the report from Agent Keller aboard the boat two miles at sea.

"Repeat that!" Moreno replied, then listened for a moment before hanging up. He punched the intercom button on his communications console and began barking orders. "Shut down the airport! We've got a level one terrorist event and a crash on the north side of the field!"

Confusion in the skies turned into chaos as air traffic controllers now had to send aircraft into holding patterns and find out how long each could remain in the air before sending them off to alternate landing sites. The impact was as large as if a boulder had been dropped into a pond; the impact spread worldwide within minutes. Based on their fuel status, flights headed for Los Angeles from places such as Honolulu or Paris were either turned around or diverted to another major airport, such as Seattle or Denver.

On the ground all planes waiting for taxi and takeoff clearances were ordered to halt and return to their departure gates as the airport police sealed off all entrances and began a security sweep to be sure no terrorists were on the grounds. High-powered weapons and bulletproof vests began appearing almost everywhere.

The biggest interruption of commercial air travel in American history since the September 11, 2001, terrorist attacks was under way.

CHAPTER TEN

F light attendants to the emergency exits! Flight attendants to the emergency exits!" Alan ordered over the plane's public-address system.

Sonja and Alan immediately started shutting down the plane. Engine control systems. Hydraulics. The auxiliary power unit. *Everything*. If it was on, it got turned off. Fast.

Out their windows the pilots could see the forward emergency exit chutes as they unrolled toward the ground and inflated, and the first passengers began sliding down them to the concrete. The touchdowns were unceremonious and lacking in dignity, with passengers sometimes landing on top of each other. Some got up and ran away from the plane; others stood by to assist those following as they reached the bottom. Some were obviously injured by their impact with the concrete or each other.

Alan was first out of his seat. He quickly unbarred the terrorist-proof cockpit door and pushed it open, only to be greeted by an inrush of choking black smoke. Instinctively he slammed it shut and reached up to open the crew emergency escape hatch in the ceiling. He pulled the hatch down and back. Doing that uncovered a compartment to one side in which a coil of rope was attached. He grabbed the weight on the end of the rope, reached up, and tossed it over the side of the plane. Using the back of his seat as a step, he pushed himself upward through the opening and pulled himself onto the top of the plane. From there he reached down to help Sonja up and out.

"Ladies first," Alan offered, handing Sonja the rope. She grasped it tightly in both hands and took a step backward as if to rappel down the side of the plane. But the curvature of the plane fell away beneath her feet and she slipped, falling hard against the metal skin and sliding downward more quickly than she wished. Landing hard on the concrete, she felt a searing pain like an electric shock shoot from her right ankle up to her hip. She felt it again as she tried to get up and put weight on that foot. So she balanced on her left foot and began hobbling away.

~

As the wheels touched the runway it became clear to Mark that the plane was in serious trouble. Though only seconds had passed since the missile had exploded behind the right engine, those seconds had been filled with incredible shock and terror for everyone aboard. Then came the swerves to one side of the runway and the other. It felt as if the plane would never stop rolling.

The flight attendants were running for the emergency exits even before the plane stopped moving, and the copilot's command was heard. Opening the emergency exit over the right wing brought an inrush of smoke and intense heat from the burning wing. That quickly turned what had been a merely frightened exodus from the plane into a panicked rush for whatever exit appeared nearest.

Mark unfastened his seat belt, stood, and looked toward the exit two rows ahead. A flight attendant was urging passengers toward the opening. "Sit and slide! Sit and slide! Just like you were in grade school!" she shouted again and again until the lowering smoke hid her from view and began choking her words.

Mark pulled a handkerchief from his pocket and covered his mouth as someone let him enter the narrow aisle. Breathing through it helped a little. Still, the smoke made his eyes water so much that it was hard to see, and it burned deeply into his lungs. Then his head began to swim.

This feeling made the door seem farther away with each breath. *I'll never make it. I'm going to die in here.* Weakness gripped his legs as panic gripped his heart. Then he was in the exit. He tried to step onto the slide, but his legs folded under him and he tripped, falling headfirst, sliding on his face and landing in a crumpled heap at the bottom. The first breath of fresh air made him want to stay where he was. Then someone landed on top of him, their shoes digging sharply into his side. Somehow he managed to roll away so the next person down the slide would not land on him too.

"Get up! Get up! Go! Go! Go!" someone was yelling. He knew the person was nearby, but in his smoke-induced daze he thought the voice sounded as if it were a mile away. He struggled to his feet and began stumbling toward the edge of the runway. Someone grabbed him and helped him the final distance to where an emergency worker was assembling the passengers. Everything seemed surreal, as if it were in a dream. To one side a young couple was embracing tearfully as the man tried to keep the woman from gazing at the scene from which they had just escaped. Ahead of him a gray-haired man helped his wife to the ground, then knelt beside her collapsed form. Two people carried a man toward the grass, his arms across their shoulders and his limp legs dragging behind. Others just stood around staring back at the plane as the flames spread.

Mark turned around to survey his surroundings. But it felt as if the world kept on turning after his head stopped. He twisted into a crumpled heap on the ground.

A moment later someone wearing a flameproof uniform like those worn by race car drivers was kneeling beside him and opening a medical aid kit. "Let's have a look at you, sir. Can you tell me where you're hurt?" the rescuer inquired.

Mark tried to form an answer but couldn't.

The rescuer placed the tips of an oxygen tube into his nostrils and threaded the hose behind his ears. "Breathe through your nose, sir. Just breathe through your nose," the rescuer instructed.

The cool, clean oxygen felt good. But, oh, how his chest and head hurt!

"Sir, can you tell me your name?" the medic asked in a voice that seemed to echo through his aching skull.

Mark heard the question but could make no sense of it. He mumbled something in reply.

"Do you know where you are?" the medic asked.

After examining him further, the medic tied a multicolored card to his left wrist and ripped off the two bottom color stripes, leaving a red stripe with a large number 1 printed on it. "The ambulance crews will be here shortly, and you're one of the first people they're going to take to the hospital," the medic declared as he picked up his gear and set off to check another patient.

≈

Alan Markland was just grasping the rope to slide down when the growing puddle of fuel dripping under the right wing erupted in flames. The blast of hot wind surged toward him, shaking the plane and yanking the rope from his hands. From 100 feet away Sonja watched him fall to the concrete and lie there like a discarded rag doll. "Alan! Alan! Get up! Get up!" she screamed as the flames raced toward him and then engulfed both the front of the plane and the ground under it. Searing heat reached out to her, and she raised a hand in a futile attempt to protect herself. Though a good distance away from the flames, she felt as if she would catch on fire.

A large crash truck halted a few yards from Sonja. The sound of its engine quickly grew to a steady roar as the nozzle mounted atop the cab articulated upward and a stream of foam came gushing out of the nozzle. The operator inside the truck swiveled it left and right several times, covering the area with flame-smothering goo. The flames at the front end of the plane subsided, and the heat diminished.

Large drops of the foam began landing around Sonja. She rolled over to try to get away from the splatter and found herself lying in a puddle of the foul-smelling flame retardant. Just then a pair of protective-suited firefighters came out a side door of the truck, grabbed her, and dragged her to safety. "Are you hurt?" one of them asked.

"My ankle," she answered as she pointed down. "I think I broke it."

One of the firefighters examined her leg and touched her foot. She screamed with pain. "Yeah, I think you're right," he said. "But we better get you out of here first. They're setting up a triage station over here somewhere. Let's get you over there where the medics can take care of you." The pair wrapped her arms over their shoulders and reached under her legs to carry her off to the side of the runway.

"What were you doing up there at the front end?" one of the firefighters asked as they helped Sonja to the grass.

"I'm the pilot," she grimaced with pain.

A medic arrived. "Looks like a broken right ankle and some burns," the firefighter reported before returning to his primary duty. The medic pulled a printed paper tag from his pocket with a string on it and uncapped a felt-tipped pen. "What's your name?"

"Cabrini. Sonja Cabrini. I'm the pilot," she answered. Just talking required what seemed an unusual amount of strength. Her lips felt stiff and did not move normally, so her last name sounded more like "Cafini," and that's what the medic wrote. Then he turned the tag over and began circling areas on a body diagram. One circle was around the right ankle. Another circle was around the head, and he wrote the word "burns" beside it. She reached up to feel her face. The touch made her yelp with pain.

The medic tied the card to Sonja's left wrist, ripped off the bottom color band, and then set about applying an air splint to her broken ankle.

Sonja looked at the card. "What's this big number 2 for?" she asked.

"You're a priority-two patient. When the ambulance crews come around they'll pick up the more seriously injured people—the priority ones—and take them to the hospital first," the medic answered.

"So what does that mean for me?"

"You get to wait a while. But don't worry," the medic said as he closed his medical kit and stood up. "We've got half the ambulances in Los Angeles coming, so you won't have to wait very long. You'll get there soon enough."

In the distance Sonja could hear the approach of sirens and the rapid wop-wopping of helicopter blades coming from several directions. "Yeah, I hear 'em." She relaxed and lay back on the grass. Then she realized that no matter which way she turned her head, she heard not a single airliner's jet engine whining. *They've shut the place down!*

~

One of those helicopters was the sky-eye for the Los Angeles MBS affiliate.

No one called Hope's attention to the row of TV monitors spread along the newsroom ceiling. Perhaps it was the collective change in mood in the room as eyes were drawn to the screen and conversations stilled for a moment. Her eyes rose, scanned past the other networks with their afternoon soap operas and talk shows, and stopped on the crash scene. As other networks' helicopters arrived on the scene, the other monitors changed too.

Banners across the bottom of each screen declared that it was live coverage of an airliner crash at Los Angeles International Airport. Hope felt her heart leap into her throat, and she let out a scream that turned heads across the room and brought several people running.

"What's wrong?" someone asked breathlessly.

Hope pointed at the monitor with a trembling finger and fought to speak. "My husband," she squeaked breathlessly.

Puzzlement painted their faces.

Hope only nodded and pointed to the monitors.

"How do you know?"

"I know. I just know," Hope answered without taking her eyes off the monitor.

Someone found the remote control and turned up the volume. The announcer from the local station was saying something about the plane involved being a Diamond Airways flight from Dallas and that there was a yet-unconfirmed report that the crash was the result of a terrorist act. At least airport and law-enforcement officials were treating it like a terrorist attack and shutting down the airport completely. The camera widened its view to include both the flaming wreckage and the mix of passengers, rescuers, and emergency vehicles milling about beside the runway. A line of ambulances was filing in and out through gates in the airport fence nearest the crash.

Hope stood frozen, her eyes riveted on the screen.

~

Keller and Henderson held on as they roared full-throttle toward Amir Al-Hamzi's boat. Henderson kept the bow aimed directly at it. Then someone aboard saw them, pointed in their direction, and shouted an alarm. Whoever was sitting in the captain's chair reacted, and the boat roared forward with the pair in back holding on to stay upright. Then one of the men bent over and came up with a large weapon.

A burst of automatic weapons fire scattered across the agents' boat even as Henderson tried to turn and still ram the escaping craft. Neither of the agents was hit by more than a few shards of flying fiberglass.

"Back off! Back off!" Keller shouted.

Henderson pulled the throttle back, whipped the steering wheel around, and let the gap between the boats grow some. Then he pulled the bow around and pushed his throttles forward to the fire wall.

"Man, that was close!" Keller called as he turned back to his video monitor. "Looks like he's got an AK-47." Doing combat against an AK-47 with his puny 9-millimeter was suicide, and the realization sent a shiver up and down his spine.

More muzzle flashes could be seen coming from the back of Amir's boat. Henderson pulled the throttles back to widen the gap.

Keller belted himself into a chair in front of the video console and reached for his cell phone. It wasn't on his belt. He unfastened his seat belt, searched the floor, and retrieved it from the lowest and farthest corner of the deck right next to a drain large enough for it to wash through and into the sea. From his knees he phoned the office to report their situation and request backup.

At the same time Henderson was using the marine band radio to contact the Coast Guard station at the airport to report the incident and request assistance. He was told to stand by, that all three Coast Guard helicopters in the area were involved in the crash rescue.

Their orders from the FBI office were about as helpful. "Maintain surveillance and active pursuit while we get help out to you."

The sea swells grew in size as the two boats left land farther behind. If it were not for the video camera and radar mounted in the superstructure, they might have lost contact with the terrorist boat altogether. Several times the agents wondered if their quarry had not managed to escape. What mostly contributed to the growing gap was the greater power and speed of Amir's boat.

"When are they going to get us some help?" Henderson wondered.

"Man, I don't know. But I don't want to get any closer to them. Do you?"

Henderson shook his head. "No. But we can kiss our careers goodbye if we break off the chase. The problem is that we can't arrest 'em. So how's that for being stuck between a rock and a hard place?"

"I'd call it between a bullet and a wet place," Keller retorted. His quip drew a tense smile in return.

~

Sweeper 5 was headed northwest and passing Monterey when the crew got the call to turn around immediately and join the search for the terrorist boat. The news from the pilot over the intercom brought every crew member to full attention. They'd been through a lot of training, practicing tracking and attacking targets. Twice a year they actually got to fire a missile and a torpedo at target ships. But while doing it for real was something that they were prepared to do, they always hoped that they would never have to do it. They had time to think as the pilots pushed the throttles to the fire wall, trying to diminish the hour travel time back to the Los Angeles area.

Something Kevin DiPlacio liked about his data system was that he could access the Internet. Typically he used that capability to send and receive e-mails while on patrol. Now he used it to view the MBS Web site and see what news they had about the event that had made them turn around. Sure enough, there was a bulletin under the "Breaking News" banner. "LAX Airliner Crash, Possible Terror Attack," it read.

"Hey! Ramon! Look at this, will you?" DiPlacio said to his partner across the aisle. "Looks as though we may be going after a real live terrorist. Think you can find him?"

Ramon Santoro got out of his seat, leaned over DiPlacio's shoulder to read the screen, and whistled after reading the headline. "Man, I'm just glad it's a Monday instead of a Sunday, or we'd never find 'em among all the pleasure craft down there. You know what it looks like down there on a weekend!"

Just then the pilot's voice came over the intercom. "Flight to crew, we've got new orders from command. When we arrive in the area, we are to establish contact with an FBI boat that is following the target boat, establish visual contact with the target, and maintain surveillance. However, we do not yet have clearance to open fire. Right now they just want us to establish contact and watch."

DiPlacio and Santoro looked at each other for a moment with the same question on their minds: America's war on terrorism had involved a lot of shooting in a growing list of places. Had the coastal waters of California just been added to the list?

CHAPTER ELEVEN

Mark felt like the circus fire-breather who'd inhaled instead of exhaled. Intense pain traced the airways of his head, throat, and chest. Breathing was difficult. He could feel fluid rattling in his lungs each time his diaphragm lifted or lowered, and it was getting worse with each passing minute. Lifting himself off the grass onto one elbow eased his distress only a little.

I wonder when those paramedics will find me, he thought as he looked around and saw an ambulance crew loading up a patient 50 or 60 yards away. It was then that he looked back toward the plane—or what was left of it. By now it was a crumpled, smoking heap covered with whitish flame-retardant foam in some places and dancing flames in other parts. The tail section, with several rows of seats still inside, rested alone on the concrete, a surprisingly pristine part of the plane that had somehow become disconnected from the carnage. The charred nose was also disconnected and resting on its right side with the attached landing gear sticking horizontally into the air.

It took only a few more sweeps with the foam to extinguish all visible flames. Now the firefighters began washing the foam away with water to expose the wreckage and enable the search for victims. The wave of wetness moved across the pavement toward Mark, soaking the ground around him and reaching through his clothing in several places. But he didn't care, not even as the malodorous scent rose around him.

"At least I'm still alive," Mark said to himself as he watched a foursome of firefighters unroll a body bag near the wreckage of the nose section and lift a limp, foam-covered form into it. A wave of sadness gripped Mark as he watched the firefighters zip the bag closed, then carry it to the edge of the runway and leave it just a few yards away from him. Moments later other firefighters added a second bag, then a third. Instinctively he knew there would be more. Many more. He did not want to know how many. The pain in his chest made him wonder if the paramedics would soon be zipping him into one instead of taking him to the hospital. Strangely, the thought was at the same time both frightening and comforting. He hated the thought of never seeing Hope and Jennifer again, but was comforted by the thought of getting relief from his injuries. He sank back onto the ground.

A moment later a shadow fell over Mark, and he looked up to see a paramedic bending over him and reaching for his triage tag. "Can you move, sir?" the man asked. Mark tried to pull himself up on one elbow, but to his surprise found he lacked the strength to do even that. The paramedic waved to unseen helpers, who soon arrived. Mark tried again to lift himself off the grass.

"Just lie back and let us do the work," the paramedic advised soothingly as four pairs of hands lifted him from the ground onto a stretcher. One of those hands pulled his wallet from his back pants pocket. Mark tried to protest, but managed only to groan as that person sorted through the wallet, extracted his driver's license, and began copying information onto a form.

"Just relax, Mr. Lancaster. We're going to take good care of you," a voice instructed. "We'll have you at the hospital in just a few minutes. We're going to put an IV into your arm, so you're going to feel a little stick right here. Go ahead and yell if it hurts, OK?"

Mark felt pressure just below his right elbow, then a stab as the needle was inserted.

The stretcher bumped and shook as it rolled across the grass, then slid with surprising smoothness into the cooler interior of the ambulance, where Mark heard a new voice. "Can you tell me where you're hurt, Mr. Lancaster?" a female voice queried as she bent over him and began checking him from the feet up.

Mark groaned.

"OK, can you shake your head yes or no for me?"

Mark nodded.

"Are you hurting anywhere in your legs?" she wanted to know.

Mark shook his head side to side.

"How about in your abdomen? Any pain down here?" She probed and watched for a response.

Again he shook his head side to side.

"Your arms?" she asked.

He shook his head.

"Your chest?"

Mark nodded and groaned. A cold stethoscope touched him in several different places as she listened to his breathing.

"You've got a lot of noise in your chest, Mr. Lancaster," the paramedic declared as she began attaching adhesive patches to his chest and wiring him up to a heart monitor. Her voice was echoing loudly through his head yet sounding very distant at the same time. He wanted to panic, to run away and have this whole experience be nothing more than a bad dream. A new, irregular beeping sound could be heard somewhere among all the other sounds around the ambulance. Was that a heart monitor? He couldn't tell.

In an instant all of Mark's panic melted away and was replaced by a powerful calm. He felt himself rising past the paramedic's face to the ceiling of the ambulance, where he turned around and watched his rescuers moving quickly.

"I'm losing him! He's gone into cardiac arrest!" he heard the paramedic shout to her partner. It was fascinating watching the second paramedic rip off the oxygen mask, slide a curved instrument down his throat, and insert a breathing tube. She connected a squeezable black bag to the tube and let her partner begin compressing it. Then she yanked his shirt fully open and reached above her to a shelf for the defibrillator paddles.

"Clear!" she shouted. The partner pulled back.

Mark watched as she placed the paddles on his chest. His body convulsed as if trying to jump off the ambulance gurney.

"He's in ventricular fibrillation. Let's get some bicarb and epinephrine into him," the first paramedic ordered. Hands darted into the supply compartments, pulling out preloaded syringes of the medications that were injected into the IV tubing.

There still wasn't a regular heartbeat, so it was time for the paddles again. "Clear!"

Mark watched as his body again convulsed, jumping off the gurney. Fascinating as it was to watch, Mark felt himself moving away, backing through the closed rear ambulance doors. For a moment he surveyed the entire crash scene before turning his view upward toward a light brighter than the sun yet easier to look at. The light enveloped him as deceased friends and relatives began appearing and welcoming him. His grandmother. An uncle. Hope's father. They were all happy to see him. They shook his hand or clapped him on the shoulder as he moved past them.

Then a glowing figure with the warmest smile he had ever seen stood before him, speaking in the most melodious voice he had ever heard. The figure was dressed in a flowing robe of the crispest white, and the brightness of his skin made him seem almost as if he were aflame. "Welcome, my child," the figure said with outstretched hands. "But your time is not yet. You must go back and tell others what you have seen and of my love for them." Now Mark felt as if he were racing back down the tunnel of light. He wanted to cry out, but all turned to blackness and silence.

∽

"Somebody find out if her husband was actually on that plane," the news director commanded gruffly from a few paces behind Hope. She and a cluster of coworkers stood with their eyes glued to the TV. A junior news producer broke away and began searching a phone list to find a contact at Diamond Airways. In moments she was back with a report that the airline could not release the names of any of the passengers. "But they'll be calling the families of the passengers as soon as they can," she reported.

"Are you sure he was on that plane?" someone asked.

Hope nodded. "I know he was," she declared, barely taking her eyes off the screen. "He was on Diamond Airways from here to Los Angeles."

A reporter went to the Internet and found the Diamond Airways Web site. "What time did he leave?"

"Uh, about 9:00. I don't remember exactly," Hope answered.

"Well, it looks like he would have been on . . ." The reporter paused, stood, and moved close to Hope. "I'm sorry, Hope. It looks like that was his flight."

For the first time in several minutes Hope broke away from the monitor. "What's that number for Diamond Airways?" she demanded as panic rose in her voice. "I want public relations, the CEO, anybody who can give me answers. I want to know if my husband was on that flight and if he's OK!"

The reporter handed Hope a note. "Here's the public relations number from the Diamond Airways Web site."

Hope glanced at the number and reached for the phone. Moments later she slammed down the receiver in frustration. "All they'll say is that

Flight 886 has been involved in an accident and that they will be putting out a press release once they have more details. That could be 10 minutes from now or a couple hours." She looked up at the ceiling in growing frustration as tears began spilling down her cheeks.

"I've got to get to LA," she said softly, more to herself than to anyone else. "I've got to get to Mark. He needs me. I need to be with him." She was comforted by the growing determination she heard in her own voice.

For several moments it seemed as if Hope's entire world was the TV monitor showing the crash site. In the distance she could hear the ringing of phones as other newsroom staffers went about their duties preparing for the evening newscast. They might as well have been a million miles away.

"Hope," a coworker called to her from several desks away. She paid no attention, so he called again more loudly. "Hope! Line 3! Says she's your mother."

Hope pulled her eyes away from the TV only long enough to pick up the receiver and punch the right button. "Hope Lancaster," she answered distractedly.

"Hope, dear. Listen—Mark was on that plane. He's badly hurt. You need to get to LA as soon as you possibly can because he needs you," her mother said. "I'll pick up Jennifer over at the day-care center. She can stay here with me until you're ready to go, OK?"

It sounded like someone else speaking as Hope heard herself say "Thank you" and reach to hang up the phone. Her eyes remained fixed on the monitor until the feed from the local station in Los Angeles changed to their first live reporter on the scene, who began talking about where the injured people were being taken. She heard something about Harbor View Hospital.

For the first time in a half hour Hope sat at her desk and looked at something besides the crash scene. She went to the Internet and soon had the phone number for Harbor View Hospital. Her fingers flew over the keypad, and in seconds she was listening to the electronic ringing. "Harbor View Hospital," a female voice answered. "How may I direct your call?"

"Uh, emergency department, I think," Hope requested.

The line went silent for a second before ringing again. "Emergency department," a male voice answered. She could hear a lot of voices in the background.

"Uh, this is Hope Lancaster with channel 3 in Memphis. I think my husband, Mark, was on the flight that crashed at Los Angeles International Airport. I wanted to see if he's there."

"Is this a media inquiry or a personal inquiry?" the man responded.

"Personal. This is personal. I think my husband was on that flight. Can you tell me if he is there and what condition he's in?"

"We're in disaster mode here. We've got casualties coming in left and right, and we're really busy right now. All inquiries need to go through the public relations office, OK?" The line went dead.

Hope stared at the silent receiver for a moment before dialing the hospital's number again. This time she asked for the public relations office. The person who answered asked for her name and phone number and promised to give her a call as soon as there was any news.

For a time Hope just sat wondering what to do. "I've got to go home," she declared as she rose from her chair. A glance at the monitor showed that the network was recycling earlier footage from the crash scene. "I'm going home. I've got to get to LA tonight," she told the news director as she passed his office.

"Keep in touch and let us know if there's anything we can do to help you," he answered.

Hope fairly flew out the door. It was amazing that she did not get a speeding ticket en route to her mother's house.

A tearful Jennifer flew into her mother's arms as soon as she was inside the front door. "Is Daddy going to be OK? I mean, Grandma says he's hurt real bad . . ." Her words trailed off into a sob on Hope's shoulder. They just held onto each other for several minutes.

"Listen. I don't know when the earliest flight for LA leaves, but we're going to get to Daddy as soon as we can," Hope tried to reassure her daughter.

"Well, let's go pack and go to the airport," Jennifer stated with new-found confidence, as if it would be that simple.

Hope shook her head. "It's not going to happen that fast. LAX is closed, and we have to wait for it to open again. And I don't know when that's going to happen. It might be tonight, and it might be tomorrow. In the meantime, let's go home, pack, and wait."

"Can I get you something to eat?" Susan offered.

Hope looked at her mother and wondered how she could be so calm at a moment like this. She started to ask the question but stopped, not wanting to make Jennifer aware of the strange source of information she had just become aware of that day. "No thanks, Mom. My stomach's in such a tight knot right now that I couldn't eat anything."

Susan nodded and turned back to something she was doing in the kitchen.

~

Hope's cell phone remained silent all the way home, despite her prayers that Mark would call to say he was OK.

"Who are you talking to?" Jennifer inquired as they turned into the driveway.

"I'm praying. I'm asking Jesus to help Daddy be OK," Hope answered softly.

"I've been praying too," Jennifer revealed as she stepped out of the car. "I think he's going to be OK."

Jennifer's confidence warmed Hope's heart, and the first smile in more than two hours crossed her face, however briefly.

"He's going to be OK. I just know it." Jennifer reached up to give her mother a hug.

Hope held her daughter tightly as her tears began falling, first as a trickle and then an uncontrolled stream.

~

Packing suitcases was a purely mechanical function for Hope. She picked a large-sized suitcase for herself and a medium-sized one for Jennifer. She packed a third medium-sized one with clothing and other items for Mark, assuming he would recover and need them. Then she sat waiting for the silent phone to ring. Jennifer watched afternoon cartoons while Hope watched the phone. Every 30 minutes she dialed the airline's public relations office, and each time got the same answers. No, they couldn't tell her if Mark had been on the plane. Yes, they would be contacting the families of the passengers as soon as they had information.

An hour dragged by, and a hungry Jennifer began digging around in the kitchen. Hope heard the door to the microwave oven open, then close.

"What are you doing in there?" Hope called out.

"I'm hungry. I'm fixing something to eat," Jennifer answered.

"What are you making?"

"One of those TV dinners you bought for Dad a while back. Want one?"

"Those things? I'd forgotten we even had them," Hope answered. "No thanks." She turned up her nose at the thought of eating such pre-packaged meals.

However, smells from the microwave began wafting through the room, awakening Hope's appetite. Maybe prepackaged food wouldn't be so bad after all.

CHAPTER TWELVE

Your Dramamine wearing off?" Henderson shouted over the roar of the engine and the wind.

Keller nodded and grabbed the fishing chair to prevent encountering the deck as the boat tipped yet again. A wave of nausea swept over him, and he dove for the starboard railing. He kept his face toward the water for several minutes before doing his old imitation of slime oozing toward the deck.

Henderson threw him a can of soda and a tablet.

Why did I have to get partnered with an old sea dog? Keller wondered as he swallowed.

"See anything when you were looking over the side? The Loch Ness monster?" Henderson had a wicked grin on his face.

Keller shook his head. "Worse. A lot worse. We've got a hole in the side from when they were shooting at us."

Henderson grabbed a support and leaned over the side as they topped a swell. As it passed him he could see the hole: maybe two inches in diameter and below the waterline whenever the bow was digging into a swell. As another swell passed he saw a second hole, slightly smaller but only occasionally above water.

He stood and looked at the control panel. A red light told him the bilge pump was running. That would remove up to 40 gallons of water per minute. Would it be enough?

Henderson moved to the aft deck, where he worked the latches on the engine compartment cover and lifted a corner access hatch. The stab of sunlight into the darkness revealed the large diesel engine with a thin layer of water sloshing around its mount.

"How bad?" Keller asked.

"Maybe an inch."

Keller's eyes were growing wide. "What're we gonna do if it gets too deep?"

"Well, if we need to, we'll radio the Coast Guard before we put on our life jackets and jump into our life rafts," Henderson said matter-of-factly. "In the meantime, we've got some bad guys to keep an eye on."

Keller looked skyward and saw a pair of Navy FA-18 Hornet fighters pass several thousand feet directly overhead. He heard them as much as saw them before they were swallowed up again by the haze. He pointed upward. "I wonder if those guys can give us a hand," he shouted.

Henderson shook his head. "I'm guessing they're the combat air patrol over the airport."

A new voice began calling them on the marine band radio. "FBI 206, this is Navy Sweeper 5. Over."

The voice repeated, "FBI 206, this is Navy Sweeper 5. Over."

"Unit calling FBI 206, say again your ID," Henderson answered.

"FBI 206, this is Sweeper 5. We are a U.S. Navy anti-submarine patrol aircraft approaching your location. Can you give me your GPS coordinates? Over."

Henderson squeezed the transmit key and slowly called off the numbers, then repeated them.

Several seconds later the voice returned. "FBI 206, radar contact. Do you have visual contact with the target vessel?"

"Uh, Sweeper 5, we've lost visual contact, but we have radar contact, so we're still in pursuit. It's pretty hazy down here, you know?"

"Yeah, we know. Can you give us a bearing and distance from your location?"

By now Keller was on his feet. He studied the radar. "Bearing 282. Range three miles."

A new sound began pounding their eardrums over the roar of their boat's engine. It was the high-speed drumbeat of four large propellers pounding the air, mixed with the whine of turbine engines. The sound passed directly overhead, and for a few seconds the agents caught a glimpse of the patrol plane.

"Sweeper 5, FBI 206. You just buzzed us. Repeat, you just buzzed us," Henderson shouted excitedly into the microphone.

"Roger that, 206. Confirm the good guys. We've got the bad guys on radar. Say, you know anything about that bigger ship that's about 10 miles past them?"

The larger ship was visible on their radar too. "Negative on the second ship. All we know is what we see on our radar," Henderson reported.

"FBI 206, we'll take over from here. Thanks for the assist. You can return to port. Sweeper 5 out."

Henderson turned the bow back toward Marina del Rey, then stepped back to take another look into the engine compartment. He shook his head as he surveyed the sight.

"We gonna make it?" Keller queried.

"I hope so. The water's getting deeper, but I think we'll make it."

The pilot brought the patrol plane around on a heading where Santoro could make a photo surveillance of both targets. In moments he had slightly haze-fuzzed photos of each.

"Photo to flight. I've got three people on the smaller craft. Two are armed with what look like Kalashnikov automatic weapons. I'd label them definite bad guys. As for the larger ship, well, that's our old friend the *Sumatra Prince* from Indonesia. It's sitting dead in the water, as though it's waiting for the smaller boat. How much of a connection do you think there is between the two of them?"

The pilot laughed. "Just put two and two together." He radioed a report to command. A moment later they responded with orders to maintain surveillance contact but not to attack unless they were fired on or given orders to attack.

"I hope everybody's buckled up tight, 'cause this could get a little bumpy," the pilot warned everyone aboard as he brought the plane around for a low-level pass, pulled the throttles back to 160 knots, and extended the flaps for slow flight. They were just rolling out of their turn as they came over the port-bound FBI boat.

The agents looked up, saw the white missiles hanging under the wings, and suddenly felt better about the whole situation.

"Weapons, let's make this a simulated missile run," the pilot ordered.

"Aye, skipper. Already on it," the weapons officer answered as he scanned his missile launch systems.

Even with the reduced airspeed, Santoro knew the haze would give him only about 20 seconds to view each of the target boats. The smaller boat came into sight first. Three people were visible: one was at the wheel, one was going below deck, and the third stood with a long tube over his shoulder aimed up at the plane. Santoro froze for an instant as his mind raced to recognize what the tube was. Then he saw a plume of smoke erupt from the back of the tube and an object begin racing toward them.

"Missile! Inbound missile!" Santoro shouted over the intercom.

Almost instantly the pilot slammed the throttles forward to full military power and jerked the plane around to the right and back toward land.

"Flares!" someone shouted. "Start dropping flares."

One of the weapons people in the rear of the plane already had his hand on the release lever, and the plane began trailing a string of magnesium flares into the air. They hoped the heat-seeking missile would lock onto a bright-as-the-sun flare and chase it instead of their plane.

~

Amir Al-Hamzi flinched and jerked away from the loud hiss of the missile launch. Three sets of eyes followed it upward as the sound of the missile was drowned by the roar of four turboprop engines.

The first problem with firing the missile head-on at the plane was that it didn't have a good heat source to lock onto. The second was that the missile did not arm until it was a half mile from the launcher and well behind the patrol plane. The third problem was that, lacking a heat source, it did exactly as it was programmed and climbed in a counterclockwise direction. That course brought it back around toward the patrol plane and above the flares falling behind it. As it did, the brightest heat source was the sun. It locked on and turned upward even more steeply. Fifteen breath-holding seconds later it ran out of fuel and turned itself into a rain of shrapnel onto the water.

"You idiot! That was our last missile!" Abdullah complained angrily.

Muhammad smiled back. "No! We have one more, and if we aim it at them, maybe they'll stay away from us." He went below and retrieved the last loaded firing tube.

~

"Photo! I want you to roll your tape back to be sure that what you saw actually happened," the pilot ordered as the plane leveled out over the open water.

Santoro rolled his tape back frame by frame until he had a freeze-frame of the missile coming out of the tube at them. "Photo to pilot. Confirm missile launch. I've got a real clear picture of a shoulder-fired missile coming out of the tube."

The intercom was silent for a moment before the pilot's voice returned. "Pilot to crew. Weapons free. Repeat. Weapons free at pilot's discretion. We've been fired on, and our rules of engagement permit us to return fire. Stand by for a missile run. Let's go harpoon us some terrorists!"

The weapons people in the back looked at each other. The one seated at the control console began flipping arming switches. Now the Harpoon anti-ship missiles on the launching rails under the wings would respond to the launch computer when the button was pushed.

"Radar, do we have any other targets in the area?" the weapons officer wanted to know.

"Negative. Closest target is range, oh, eight miles and widening."

It was taking some time to set up the attack. Sweeper 5 could attack from any direction, but they needed to start their missile run from at least a 10-mile distance. In the time it took them to do that the smaller boat's blip on the radar moved toward the shape of the larger ship and then stopped.

"Pilot to weapons, you may fire at will. Repeat. You may fire at will. Confirm when you are locked on target and ready."

"Weapons, aye."

~

Amir pulled the boat under the boarding ladder. Muhammad used the fishing chair as a step to lift himself up high enough to catch the ladder as the boat topped a swell. Abdullah followed several swells later. Amir cut the engines and stepped back quickly to follow his comrades. A swell pushed the stern of the boat hard against the side of the freighter. The impact sent him sprawling across the deck. He picked himself up in time to reach up and grab the bottom rung of the ladder, only to find himself dangling in the air as the boat fell away beneath him.

Abdullah turned around to assist him, but the boat rose again before he could arrive. The stern rail came up under Amir's left foot and pushed him up enough so that he could pull himself halfway onto the step. Abdullah's strong hands helped him the rest of the way.

"Quickly!" Abdullah admonished as Amir gained his footing and began climbing.

The sound of turboprop engines was approaching from somewhere off in the haze.

～

"First target is the smaller boat," the weapons officer said, then announced words that sent a thrill up everyone's spine. "Fox 1! Fox 1!" The first Harpoon missile was away.

DiPlacio glanced out his window and saw the smoke trail before it disappeared in the wind.

The missile flew level until almost a mile short of the target, then turned sharply upward to gain altitude before turning over and spearing downward into its target. Designed to puncture steel, the nose of the missile had no trouble going through layers of fiberglass and wood. It punched through the boat before exploding several feet under it. The boat disintegrated into shards of debris as it rose upward on the geyser.

Santoro caught the explosion on videotape.

～

The terrorists were already up the ladder and inside the aft superstructure of the boat when the missile detonated. They felt the explosion as much as heard it as it knocked them off their feet.

Muhammad was first out the door to see what had happened. He ran to the rail, saw the debris raining back onto the water, and ducked back inside. "They missed us! They hit the boat, but they missed us!"

Abdullah and Amir ran out the door to survey the sight.

"Allahu Akbar!" Abdullah began shouting. "The infidels can't shoot straight!"

Amir suddenly felt sick to his stomach as he realized it was his boat, his pride and joy, that was raining down on them in little pieces and slipping below the waves.

～

"Let's make this a photo pass," the pilot ordered as Sweeper 5 let the distance to the *Sumatra Prince* grow. Four minutes later their nose was pointed back at the ship.

"Looks like they're moving," DiPlacio reported. A minute later he added, "Their bearing looks like 255 degrees, and their speed's about 10 to 12 knots."

"Fox 2!" the weapons officer called at the 12-mile mark. "Fox 3!" he called at the 10-mile mark. The first missile would spend 18 seconds in flight. The second would arrive less than a minute behind it.

The pilot banked the plane left, then put it into a standard-rate turn to the right so the targets would be at the center of their circle and within photo range.

~

The trio heard the patrol plane somewhere off in the haze. *What's it going to do?* was the unspoken question on everyone's mind. All faces followed as the sound grew louder in the distance, then changed direction.

"They're turning away!" someone shouted. Smiles of relief spread across their faces. Then the roar of the missile captured their attention, and their eyes locked onto the rising streak until it tilted over. They followed it downward as it drilled a hole through the cover over the forward cargo hold. A split second later they were knocked off their feet as it exploded, buckling the hold cover upward and cracking the keel.

Abdullah recovered his balance, then prostrated himself on the deck toward the east and began shouting the martyr's prayer.

Muhammad pulled himself to a sitting position against the wall of the aft hold and just looked at his partners. "If they can't shoot, what was that?" he asked no one in particular.

The roar of the third missile caught their attention. They looked up in time to follow the smoke trail as it turned downward from 2,000 feet overhead. This one rammed through the cargo cover closest to them. This explosion finished breaking the ship's keel and sent all three terrorists flying over the side. Most of the ship's crew below deck were either killed by the blast or too seriously injured to escape as the ship began breaking apart and taking on water.

~

"The ship is dead in the water," DiPlacio reported.

"The *Sumatra Prince* is starting to burn and looks like it's breaking in two," Santoro reported. The image on his screen turned upside down as the plane flew over the ship and the camera remained locked on. "I've got three people over the starboard side and one person in the water on the port side. Wait a second. Two more just went into the water off the stern."

A billow of smoke began rising around the stern. "The ship is on fire," Santoro reported.

The pilot banked Sweeper 5 into a right-hand turn, the idea being to fly a figure-eight pattern that would bring them back over the ship at the intersection of the circles. On their first return pass the ship was obviously breaking apart just ahead of the aft superstructure. By the second pass two minutes later the breakup was complete, with both sections sinking quickly. By their fourth pass at the eight-minute point the stern was gone and the bow barely visible.

Santoro switched to his thermal imaging system to scan the area for survivors. "Looks like several survivors in the drink, and no life rafts," he reported on their fifth pass.

"Should we call the Coast Guard and ask them to drop a life raft?" the pilot asked.

Santoro waited a moment before answering and watched as the stern section slipped under the waves and pulled all but one of the survivors down with it. "I'm not sure they can get here in time."

A half hour later the last warm body disappeared below the waves.

"No survivors," Santoro reported on their last pass. *The sea is the ulti-mate avenger.*

~

"I wish Mom would answer her phone!" Hope hissed in frustration for the umpteenth time. A new round of tears began as quickly as she punched the "off" button on the cordless handset. Hope yelled to the empty room, "She's the one who got me worrying by telling me not to let Mark get on that plane! Now I can't reach her on either her cell phone or at home!"

Hope looked at the cordless telephone in her hand and fought the temptation to throw it at something. She was glad that Jennifer was quietly watching television in the other room, unable to see or hear her tirade.

Then, as Hope's emotions swung to the other extreme, she found herself wishing that her mother would not call. That way Hope could avoid the possibility of her mom delivering another message from her deceased father. This whole situation was more than Hope could handle. She was a wreck.

Hope's fingers punched the memorized pattern of numbers for the airline, and she listened for the ringing that followed. This time the airline had a little bit of news: they expected to have a compiled list of victims from the crash within a few minutes and would soon begin notifying relatives. If Mark was on the list, they would be calling, the woman told her. Strange as it seemed, even this tidbit of nonnews gave her a little bit of comfort, because her wait for some sort of information was almost over.

"I'm going upstairs to check our suitcases," Hope called into the other room. Somehow her voice sounded a bit stronger than before the call, and that made her feel just the tiniest bit better too.

"OK, Mom," Jennifer answered. Then after a slight pause, she added, "Any more news about Daddy?"

"The airline said they would be calling the family members of the passengers shortly. I expect we will find out something in the next hour or so. I'll let you know as soon as I hear from them."

CHAPTER THIRTEEN

Another hour passed before the call from the airline finally came. The good news was that Mark was among the living. They couldn't give her details of his condition, but they did have a phone number for Harbor View Hospital.

～

After receiving news from the Navy about their attack on the terrorist boats, the Department of Homeland Defense decided that Los Angeles International Airport could reopen at 8:00 p.m. The disruption caused by the closure had been enormous. Delayed flights waiting at other airports had to be rescheduled. Diverted flights meant that planes that were supposed to be in Los Angeles weren't there and ready to go to other cities. It would take two days to get everything back to normal.

The reservations agent that Hope called at Diamond Airways assured her that the airline would get her and Jennifer on the first possible flight into Los Angeles. The only problem was that no one had any idea when that would be. The airline promised to cover all travel and lodging expenses for both of them until Mark could return home.

Hope's hands were trembling so much that she misdialed the hospital's number twice. Finally she asked Jennifer to do the dialing.

"How is he? How's Daddy?" Jennifer asked again and again as Hope waited for someone to answer the phone.

"Harbor View Hospital," someone finally answered before switching Hope to an unnamed extension.

"Intensive-care unit," a kind voice answered.

Hope's heart had been about to beat out of her chest; now it leaped into her throat and choked her voice. She barely managed to say who she was and whom she was inquiring about. "Is he going to live?" was her biggest question.

"He's very ill, and we're doing all we can to help him. We've got him sedated right now to help him rest, and he's on a ventilator to help him breathe," the nurse advised. "How soon will you be here?"

"I . . . I don't know. As soon as I can . . . I guess." Hope heard her voice quivering. "I mean, the Los Angeles airport is still closed, and I'm in Memphis, and I don't know when I can get a flight."

"If I were you, I would try flying to Ontario or Orange County and renting a car," the nurse concluded. "It might be faster than waiting for everything to get back on track at the Los Angeles airport."

Hope related the news to Jennifer before announcing that they would simply go to the airport, see what flight they could get, and wait for it to leave.

"How long will we have to wait?" Jennifer yawned.

"As long as it takes," Hope said with resignation.

They made a quick circuit of the house. A trio of bananas that would surely spoil before they returned went into the trash, and Hope rolled the trash can to the street even though it wouldn't be picked up for two days. Jennifer had dragged their suitcases out to the SUV by the time Hope got off the phone with a neighbor, who agreed to watch the house until they returned.

"I even packed a sundress, my swimsuit, and sunscreen because the weather guy on TV said it's going to more than 100 degrees there during the next few days," Jennifer announced as they backed into the growing darkness.

Hope smiled proudly at her daughter. A few days from her ninth birthday, she was still so young but at the same time so mature. "Did you pack your toothbrush?"

Jennifer nodded; then her face became sad once again. "I just want to be with Daddy," she said softly.

Another round of tears welled up in Hope's eyes, and she held out her hand to squeeze Jennifer's.

~

Their wait was surprisingly short. Diamond Airways had a flight leaving for Dallas an hour after they showed up at the ticket counter, and from there they were booked on a connecting flight to Los Angeles. The unknown was if that flight could be given a landing slot at Los Angeles during the first hours after the airport reopened.

"We'll at least get you to Dallas, but we can't promise how long you'll have to wait once you get there," the ticket agent apologized.

After passing through security, Hope looked at their boarding passes to see which gate they would depart from. It was then that she saw their seat assignments: 2A and 2B. First class! She'd always traveled coach, even when flying overseas.

"That's because you're priority passengers," the agent at the gate explained.

Exhaustion overtook Jennifer shortly after they boarded. She leaned her head against her mother's arm and was asleep barely after takeoff. She roused enough to return her seat to the upright position for the landing in Dallas, but then leaned back over against her mother and once again fell asleep while they landed and taxied to the gate. Their flight to Los Angeles departed without delay. Fortunately, they did not have to change planes, so Jennifer slept through the entire transition.

In contrast, sleep evaded Hope the entire way.

As the plane tipped forward for its descent Hope found herself staring out the window and thinking, *Is this the path Mark's plane took?* The winds had eased and the visibility had improved, so lights could be seen reflecting off the water as the plane dropped lower. Two boats with bright searchlights could be seen poking into the darkness around them. Then they were over the beach, and the runway flashed beneath them.

Jennifer roused enough to walk off the plane to the baggage claim area. Once there she again wrapped her arms around her mother and tried to use Hope's stomach as a pillow.

In the idle minutes waiting for the luggage carousel to begin moving, Hope looked around the baggage claim area. At first she was surprised by how many others looked as tired as she felt. *This must be why they call them red-eye flights.* As she continued to scan the faces around her, she saw a sign with her name being held aloft by a tall, young African-American man with Hollywood looks. Hope walked toward him and held out her hand. "I'm Hope Lancaster."

"Good morning! I'm Andrew Camacho," he said in a voice too cheerful to be legal at that hour as he pumped her hand. "I work with Diamond

Airways, and they've assigned me to be your helper, aide, and all-around guide during your time here."

"What exactly do you mean by that?" Hope asked as she stifled a yawn.

"It means that, well, whatever you need, I'm here to provide it. Because of the circumstances, you and your daughter are guests of Diamond Airways, and we want to make sure that you are well cared for. Do you have a rental car reserved?"

That was something Hope had not considered in her rush to depart. She shook her head.

"That's OK. We've taken the liberty of renting one for you. I've got it parked in the short-term lot right across the street. What about hotel reservations?" he asked.

She hadn't considered that, either. This was totally unlike her typically well-organized self. Once again, she shook her head.

"We've got that covered too. We've got you a room reserved at the Radisson just east of here. It's so close that you can look out your window and watch the planes as they land." Andrew studied Hope's face. "You feel up to driving?"

She shook her head.

"OK, I'll drive if you want," he offered.

"That'll be great, because I don't know my way around. How far is it to the hospital?"

Andrew thought for a moment. "At this hour, oh, 20 to 30 minutes. But in rush hour, multiply that by at least three."

A half hour later mother and daughter were riding the elevator to their room at the Radisson. They stayed just long enough to drop off their luggage.

"You sure you don't want to rest awhile first?" Andrew asked as they stepped out of the elevator.

"I can sleep later. Right now I just want to see my husband," Hope declared.

The first rays of sunrise were lightening the sky as the trio headed for the car. Because of the haze there was no glowing orb in the sky, only a generalized brightening, a realization that things were not as dark as they had been. The sky was fully alight as the car entered the relative darkness of the hospital's parking garage.

Minutes later they were at the door to the intensive-care unit, where they found a sign listing the visiting hours. Hope looked at the sign, glanced at her watch, and began crying.

"What's wrong?" Andrew inquired.

"I flew all night to be with my husband, and I've just missed the visiting period. The next time's not for two hours," she wailed.

Jennifer's visage reflected her mother's, and she began clouding up as though she might begin crying too.

Andrew snatched tissues from a box resting on a nearby table and distributed them. "Uh, what time do you have?" he inquired.

"Eight-twenty-five," Hope cried. "The last visiting time ended 10 minutes ago. If we'd come straight here from the airport, we could've made it. I could've seen him!"

Andrew shook his head. "Uh, is your watch on Central time?"

Hope nodded.

Andrew smiled. "It's 6:25 here. Pacific time." He glanced at the visiting hours' sign. "The first visiting time starts in a half hour."

"Excuse me," a voice interrupted. The trio looked around to see a middle-aged man in a tailored business suit holding out his hand. The warmth of his smile and the sympathy in his eyes instantly made Hope like him. "I'm Chaplain Taylor Steiner. Are you related to one of the crash victims?"

Hope nodded as she choked on a tear. "Yes. Mark Lancaster. He's in ICU, and we just arrived from Memphis, and we haven't been able to see him yet." She pointed toward the closed doors.

Chaplain Steiner held up a hand and smiled warmly. "Give me a minute and let me see what I can do for you," he said softly. He walked over to the security card scanner pad next to the visiting hours sign and waved his photo ID badge in front of it. The door unlatched with an audible metallic click and swung open with a pneumatic swoosh. "Wait here," he said as he stepped through and the door closed behind him.

Hope and Jennifer stared in silence at the door as they waited. After what seemed an eternity, the door opened again and Chaplain Steiner reappeared, this time waving his hand for them to enter. "The nurse said you could have 10 minutes with him. Follow me."

Jennifer's eyes grew wide, and she began stepping warily around the medical equipment and patients they passed. Her grip on Hope's arm tightened as they paused at the door to one of the cubicles.

Chaplain Steiner waved them inside. "Here he is," he smiled kindly. The turned-up corners of his mouth accentuated the deepening lines across his face and made his eyes seem to twinkle. Jennifer wondered how he could smile in a place like this, where her eyes were growing wider by the second. Then her entire world became focused on the form lying in the bed in front of her.

Mark lay still except for the rhythmic rising and falling of his chest that was driven by a mechanical ventilator sending air through a tube in his mouth. A pair of IV bags hung from a pole on one side of the bed. An IV pump on the pole hummed for a few seconds, causing Jennifer to turn in fright and grab her mother's hand with both of hers.

Wife and daughter stepped cautiously to Mark's side. Hope leaned over and gave him a kiss on the forehead. "We got here as soon as we could," she said with a quiver in her voice. He did not respond.

Jennifer reached through the bed rails and stroked her father's arm. "I love you, Daddy," she said with a matching quiver in her voice. She choked on her words. "I just want you to get better and come home soon." She threw her arms around her mother's waist and buried her face in Hope's blouse.

It was such an odd and uncomfortable moment. They were so happy to see Mark, yet so stricken with fright at the sight of him in this condition. They talked to him, yet he did not answer. He was receiving the best of care, but they were helpless to do anything to assist him. All they could do was wait. It was then that Hope realized just how noisy this place was, with heart monitors beeping, nurses talking, and the varied sounds of machines keeping people alive.

"Excuse me, folks," a middle-aged male nurse with thinning hair said as he slipped into the room to check the IV pump, study the display on the heart monitor above the head of the bed, and make some notes on Mark's chart. "Are you his family?"

"He's my daddy," Jennifer answered in a voice stronger than Hope could muster right then.

"Has anyone told you what's going on with him?" the nurse asked.

Mother and daughter both shook their heads.

"OK. Here's the story. He was brought in yesterday after the plane crash over at the airport. Apparently he inhaled a lot of smoke while getting out of the plane. Of course, the smoke contained a lot of chemicals and acids from the burning plastic and other materials on the plane. Things like that cause severe irritation to the airways and lungs. As a result, his lungs filled up with fluids. The reason he's on the ventilator is to keep enough pressure in his lungs so all the little air sacs in his lungs won't fill up with fluid."

"How long will my daddy have to be here? How long will he have to use that machine over there?" Jennifer pointed to the ventilator.

The nurse's deep breath and body language told them he was being guarded. Mother and daughter instinctively grabbed each other's hands.

"Hopefully not more than a few days. In here, I mean. Right now he's got a lot of fluid in his lungs, but he's getting enough oxygen, and the fluid's not getting worse. So that's a good sign," the nurse revealed.

Jennifer studied her mother's face for some assurance.

Hope knelt down to look Jennifer in the eye. "Listen. We've just got to give Daddy some time to heal. All we can do now is wait and pray that he will get better," Hope said softly.

Mother and daughter studied each other's face in silence. "Let's go get some breakfast," Hope said, almost in a whisper.

"But I don't want to go. I want to stay here with Daddy," Jennifer protested.

"We'll come back in a little while. I promise. Let's let him rest. Remember what I told you about your body healing when you're asleep?"

Jennifer nodded. "Uh-huh. But what's that got to do with Daddy?"

"Everything, sweetie. Everything. The doctors have given him some medicine to make him sleep so he can get better," Hope declared firmly, then softened her voice. "You know what? My tummy's starting to rumble. What about yours?"

Jennifer nodded. "Mine too."

"We'll come back in a little while. I promise." Hope stood and turned to the door.

"Thank you," Hope mouthed toward the nurse as they turned back down the row of cubicles and heard the myriad of sounds from the unit.

Chaplain Steiner and Andrew rose from their seats to greet the pair as they came through the double doors.

Chaplain Steiner held out a brochure with a business card sticking out of it. "I want you to know that the other chaplains and I are here to help you anytime you need us. My cell phone number is on the card. Please don't be afraid to use it, OK? You're not bothering me when you call. We have a chapel just a couple minutes' walk from here, and my office is right next door. There's also a list of phone numbers for area churches if there's anyone in particular you want to contact."

"Thank you," Hope said weakly as he turned to leave.

A moment later Andrew was leading them back to the car. "I've heard that there's a restaurant just down the street that serves really good breakfasts. Anybody hungry?"

Jennifer's stomach growled loud enough for everyone to hear.

"I guess that's a yes," Andrew smiled.

Over the course of the morning Hope and Jennifer made the acquaintance of three other family members of crash victims. Actually, Jennifer made the first contacts. Hope's attention was focused on pacing the floor and counting the minutes until the next visiting period, while Jennifer was looking for something to do. In one of the other family groups she spotted a girl about her age who looked equally bored, and they were magnetically attracted. The parents soon followed. Others overheard the conversation, and the community grew.

Their conversations were filled with details of injuries, medical expectations they had been given, and fears. Fortunately, it helped fill the hours between when the doors opened for visitors.

As chairs went, the ones in the waiting room were nothing to brag about. They were comfortable if you were sitting erect, but when it came to providing a place to nap they were difficult. Despite her resistance, exhaustion overtook Hope as she settled into one of them after the mid-morning visitation period. Within seconds she was leaning over at an odd angle with her eyes closed.

Andrew was entertaining Jennifer with a magic trick when he noted Hope's posture and drew Jennifer's attention to it. "I think we need to get your mother back to the hotel for a nap," he declared.

Jennifer tried several times before she was able to rouse her mother. Once in the car Hope managed to stay awake all the way to the hotel, where she stretched across the bed.

"If you want to watch TV, just keep the volume down, OK?" Hope mumbled as she tugged at her pillow. "Maybe Andrew can help us find something for you to do later."

She was asleep before Jennifer found the remote control.

Somewhere off in the distance Hope could hear a telephone ringing. As consciousness crept into her cranium she first realized that the ringing was different from the phone at home. Next she realized that she had been sleeping fully clothed, that sunlight was streaming through cracks in the draperies, and that a television was on somewhere beyond her sleepiness. The ringing was from her cell phone buried somewhere in her purse. Where was she? That's right, Los Angeles! She managed to awaken and retrieve the phone just after it quit ringing.

"Maybe they left a voice message," she muttered to no one in particular as she pushed hair back off her face and punched the buttons to check her messages. There were several from family members asking about Mark. She called her brother, David, gave him a short report, and asked him to relay it to the rest of the family so she wouldn't have to call and repeat the same things to everyone. He agreed.

Another was from Bob Knoller, the usually grumpy news director back at channel 3. She was about to dial his number when she realized with alarm that Jennifer was not around.

"Jennifer! Jennifer!" she nearly screamed in panic, and instinctively headed for the door to look outside. The hallway was empty. Back in the room she headed for the house phone to call the front desk when the bathroom door opened and Jennifer stepped out. Hope clasped her hands across her chest and let out her breath. "Whew! There you are! Don't scare me like that!"

"But you were asleep, Mom, and I had to go to the bathroom."

"I'm sorry, dear. I . . . I guess I'm just really uptight right now."

"That's OK, Mom," Jennifer consoled her mother. "I know you're worried about Daddy. I am too. I'm really, really worried about him. Those machines at the hospital really scared me."

The last message on Hope's cell phone was from Peter Leventhal. "How are you? How is Mark?" he wanted to know.

Hope called him right back and gave him a quick review of Mark's condition. "Right now all we can do is wait and see what happens," she said.

"Is there anything we can do for you?" Peter wanted to know. "Anything at all? Just say it," he pressed.

"Just pray," Hope answered. "He's really, really sick. The staff think he's going to recover, but he's going to spend several days on the ventilator. Right now we're in wait-and-see mode. That's all we can do. Just wait and see."

"Our prayers are with you. I'm here if you need me, OK?" Peter implored.

Had she heard him right? Had Peter just used the word "here"? Hope wondered. "Uh, Peter. Where are you exactly?"

He laughed. "You're not going to believe this, but I'm downstairs outside the ballroom with a crew waiting to see who all comes to this meeting the airline's holding. Believe it or not, we were changing planes here yesterday when the crash happened and the airport got shut down. Since we weren't going anywhere, Brandon Campbell decided we might as well stay and cover the story. Nothing like being there, right?"

"What meeting are you talking about?"

"The one the airline is holding for the families of the crash victims. Didn't you know about it?" Peter answered. "You know, the one that starts in about an hour."

Hope's eyes darted to an information sheet Andrew had left with her earlier. Sure enough, the meeting was listed. How had she overlooked it? Well, she'd been sleeping. Her mind began racing over the dozen things she had to do between now and then. A glance in the mirror showed her hair in frightful condition, her makeup streaked from crying, and her blouse and slacks wickedly creased from sleeping in them. On top of that she needed a shower, and her stomach was tied in a tight ball that felt as if it were climbing into her chest.

"I've got to run if we're going to be ready," Hope excused herself. "Maybe I'll see you downstairs."

Imagine the probability of meeting Peter like this! she thought. *What a coincidence!* Only this would be different, Hope knew instinctively, because the tables would be turned. Instead of being the hunter pursuing the story, she would be one of the pursued. What would it feel like being the prey?

～

"He's sedated so he can rest and let the ventilator help him breathe," Hope reported to her mother.

"Do you know who else from here is in the same hospital?" Susan asked.

"Who?"

"Robert Ingersoll. The report I heard said he was in critical condition."

"Really? I've already met some of the other families. Maybe I'll meet his wife here, too," Hope answered. She started to ask her mother another question, then hesitated and reconsidered.

"You were saying something?" Susan prompted.

"Oh, nothing," Hope answered. In reality she knew exactly what she wanted to ask, but was afraid to ask it for fear of what the answer might be.

"In case you're wondering, dear, your father hasn't told me anything new."

That answered the question she'd been afraid to ask.

Chapter Fourteen

A solid wall of reporters flanked the path between the trio and the hotel meeting room. "Don't say a word to any of the newspeople—at least until after the meeting, OK?" Andrew cautioned before launching them straight toward the outstretched microphones and shouldered TV cameras.

"How do you feel about how the airline is handling the situation?" the first reporter shouted in what turned into a barrage of inquiries.

"Where are you from?"

"Who in your family was on the flight?"

Someone ahead of them stopped to talk to the reporters, who circled to get camera angles and blocked the path to the meeting.

A barrage of camera flashes blinded Jennifer. She tripped and would have fallen had she not been holding tightly to both her mother's and Andrew's hands. He responded by turning a shoulder into the group and parting the press like a football linebacker cutting a hole through the defense for a ball carrier. In one big rush they were through the double doors and inside one of the large banquet rooms.

It was quieter in here, if for no other reason than that people were speaking in polite volumes instead of shouting over each other. Hope and Jennifer looked around, fearful of staring into a camera lens but finding only the polite faces of people from Diamond Airways and the Red Cross and assorted family members wearing a universal mask of stress. They were asked to fill out some registration papers and have their picture snapped for a photo ID badge before taking a seat for the briefing.

An airline official gave the tally of the wreck: of the 207 people aboard the plane, 58 had died, including one who had passed away overnight. Another 62 were scattered among five area hospitals. The rest were not injured or had been treated and released.

There was no doubt that it was a terrorist attack, a senior FBI administrator declared, while declining to say exactly how they knew. Already pieces of the missile had been recovered from the wreckage of the plane. Agents were working on identifying and rounding up anyone who had supported the terrorists. Earlier that morning they had raided an apartment and pizzeria in Venice Beach believed to be owned by one of the conspirators.

Officials believed that all the terrorists were dead, the result of an attack by a Navy patrol plane that had sunk both the boat used by the attackers and an Indonesian freighter to which they had fled. There were no known survivors, the FBI administrator added.

"But we get to live with the aftermath," Hope muttered to herself.

"What did you say, Mommy?" Jennifer whispered.

"Oh, nothing."

"But you sounded angry, Mommy. Real angry," Jennifer pressed.

"I guess you're right, dear. I'm angry, and I'm hurt. All I want to do is hug Daddy and take him home and be able to tell him everything's going to be all right." She fell silent for several seconds as she fought tears. "But I can't."

⁓

The next morning Andrew spotted Hope and Jennifer at a table in the hotel's restaurant. "Mind if I join you?" he asked politely as he approached.

"Pull up a chair. Had breakfast yet?" Hope waved him toward one of the empty chairs at their table.

"Yes. I've already eaten, thank you. But that coffee smells really good." He flagged a passing server and requested a cup. "And how are Hope and Miss Jennifer this morning?"

"I'm OK, I guess," Jennifer stated with a note of uncertainty. "Kinda sleepy."

"She's not too excited this morning. I mean, she wants to see her daddy, but she's not excited about all those hours in the waiting room between visits."

Andrew thought for a moment and shook his right index finger in the air. "I might have a solution. Let me go make a call and see what we can do about that." He excused himself and disappeared in the direction of the lobby. He returned minutes later with an extra twinkle in his eyes and a mischievous grin.

"Out with it, Andrew," Jennifer ordered. "Like my mommy says, you look like you've got a secret and you're dying to tell it."

"Well, it's up to your mother." He glanced in Hope's direction. Hope felt her defenses go up. "Can we go outside and talk for a minute?"

Hope nodded and rose from her chair.

"I was checking in with my boss and found out that there are several other families here with kids about her age who are feeling the same way, so the airline's sponsoring an outing for them today over at Universal Studios. It's a really fun place where you get to see how movies are made, and there's even a preteen pop concert there this afternoon."

"Who's going to be with them?" Hope demanded.

"We've got a group of flight attendants who are either off flight duty or assigned to the families who will be going. Oh, and don't worry about the expense. The only thing she might need is some money for souvenirs."

"Sounds good to me," Hope declared after considering the details. They returned to the table.

Jennifer started wiggling in her chair and was bouncing up and down by the time Andrew had finished his sales pitch. "Can I go, Mommy? Can I? Can I?"

"Yes, you can go. We just need to go back up to the room so that you can brush your teeth and put on some sunscreen. I don't want you getting a sunburn," Hope instructed.

Jennifer sprang from her seat and threw her arms around her mother's neck. "Thank you! Thank you!" she squealed. "I promise I'll be good. Best behavior."

Andrew smiled. "The bus leaves from the front entrance just after 9:00. That way we'll get there right when they open. We'll probably be back around 5:00 or 6:00. I expect she'll be absolutely worn-out. We'll buy them lunch there along with snacks."

Jennifer was still doing a victory dance. "Thank you, Mommy! Thank you! Thank you! I promise I'll be good."

Hope held up a hand for Jennifer to stop, and a look of concern covered the child's face. "OK, time to settle down. Before you leave for the day we're going to see Daddy. It's early enough that we should be able to get over there, see him, and get back in time for you to meet the bus."

Jennifer jiggled and wiggled with excitement.

"You have my cell phone number, right?" Andrew asked.

Hope double-checked the pocket of her purse. "Right here."

"Call me if you need anything. I'll try to have her call you, oh, mid-afternoon just to check in," Andrew promised as Hope turned back to her breakfast. Unlike her mother, Jennifer couldn't eat another bite.

～

The ICU staff were hurrying quietly about their duties as the 7:30 a.m. visiting period began. The machine that Jennifer once regarded with fear now aroused benign curiosity as she made a beeline for her father's side.

Hope, on the other hand, was reading the names on the outside of the cubicles as they passed. She noted that the name outside the third doorway was "Ingersoll, Robert M." A few doorways down, she paused at Mark's cubicle, took a deep breath, and put on a brave face before stepping inside.

"Hi, honey!" she greeted his still form as cheerfully as possible as she stepped to the head of the bed. He responded just enough to turn his head and open his eyes a little. Surprise registered on Hope's face for a moment until she realized that he was not looking at her.

"Can you hear me, Mark?" she asked.

His head moved a little bit, and his eyes opened for a few seconds before closing again.

Hope reached out to stroke stray hairs away from his forehead. Unexpected warmth reached up to her fingertips. At first she recoiled in surprise, then gently laid her palm across his forehead to confirm her fears. His fever melted the bravery off her face.

"Oh, Mark! You're burning up!" she whispered barely loud enough to be heard above the cardiac monitor and the ventilator.

"What's wrong, Mommy?" Jennifer reflected the fear on her mother's face.

"Your daddy has a fever. I'm going to go get a nurse and see if they know about it," she said as she turned and exited the cubicle. She had to wait a moment at the nurses' station before one of the staff returned.

Yes, they knew about the fever. It had been elevated for several hours and was nothing unexpected or unusual in a situation like his, the nurse said. Mark was being given an antibiotic in his IV to help combat the infection.

As she turned to return to her husband's side, something caught Hope's gaze, and she stopped to look again. Theresa Ingersoll was entering the intensive-care unit and walking to where her husband lay. Except for the look of concern on her face, her appearance resembled that of someone who'd just stepped from the pages of a fashion magazine. Her makeup was perfect. She wore a tailored suit and multicolor printed blouse with coordinated jewelry that fairly shouted the word "money."

In a second she was out of sight. In that same second Hope realized she wanted very much to meet Theresa Ingersoll. But why? Why did she feel this compulsion to meet the wife of a man about whom she'd aired a negative story just days before? Would Theresa even talk to her? What was she like?

"Are you Mrs. Lancaster?" an authoritative voice inquired from the cubicle entry.

"Uh, yes. Yes, I am," Hope answered as she surveyed the man addressing her. The white lab coat with his name sewn above the left pocket looked three sizes too big for the suntanned and athletic form. *How could someone who looked so young be a physician?* she wondered.

"I'm Dr. Purcell." He smiled broadly as he held out his hand to shake hers, then Jennifer's. "Have the nurses updated you on your husband's condition?"

"Not yet," Jennifer answered for her mother.

"He's getting better. I expect we're going to see a dramatic improvement over the next day or two. He's got a fever from an infection right now, but his lungs are clearing up and he's working at breathing on his own, so we've been able to reduce the pressure on the ventilator some. With any luck, by this time tomorrow I expect he could be breathing on his own," Dr. Purcell declared. "When he does, we'll cut back on the sedative and let him wake up."

The news made Hope smile. "A minute ago when I got here he responded when I spoke to him, but he wasn't looking at me."

Dr. Purcell nodded. "Responding to such stimuli as someone calling your name is an instinctual response. But he's still sedated too deeply for him to begin responding coherently. That'll all come back as we ease up on the medication."

"I don't understand," Jennifer piped up.

Dr. Purcell turned toward the child and bent down to talk on her level. "It means your daddy's getting better, and I think in another day or two he will be awake and we can move him out of here into a regular room. What do you think of that?"

Jennifer smiled broadly. "I like it a lot 'cause I want him to get better. I don't like hospitals, so I've been praying for him to get better."

Dr. Purcell returned the smile and patted her shoulder. "Well, I think your prayers are being answered."

He straightened up and turned again to Hope. "I'll be checking on him this afternoon." In an instant he was out the door and heading to the nurses' station, where he began writing something on Mark's chart.

⁓

Hope made the trip back to the hotel just in time to rub some sunscreen on Jennifer's face, neck, arms, and legs before putting her on the bus to Universal Studios. Then she was back in the car driving north toward the hospital. Arriving back in the waiting room, she realized that she had almost an hour to wait before the 10:00 a.m. visiting time, so she found a chair next to a table and began sorting through the selection of outdated and well-thumbed-through magazines. Issues ranged from racy women to celebrities and men's fitness to skiing—nothing high on her interest list. Finally she found an old issue of *Ladies' Home Journal.*

Every few paragraphs Hope would glance at either her watch or the clock on the far wall. The hands on each seemed glued in place. The volume on the public-address system was low in this area, but the pages she heard always seemed to come in midparagraph, as if calculated to interrupt what little attention she was giving to the print. Then there were the snatches of conversations between anxious family members regarding a loved one on the other side of the locked doors. Finally she tossed the magazine back on the table, arose, and began pacing the room.

Wandering aimlessly back and forth between the potted plants in the windowless room, Hope began wishing for a Bible. Had she packed one in her suitcase? She couldn't remember. If she went back to the hotel to get it, she might not make it back before the next visiting period. Maybe Chaplain Steiner could provide her with one. She dug his business card from a side pocket in her purse and eyed the phone number before glancing up and seeing one of those "No Cell Phones Allowed" signs that seemed to be posted everywhere. Instead of calling him, Hope flagged down a person wearing hospital garb and asked for directions to his office.

Chaplain Steiner was out, but the receptionist provided her with a Bible and a sympathetic ear for the latest report about how Mark was doing.

Back in the waiting room, Hope found a chair and began thumbing the pages to decide where to begin reading. For no particular reason she opened to the latter chapters of John, where she began reading the scenes surrounding the crucifixion of Jesus. She read of His trial, of how He was beaten and nailed to the cross, of His death and burial. Then came the scene outside the tomb where Mary of Magdalene met Jesus without recognizing Him.

123

Hope read John 20:16-18:

"Jesus said to her, 'Mary.'

"She turned toward him and cried out in Aramaic, 'Rabboni!' (which means Teacher).

"Jesus said, 'Do not hold on to me, for I have not yet returned to the Father. Go instead to my brothers and tell them, "I am returning to my Father and your Father, to my God and your God."'"

Something about the passage seemed puzzling, so she read it again. There it was: "for I have not yet returned to the Father." She'd read it before. Many times. So why was it catching her attention now? "Father," she prayed silently, "what is in this text that You want me to know about right now? Please show me why it's jumping out at me like this."

Hope looked up. Ah! The hands on the clock seemed to be moving faster. Or had she just not looked for a longer period? Whatever the case, the next visiting period began in another five minutes. Already several people were clustered by the door so they could be the first through when the security lock was released.

～

Feeling Mark's feverish forehead, hearing the mechanical sounds of the ventilator, and seeing his blank stare all increased Hope's anxiety level. She didn't want to be anywhere else, yet at the same time she began to feel trapped. Dr. Purcell's earlier words gave her hope that this soon would be over, so why wasn't it happening faster? Why hadn't his fever broken yet? How much longer would this continue?

She returned to the waiting room a minute before the visiting period ended. She wanted to be close to Mark. But with him being in a drugged sleep, there was nothing she could do to help him, and in that state of uselessness a single minute seemed unimportant. Oddly, the chair to which she returned was beginning to feel comfortable. Well, at least familiar.

Reading and really paying attention to what she was reading was a challenge, with the people milling about and muffled conversations drifting on the air. Still, Hope managed to pick up where she'd left off in the Gospel of John and finished the book before being distracted by someone claiming the chair directly across from her. This had happened several times before. Sometimes she looked up just enough to recognize that the motion in her peripheral vision was a person. Sometimes she made eye contact and even shared a greeting nod before returning to her private space. This started out to be one of the quicker glances until she saw the tailored suit and multicolored blouse as the air finished squishing out of the vinyl-covered seat cushion.

Her gaze rose to take in the tear-stained face of Theresa Ingersoll. Hope felt her jaw begin to go slack, then caught herself and contained her surprise.

Fortunately, Theresa Ingersoll was lost in her own thoughts and staring off into space, so she did not notice Hope at all. Then sobs captured her frame, and the tears began flowing freely.

Hope sat transfixed for a few seconds. She could not believe that Theresa Ingersoll was sitting directly across from her! After overcoming her surprise, she scanned the table for a box of tissues. There were none. She dug into her purse, pulled out a travel-sized packet, extracted several, and held them out where they brushed the back of Theresa's hand.

Theresa looked up long enough to take the tissues and whisper a muffled thank-you as she wiped her eyes and cheeks. She held her face in her hands for a long moment before realizing that Hope had moved to the chair beside her and had wrapped a sympathetic arm around her shoulder.

Theresa sobbed for an extended time before regaining some of her composure. "Thank you. That's really kind of you," she said with a shaky voice.

"How is he?" Hope inquired softly.

Theresa shook her head, sniffled, and wiped her nose. "Not good. The doctor says he's inhaled all this stuff and his lungs are filling up with fluid, and there's nothing more they can do for him." She buried her face in her hands again as a new round of sobs began racking her frame.

Hope offered another clutch of tissues, kept a hand on Theresa's shoulder, and waited. After a time Theresa sat up and dabbed away the tears.

"They said he can't live more than a few more hours," Theresa said in a raspy whisper. "What am I going to do without him? I can't imagine being without him!" she sobbed.

Hope pulled Theresa close and felt tears wetting her blouse.

Theresa pulled herself together again. "Thank you. Thank you for being here for me," she whispered hoarsely. She held out her hand to Hope. "I'm Theresa Ingersoll. From Memphis. What's your name?"

Hope kept her right hand on Theresa's shoulder while reaching out with her left hand to shake Theresa's. "I'm Hope Lancaster. Also from Memphis," she answered almost reluctantly.

"Your husband's in there?" Theresa asked as she shook her head toward the ICU entrance.

Hope nodded. "Same sort of situation."

Theresa suddenly looked shocked. "Your husband's not . . . dying? Is he?"

Hope shook her head. "Oh, no! What I meant was, well, the doctor said he inhaled a lot of the hot gasses into his lungs too. But he's starting to get better."

"Oh, that's *good* news! I'm sure you're excited." Theresa managed a bit of a smile. "I'll bet I'm a real sight, don't you think?"

Hope surveyed the tear-streaked face with its stress lines and mussed makeup. "Not ready for prime time, but I probably don't look that good either."

That made Theresa smile.

"Listen, there's a snack machine down the hall. Can I get you something?" Hope offered.

Theresa started to decline but changed her mind. "Thank you. Some of those crackers with the cheese in the middle would be good."

Hope returned a minute later with a pack of crackers for each of them.

"When did you get here?" Theresa inquired.

"Yesterday morning. The airline got us on a flight out of Memphis Monday night. We didn't know if we were going to get into LA until we got to Dallas and the pilot announced that we were one of the first flights allowed to come in after they reopened the airport. What about you?"

Theresa finished a cracker before answering. "I just got here a couple hours ago. I was in Paris when it happened. You wouldn't believe what closing the airport for a few hours did to travel plans! It took me 24 hours just to get reservations and almost another day to get here! I mean, I don't even know my room number over at the Radisson by the airport. I just dropped my bags off and told the driver to get me over here as quick as he could."

Theresa dissolved into another round of sobs that emptied Hope's supply of tissues. Hope excused herself just long enough for a trip to the hospital lobby and the gift shop, where she purchased a multipack bundle. Returning to the ICU waiting room, she pressed one of the packs into Theresa's hand.

"I can't believe it's another hour before they let us back in. I just hope he's still alive when I get there," Theresa said as she stared somewhere past Hope.

"You know, we're in this situation together, so how about if we stick together?" Hope suggested.

"I'd like that. I'm so glad you're here," Theresa responded with a hint of a smile as she reached for her purse. She extracted her billfold and from it removed a business card and a pen to scribble something on the back before handing it to Hope. "That's my cell number. Call me anytime—and I mean anytime, OK? You're my only friend here right now, and heaven knows how much I need a friend."

Hope glanced at Theresa's card and saw something about RMI Industries before flipping it back over to memorize the cell number. Then she borrowed the pen to write her cell number on the back of one of her own business cards. "There's my number. Likewise, call me anytime, OK?"

Theresa squeezed both of Hope's hands between hers. "I just can't believe we're both from Memphis and both our husbands are in the same ICU! What a coincidence!" she exclaimed before falling silent for a moment. "Only my husband's dying, and your husband's going to survive." She dissolved in another round of tears and sobs as Hope offered tissues and kept a comforting arm around her shoulder.

CHAPTER FIFTEEN

W hat does your husband do for a living?" Theresa Ingersoll inquired during one of her less-emotional periods.

"He's a computer programmer. Works for Featherweight Software. He got laid off last year, and they called him back only a few weeks ago." Hope paused for a moment. "He and some others came out here to meet with a client this week. Except, well, you know what happened Monday afternoon." Her words trailed off until the last sound was barely audible.

This time it was Theresa offering Hope a tissue to wipe the tears welling up in her eyes.

"What do you do?" Theresa wanted to know. "What do you do for a living?"

"I'm a news anchor with channel 3 in Memphis. I'm also the area network correspondent for MBS News."

"Really!" Theresa exclaimed as she began digging in her purse to extract Hope's business card. She studied the card for a second before pushing it back into a side pocket. "I thought your name sounded familiar. Weren't you that reporter who was on the air a year ago when Jerusalem got nuked?"

Hope smiled and nodded. "Yes, that was me. Cuts and all." She shook her head. "My husband cut that picture out of the newspaper, the one where I'm all bandaged and bleeding but still on camera. I can't believe the newspaper ran that picture on the front page!"

"I guess he's proud of you for being so gutsy," Theresa answered softly.

"It wasn't gutsy, believe me. I was so scared I didn't know what I was doing," Hope replied.

The pair chatted for several minutes about children and places they'd been.

In another 10 minutes the ICU doors would open again, so Hope excused herself and returned to the hospital lobby, where she could use her cell phone. There were several voice messages from family members asking for updates about Mark's condition. Yet the message she was hoping to find, one from Andrew or Jennifer, was not there.

She dialed Andrew's number. When he answered, they could barely converse over the squealing and yelling of children. Everything was fine, and they'd be staying at Universal Studios for several more hours, Andrew reported.

Hope scrolled down through the address book on her cell phone until she found Peter Leventhal and pressed the "dial" button.

"Leventhal," he answered gruffly.

"Hey, Super Scoop!" Hope greeted him playfully. That softened his demeanor considerably. "I've got a favor to ask of you. A personal favor."

"Whatcha have in mind, shweetheart?" he answered in his best Humphrey Bogart imitation. "You know me. I'll do it if I can."

"Two things, actually. First, I'm going to give you some information on background. No quote. No source. You got that?" Hope declared.

"Depends on what it is," Peter answered.

"No depends. It just is," Hope insisted. "No name. Just a reliable source."

"OK, Reliable Source. Whatcha got for me?"

Hope took a deep breath. "Robert Ingersoll, that industrialist whose company is under investigation by the SEC—he was on the Diamond Airways flight that crashed. He's in the intensive-care unit up here at Harbor View Hospital, and he's dying. Could be dead in a matter of hours."

"Got it," Peter answered. "What else?"

"Second thing. The favor I need. Theresa Ingersoll is here. Just got here a little bit ago from Paris. I met her in the waiting room, and I've gotten to know her. She's a really nice woman who's in a lot of emotional distress right now because her husband's dying. I want you to stay away from her. Just leave her alone, OK?"

It was Peter's turn to take a thinking breath or two. "I can't promise that. If she's part of the story, then I want you on it."

"Hey! Whoa! I'm on personal leave, remember? So I'm not on the story. *You're* on the story. Now, here's the second favor that I need. Take me off the RMI story. Completely off. I'd be betraying a friend if I kept working on it," Hope declared. "Put somebody else on it."

"You're suddenly calling her a friend, are you? You didn't know her yesterday, and today you're calling her a friend and asking me to protect her. That creates a real problem, don't you think?" Peter was becoming argumentative.

"I guess it does. It creates a real problem for me. She's become my friend, so I can't be objective. Plus, we go to the same church back in Memphis. Look, Peter, you've got other reporters you can put on the story. Plus, you know everything I know about this RMI story, so you can run with it. Just give the story to somebody else and leave Theresa Ingersoll alone." It was a demand, not a request.

The line was quiet for a long moment. Peter's voice was firm but not as argumentative. "Just do me one favor, will you?" Peter asked.

"What's that?" Hope said.

"Just don't get involved in the story, and don't get between my crew and her, OK?" Peter commanded.

"Only if you don't ask me for any personal information about her," Hope countered.

"Agreed." Peter's voice softened. "How's Mark doing?"

"Getting better. He's still in ICU, but they might move him out in a day or so if he keeps improving."

"Keep me posted. Let me know if there's anything we can do for you," Peter offered.

"I'll do that. Oh, a thought just crossed my mind," Hope answered.

"What's that?"

"If he's well enough to get out of the hospital but not well enough to fly on a commercial airliner, is there any chance we could use one of the company planes as an air ambulance to take him back to Memphis?" Hope queried.

"Let me check with the brass in New York and see what they say about it. You're part of the MBS family, so I don't know why not, but let me check with them first."

The clock was marking the start of the next visiting period when Hope came off the elevator. Across the room she saw Theresa going through the doors into the ICU, and Hope followed a few seconds behind. Mark remained in a drug-induced sleep.

As the period expired, Hope stopped outside Robert Ingersoll's cubicle and waited for Theresa to leave her husband's side. It was obvious that she had been crying again, and she left with great reluctance when a nurse insisted that it was time to go.

"We'll come and get you if there's any change," the nurse told Theresa as she left.

Hope put an arm around Theresa's shoulders as they turned toward the waiting room. It was a time when touching said more than words. Outside the unit Theresa spotted a familiar face across the room and raced toward him with outstretched arms.

"Tim! Tim! Oh, I'm so glad you're here!" she exclaimed as she embraced the tall, middle-aged figure. They hugged for a long moment; then she stepped back to survey him. "You're a sight for sore eyes!" She ran a hand over his balding pate. "Still a poster child for Rogaine, huh?"

He smiled. "Who's your friend?"

"Tim, I want you to meet Hope. Hope Lancaster. Hope, this is my big brother, Tim Borchard."

Tim started to extend a hand to exchange greetings, then pulled back. "Hope Lancaster? MBS News?" Suspicion tinted his words.

"Yes," she answered, suddenly guarded.

Tim pulled his sister away from Hope. "Just how far will you go to get an inside scoop on a story?" There was acid in his words.

"I . . . I . . . I don't know what you mean," Hope stammered in surprise. "What are you talking about?"

"You know what I'm talking about," Tim snarled. "First you go and air that awful report about Robert and his company. Then you come in here and make friends with Theresa just so you can get inside information to put on the air."

"Tim!" Theresa tried to interrupt him.

"I'm not going to let you take advantage of my sister this way!" he continued as he pushed Theresa behind him.

"Tim! You stop that!" Theresa shouted. "It's not that way at all. Her husband's in the ICU too. He was in the same plane crash."

"You don't expect me to believe that, do you?" While he was angry before, now he was livid. "C'mon, Theresa. We're getting you out of here and away from her." He grabbed her by the arm and began pulling her toward the elevator.

Hope felt her jaw going slack and saw Theresa's jaw doing the same as she was dragged away.

~

A totally worn-out Jennifer stumbled off the bus and into her mother's arms with an only slightly more energetic Andrew right behind her.

"I'll tell you what. These kids absolutely wore me out today," he said wearily.

"Did you have a good time?" Hope asked the body wrapped around her waist.

Jennifer's answer was mostly an up-and-down movement of her head against Hope's abdomen. "Uh-huh," she mumbled. "But I'm tired; I just want to go to bed."

"Thank you, Andrew." Hope hugged his neck. "You don't know what this means to me."

"That's what I'm here for." Andrew stifled a yawn. "Listen, tomorrow we're planning an outing to a water park. A half-day outing in the afternoon. Then the airline is having a sunset memorial service on the beach out by the airport. You're invited, of course, if you want to come."

"That sounds nice. Let's see how tomorrow goes," Hope answered as she guided an exhausted daughter toward the elevator.

~

Sometime in the night Hope awoke to the trilling of her cell phone. She fumbled around in the unfamiliar hotel room until she located the source deep in her purse on the bedside stand. "Hello," she croaked sleepily.

"Hope? This is Theresa."

The emotion in her voice brought Hope wide awake. "What's wrong?"

"Robert," Theresa struggled to speak. "He just died. A few minutes ago. The nurses let me spend the last couple hours with him before God took him."

"I'm sorry. I'm so very sorry," Hope said. "Is there anything I can do for you? Anything you need right now?"

"No. I really can't think of anything right now. Tim's here, and he's taking care of me."

"I'm glad he's there for you. Theresa, if there's anything, anything at all, that I can do for you, please let me know, OK?" Hope pleaded.

"I just wanted you to know. Maybe we can get together when we both get back to Memphis," Theresa offered.

"You know, I'd like to do that. I guess you'll be going back home pretty soon?" Hope queried.

"I guess so. First we're going to try to get a few hours of sleep. Then Tim's going to help me get the funeral plans started. I'd like it if you could be there, but I'm guessing you'll still be here with Mark, right?" Theresa observed.

"Yeah, I don't plan on leaving until Mark is better. Hey, I'll be praying for you."

"Thanks. I just wanted you to know about Robert," Theresa said softly.

"I appreciate that. I'll talk to you when I get back," Hope promised. "Hey, is Tim still mad at me?"

Theresa paused before answering. "Let's just say that if you meet him again, he'll be more polite. Just don't expect any favors."

∼

"What does *Vista del Mar* mean, Mom?" Jennifer asked as their bus approached the site of the sunset memorial service. Close ahead they could see planes from Los Angeles International Airport racing for the sky. The winds were now off the ocean and the view limitless, the opposite of three days before.

"You would ask that!" Hope exclaimed. "It's been years since I last studied any Spanish. I don't know!"

"It means 'view of the ocean,'" the woman across the aisle chimed in.

"Thanks. Sounds like a logical name, doesn't it?" Hope answered.

A row of palm trees and a wide band of grass marked the west side of the road. The line of buses passed through a police roadblock and into a parking area. Police officers directed everyone toward an area of chairs set up in front of a large canopied stage next to where the grass gave way to sand. Reporters covering the event were kept at a discrete distance on a set of risers behind the seating area.

Family members of the passengers, as well as airline employees, emergency workers, public officials, and clergy, attended the multifaith memorial service. It was a somber event until Captain Sonja Cabrini was brought onto the stage in a wheelchair, her right leg in a cast extending straight out into space. Her appearance brought the entire audience to their feet in a standing ovation. She blushed as she acknowledged the adulation.

Clergy of different faiths made soothing and encouraging remarks about eternity, family, and getting through difficult times. A choir sang hymns, including a rendition of "Amazing Grace." At the end of the service the invitation was given for those who wished to do so to take a flower from the table beside the stage and toss it into the surf as a way of remembering and saying goodbye to those who had died in the crash.

Jennifer saw others picking up flowers and wanted to do the same.

"Sure. Why not?" Hope stood and took her daughter's hand to join the line. Jennifer selected a rose, Hope a carnation.

"Is this really the ocean?" Jennifer whispered as they followed the crowd of people down the sandy beach toward the water.

"Sure is. The Pacific Ocean," Hope said as she listened to the gentle sound of the waves and the crunching of sand under their shoes.

Suddenly Jennifer stopped and pulled off her shoes. "I want to get my feet wet in the waves."

"Hey! That sounds like fun," Hope responded as she reached down and pulled off her own shoes. "First let's throw our flowers in the water."

Jennifer led the way into the twilight. Only she didn't stop at the wet line where the waves began their retreat. With shoes in one hand and a rose in the other, she stepped forward until the waves washed above her ankles. Only then did she launch her rose toward the back of the next wave.

"What's out there? I mean, *way* out there?" Jennifer waved her arms toward the sunset.

"Hawaii. Japan."

"How far? Can I swim there?"

Hope smiled at the thought. "That's a bit too far to swim. We're talking a long way. A really long way."

The water was too cool for them to wade longer than several minutes. Plus, darkness was settling in. Hope took Jennifer's hand and steered her toward the refreshment table, where they each were given a cup of punch before turning to mingle with the crowd.

Jennifer pulled her mother down to whisper a question in her ear. "Who are all those people in uniform?"

"I think they're the rescue workers who were called to help when the plane crashed," Hope whispered back.

"I wonder which ones helped Daddy."

Hope shrugged her shoulders. "I don't know. I guess all of them."

"Then I want to thank all of them," Jennifer declared. She surveyed the clusters of people illuminated by the lights around the stage and made a beeline toward a trio of paramedics. They turned from their conversation as she approached with her mother three steps behind.

"I'm Jennifer Lancaster," she announced as she extended a hand to each of the paramedics. "Are you the people who helped my daddy?"

The trio looked at each other to decide who would answer the question. A man with two-rank stripes on his sleeve spoke for the group. "We helped a lot of people that day, so we can't say for sure. Somebody here tonight helped him, I'm sure. How is your daddy doing?"

"A lot better. He's awake now, and they took him out of the ICU. The doctor says he might be able to go home in a few days." Jennifer smiled broadly as she shared the news.

"That's wonderful!" a second paramedic exclaimed. "Thank you for telling us."

"Thank you for helping him." Jennifer fairly bounced as she turned away from the trio and made a beeline for another group of rescue workers.

"Hi. I'm Jennifer Lancaster, and I want to thank you for what you did to save my daddy," she announced.

Late on Sunday morning an ambulance was waved through the security gate onto the corporate aviation ramp on the south side of Los Angeles International Airport. It moved slowly along the rows of corporate planes and stopped beside a Gulfstream jet where the pilot was finishing his pre-flight walk-around inspection.

Hope and one of the paramedics assisted Mark up the ladder and into one of the overstuffed executive seats, where he reclined and found a comfortable posture. A few minutes later the door closed, the engines spooled up, and the plane moved toward the runway. The pilot took his turn among commercial airliners of various sizes cuing up at the east end of the southern runways and soon was pushing the throttles forward for takeoff.

"Quite a ride, don't you think?" Hope asked as she reached across the aisle and squeezed Mark's hand.

"How much is this costing us?" he wanted to know.

Hope shook her head. "The brass at MBS arranged this. Officially this is an 'angel flight.' But you can bet I'll be writing thank-you notes for at least a week."

"You know, yesterday when I asked you about the other members of my team, why didn't you answer me?" Mark questioned.

Hope looked away and hesitated. "I didn't want to tell you because I wasn't sure how you'd take it."

"OK, how many of them died?" Mark asked.

"One."

"Who?"

Hope hesitated. "Art. Art Whitfield."

"I can't believe it. He was ahead of me going to the emergency exit. How did he die and not me?"

"I don't have details," Hope answered. "All I know is that I found his name on the fatalities list."

"Terri Pelosi? Did she make it?"

"Now, there's some good news," Hope smiled. "She was home with her child Tuesday night."

Mark lay back and relaxed. "I'm glad she's OK. What about the others? Mike? Tony? Sharon? Wayne?" He counted the list on his fingers.

"Tony and Sharon were in the hospital overnight and sent home. Wayne was unhurt. You're the last one to go home," she reported.

"That's good. That's real good," he said.

CHAPTER SIXTEEN

"Hey, look at you!" Mark exclaimed as Hope set two bags of groceries on the kitchen counter.

She looked at him with a puzzled expression, then began checking herself to see if something was wrong with her clothes.

"Your hair," Mark declared.

"Oh, that." She grinned broadly and turned a pirouette so her husband could survey all sides of her new hairstyle. "You like it?"

"Yeah. You know, aside from its being a little shorter, I'm not sure what they did to it, but I like it. I really do."

Hope rose up on her tiptoes, looked Mark straight in the eye, put her arms around his neck, and gave him an extended kiss. "Well, so long as you like it, I guess you don't have to know what they did. Question is, will I be able to keep it this way, or will I be back in the salon every other day? Uh, did you happen to notice anything else different?" She stepped back, struck a model's pose, and batted her eyelashes rapidly.

He reached into one of the grocery bags and pulled out a jar of spaghetti sauce before looking up. "Aside from you acting silly, no," he answered with barely a glance, then turned toward the cupboard. He must have felt her gaze on his back, because he stopped midcourse and slowly turned back her direction.

"You are *so* male. I mean, you can't see it when it's right in front of you," she declared with mock frustration. "My makeup! Besides my hair, I've had a whole new makeover. Don't you like how it makes me look?"

Mark thought quickly for a proper comeback that would keep him out of the doghouse. "Well, dear, I've been so spoiled by seeing your natural beauty all these years that I'm not sure the makeup makes that much difference."

Hope moved to block his path as he turned back toward the cupboard with a canister of chocolate milk mix in hand. "If that isn't the slyest line I've heard in years, I don't know what I'm hearing. But I like it." She planted another kiss on his lips. "How are you feeling tonight?" she asked. "Is your chest still hurting?"

"A lot better. The doctor says he wants me to take it easy another week, but I'm getting a good case of cabin fever. I think I need to go back to work," Mark said.

"So you want to violate doctor's orders and go back to work early, do you?" A commanding scowl erased Hope's smile, and she waved her up-raised hands back and forth for emphasis. "I don't like that idea. Not one bit. We nearly lost you out in LA, and I don't want you going back until the doctor says you're ready."

"But I've got to get back to work. Gene Mitchell's coming in from California to take over the project for a time, and he said he wants to meet with me on Thursday."

"Well, Gene can just come here if he wants to meet with you."

The corners of Mark's face turned downward as his face hardened. "I can at least go in for a couple hours. You know, just go to the meeting."

"Why do you think Gene wants to meet with you? What is he going to say that can't wait for you to get well?" Hope began pushing the empty plastic grocery bags into the trash can.

"I really don't know for sure. But since Art Whitfield died . . ." Mark's words trailed off for a moment. "We've got to have a new team leader. Gene says he's going to take over for a while. One of the first things he's got to do is decide who will take Art's place."

"So do you think Gene wants you to take over the project? If you ask me, I think you ought to be the lead. You've worked hard for a lot of years, and you used to be a leader when Gene owned the company. I think you ought to pursue it aggressively. You know, make Gene pick up and notice you and think about you for the position."

Mark smiled. "I appreciate your vote of confidence, but I don't know. God is in control, and whatever He wants to happen will happen."

Hope stared at him. "Where'd this attitude of faith come from? This isn't like you. What happened to my old go-getter husband?"

"Hi, Mom!" a pajama-clad Jennifer greeted her from the stairway. She crossed the space to the kitchen quickly and embraced her mother, who knelt to get a neck hug. "I'm glad you're home. I missed you today."

"Well, I missed you, too. Did you and Dad have a good time together?"

Jennifer took a step back and looked her mother in the eye. "We had a great day. We played games together. Then Daddy took me swimming, and we rented a DVD on the way home. After we watched it, I went over to the Martins'—when Daddy told me to—and played with Emily."

"You told her to go to the Martins'?" Hope asked with a wry smile and a glance in Mark's direction.

He shrugged his shoulders. "Let's say it was a mutual decision. She wanted to go, and I wanted to take a nap."

"And what did you do at Emily's house?" Hope wanted to know.

"Oh, we played with her dolls and stuff like that."

An hour later the parents were tucking their daughter into bed. "And thank You, Jesus, that my daddy is home safe and getting well," Jennifer prayed before the light was turned off.

The parents' footfalls were absorbed by the thick pile carpeting as they made their way along the hallway and down the stairs to the den, where they settled onto opposite ends of the couch with their respective books. For Mark it was a spy novel from the library. For Hope it was her Bible.

"Oh, your mother called this afternoon," Mark interrupted her reading.

"Really? What did she have to say?"

"Something about when you go shopping for maternity clothes to go to Saks. She kept saying Saks, only Saks. Didn't say why," Mark said.

Both returned to their books. After several minutes of reading, Hope looked up to see her husband looking at her. They exchanged smiles before returning to their respective pages. A few minutes later she looked up again to see him staring at her.

"Why are you looking at me that way?" she wondered aloud.

"Oh, I was just enjoying looking at you. That new hairstyle really makes you look good."

Hope smiled. "Thank you. Hey, you'll never guess who called me at work."

Mark looked over the top of his book.

"Theresa Ingersoll."

Mark's eyebrows went up. *"The* Theresa Ingersoll? As in the widow of Robert Ingersoll?"

Hope nodded. "One and the same."

"I thought she'd never speak to you after that report you aired about her husband's being under investigation."

139

Hope shook her head. "No. You don't understand. Robert Ingersoll was in the same intensive-care unit where you were, and I met her in the waiting room. I think I was the first person she called outside of her immediate family after he died. She woke me up at something like 2:00 or 3:00 in the morning to tell me."

"Will wonders never cease!" Mark exclaimed. "Well, what's the news from her?"

"You're not going to believe this. She wants us to come over to their house on Saturday. They're having a pool party and cookout. Starts at 10:00. You want to go?"

Surprise painted Mark's face, and he puffed a spurt of air through his lips. "I guess so. We're not doing anything else, are we?"

"OK. I'll call her tomorrow and tell her we're coming." Hope returned to her Bible.

A few minutes later it was Mark's turn to glance over his page and see his wife looking at him. He read a few more paragraphs before looking up again and realizing that she was still staring at him.

"What?" Mark asked.

"I'm enjoying seeing you here instead of being on a ventilator back in the hospital. You know, that really scared us. We were afraid we were losing you," Hope said softly.

For a moment he seemed lost in thought. "Well, you need not have worried," he finally said.

"Don't tell me I shouldn't have been worried about you!" Hope flared. "I'm your wife, and I love you. I'll worry about you if I want to!"

He held up a hand for her to stop. "That's not what I mean. You see, God told me I was going to survive."

Hope looked at him with disbelief. "God told you . . . that you were going to survive? How? When?"

"After the crash. After I was taken to the ambulance."

"But I didn't know that, so I had every right to worry!" she declared.

"I know. I know. That's OK, dear. I just haven't told you about it yet." They sat in silence for several seconds as she waited for him to continue.

"When the plane landed, it was already on fire. On the right wing. That's where the missile hit with this really loud bang!" He clapped his hands for emphasis. "The inside of the plane started filling with smoke even before we touched down, and by the time we stopped and got the exits open it was getting really thick. I thought for a time that I wasn't going to get out. When I got to the exit, I must have tripped or something, because I fell down it instead of sliding down on my bottom the way I was supposed to."

Mark paused to compose himself. "I was over on the grass beside the runway for a time waiting for the paramedics to come. Then they loaded me up in the ambulance, and the strangest thing happened."

Mark paused again as he searched for the right words. "I felt myself lifting outside of my body and rising to the ceiling of the ambulance, where I watched them working on me. I mean, I actually was up here"—he held a hand high with fingers pointing downward—"and I was watching them trying to resuscitate me. Then I floated out through the back doors and turned around."

Hope stared at him with fascination.

"I felt myself being drawn toward this really bright light. As I moved toward it, people started coming up to me and welcoming me. I mean, it was people like my grandma Nelson, the one I remember baking those really great apple pies when I was little. And my uncle Jason. And your dad."

Hope's face registered surprise when she heard mention of her deceased father.

Mark nodded for emphasis and kept gesturing. "He was there. Then I saw this really bright being. I guess it was Jesus. He was surrounded by light, and he was glowing really, really bright. Brighter than anything I've ever seen, but it didn't hurt my eyes. And he spoke to me in this really beautiful voice and told me that it wasn't my time yet. Then everything went black, and the next thing I knew I was waking up in the intensive-care unit . . . and you were there holding my hand." Mark smiled broadly at his wife and reached to caress her arm where it rested on the back of the couch.

"I love you, Hope," he said softly.

Hope took his hand in hers and squeezed it. "I love you, too. And I'm so thankful to have you back with us."

They sat in silence for several minutes just looking into each other's eyes and holding hands.

"That's really amazing. What you just told me. I've heard of it happening, but you're the first person I've known who's actually had one of those experiences," Hope said softly.

"It was unbelievable. I mean, actually getting to meet Jesus. I still can hardly believe it," Mark said as he studied his wife's face. "Hon, you look like something's on your mind."

Hope reached up with her right hand to wipe a stray hair away from her eyes. "There's something I haven't told you. Something that happened the same day." She paused to collect her thoughts. "You know that strange feeling we both got during first Sunday dinner over at Mom's that one time? And how Mom seemed to know I was pregnant before I told her?"

Mark nodded and waited for her to continue.

"Well, I found out what was going on right after I dropped you off at the airport. Remember how we turned off the ringer on the phone so we could be alone that night? Well, I didn't turn the phone back on until later, and I didn't turn on my cell phone until I was at work, and then there were all these really urgent messages from Mom saying she had something really, really important to tell me." She paused to swallow hard and stifle a cry.

"Go on," Mark said after a moment.

"Mom was calling with a warning to tell you not to get on that plane—that you were in great danger."

"Wow!" Mark exclaimed. "How did she know?"

Hope nodded and cleared her throat. "She knew because . . . I can hardly believe I'm saying this . . . because Daddy's been visiting her and telling her things that only someone who's in heaven would know."

Mark's face registered shock and disbelief. "I don't believe it! No! I can't believe it! You mean to say that your father has been appearing to her?"

Hope nodded. "Apparently this has been going on for some time. Oh, and what we felt that day—apparently that was Daddy in the room standing right behind us . . . and only she could see him."

Mark just looked at his wife for a long moment as he tried to make words come out of his mouth. "I've heard of this happening," he finally said, "but it's always been in a sermon in which the preacher was talking about being deceived by evil spirits. I remember your dad talking about it. Something about King Saul in the Old Testament and how he went to . . ."

"The witch of En-dor," she completed his sentence.

"Yeah. That's who it was. The witch of En-dor, and she supposedly brought up the dead prophet Samuel from the grave to tell Saul that he was going to die the next day." He paused to collect his thoughts. "And now the preacher is appearing to his wife. Can you beat that?"

Hope just shook her head.

"Well, we can be sure of one thing," Mark said with sudden confidence.

"What's that?" she asked.

"We know this isn't a deception, because I saw your father just before I saw Jesus, so I know he's in heaven. And if he's there, what's to keep him from appearing to her?"

"You know, this is all so amazing! But I'm not sure what to make of it. There's something about it that makes me not want to believe you. It sounds good, but there's something about it all that just doesn't add up," Hope declared.

"Are you saying there's something fishy about what I saw and felt . . . and heard?" Mark asked. "OK, dear. Let's review. Your mother is getting visits from your father, who's in heaven with God. And I have a vision in which I see your father in heaven and meet Jesus. Now, what could be deceptive about that? If it's coming from God, what could possibly be fishy or deceptive about it?"

Hope took a long breath. "You raise a good question, and I'm not sure how to answer it. But you know what sticks in my mind? It's something that I read while you were in the ICU. It's a text that, when I read it, just seemed to jump out at me."

Mark scooted down to her end of the couch, slid his arm around her shoulder, and began nuzzling her neck.

"Stop that! You're distracting me!" she giggled.

"I hope so," Mark mumbled in her ear as he continued nuzzling.

She thumbed a few more pages, then closed the Bible. "I can't find it right now. But it was the scene outside the tomb on the resurrection morning when Mary finds Jesus and grabs Him. Remember?"

"I think I've read it," Mark said as he kissed his wife's neck.

She pushed him away. "Mark! I'm trying to have a serious discussion with you. Stop that!"

He backed away with a hint of a pout on his face.

"Remember the scene? What was it Jesus told Mary?" Hope pressed.

"I don't remember," Mark confessed.

"He told her to let go of Him because He had not yet ascended to His Father in heaven. That's what Jesus said. He hadn't gone to His heavenly Father, and this was after He'd been in the grave since Friday."

"So?" Mark dismissed.

"What do you mean, 'so'? If Jesus had been in the grave and hadn't gone to heaven, how could anyone be there? If Jesus hadn't been there yet, how could my father be in heaven? How could you have seen Daddy in heaven if Jesus didn't go there after He died?"

"But the Bible teaches that you go to heaven when you die—if you're good, that is," Mark countered.

"Then tell me this: If you're good and you go to heaven when you die, why does Jesus have to come back and resurrect the dead later?

Answer that one, will you?" Hope argued. "I mean, if you're already up there," she pointed upward, "and God's going to give you a new body, why does He even have to come back here and raise our old body back to life? It just doesn't make sense."

"I can't explain it, dear. All I know is what I saw and what I felt and what I heard. I saw your dad in heaven. I saw Jesus. I felt that I was in the presence of something I'd never felt before. I've been there, Hope. No, I didn't come back with a T-shirt, but I don't need one."

"Ha!" The thought of coming back from heaven with a T-shirt made Hope laugh.

Mark moved closer to his wife, took the Bible from her hands, and laid it on the coffee table. Tenderly he slid his hands along her waist and around her back as he pulled her closer. He felt her arms wrapping around his neck as they moved together for a passionate kiss.

Suddenly Hope pulled away and convulsed with laughter. "A T-shirt! You came back without a T-shirt! You're funny!" She turned her face upward for another kiss but turned away just as suddenly with a convulsive laugh. Even Mark was tickled by the thought.

Several more attempts got interrupted by laughter before passion took over. "What do you say we go upstairs?" Mark mumbled in her ear.

"You really are feeling better, aren't you?" Hope answered softly as she allowed herself to be pulled from the couch.

CHAPTER SEVENTEEN

The Lancasters had driven a half mile since being admitted through the guarded gate leading into the Ingersoll estate. The bright sun made waves of heat rise off the asphalt driveway, promising a broiler-hot late August day. To either side horses grazed in bright-green pastures. Although they were sheltered in the shade of giant oaks and pines, a sheen of sweat already glistened on their muscular forms.

"I hope I get to ride a horse," Jennifer squealed as her eyes grew wide with excitement.

"Let's just wait and see, OK, honey?" Hope cautioned. "We were invited to come swimming and for a cookout, so don't even ask about the horses."

"Yes, Mom," she agreed with obvious reluctance. "But it's that I've always wanted to—"

"I told you, don't ask," Hope cut her off. "Is that clear? We're here to have a good time *swimming.*"

Mark whistled loudly as they passed a line of trees and caught sight of the Ingersoll mansion. "Reminds me of something we used to see on that old TV show *Dynasty,*" he exclaimed.

"Or *Lifestyles of the Rich and Famous!*" Hope added. "I wonder if there'll be some other kids around for Jennifer to play with."

Hope surveyed the scene as she stepped out of their Mercedes M-class SUV, taking in the high-dollar sports cars, oversized SUVs, and top-of-the-line minivans around them. *At least we aren't driving Mark's 10-year-old Ford that he traded in last year. That would've really stuck out like a sore thumb!*

A uniformed attendant answered the eight-note doorbell and invited the family inside. She led them through the opulently furnished foyer and an equally eye-popping living room toward a patio. "Mrs. Ingersoll will be down shortly," she announced as she led them through doors decorated with engraved and stained glass and onto an expansive patio surrounding a large swimming pool. Already a number of adults and children were splashing around, chatting, or catching rays on chaise longues. A volleyball net across the shallow end of the pool promised future competition.

"If you wish, you may change in the pool house over there." The attendant pointed toward a building just beyond the pool that looked as large as the Lancaster's home.

To one side picnic tables were set up under a large tent pitched for the occasion. Just outside it a man in a cook's uniform was nurturing a fire through the charcoal on a grill that must have been at least 10 feet long. An assortment of coolers offered canned drinks buried in ice, and a table offered a variety of foods. A bartender mixed drinks for the adults.

"The Ingersolls sure know how to entertain a group," Hope said just above the music pulsating from somebody's boom box.

Inside the pool house they found dressing rooms and set about changing into their swimsuits. "Looks like this is the last time I'll be able to wear this swimsuit for a while," Hope observed as she surveyed her barely enlarged abdomen in the mirror. "I hope I don't look too funny."

Outside, Mark's eyes went quickly to Hope's belly. "Won't be able to hide it much longer, will you?"

"I think I'm going to change back and sit this one out."

Mark grabbed her arm and prevented her from turning around. "Dear, you're pregnant and you're barely showing. So what if your tummy has grown a little? It goes with the territory. Let's just relax and try to have a good time."

"Right. How am I going to have a good time when I'm about to bust out of this swimsuit?" Hope argued.

"Honey, I think you are exaggerating things," Mark countered.

"I guess I'm remembering how big I got when I was pregnant with Jennifer," Hope said. "I could've won the Miss Blimpie title at six months."

"No. Mrs. Blimpie," Jennifer interjected.

"Oh! There you are! You ready to get wet?" Mark challenged Jennifer.

"Last one in is a rotten egg!" she squealed as she headed for the water with Mark in hot pursuit.

~

It turned out that most of the people at the pool party were senior executives at RMI Industries and their families. A few were familiar faces from church. Two clusters turned out to be Robert Ingersoll's son and daughter from his first marriage, with their spouses and children. Several of the kids soon paired up with Jennifer for impromptu races and diving competitions.

"Hi! I'm Connie," an obviously pregnant woman in her 20s with a megawatt smile and long blond hair greeted Hope. "This is my husband, Paul, Theresa Ingersoll's son, and this"—she patted her expanding abdomen—"is Theresa's first grandchild."

"Oh, how exciting!" Hope cooed. "I'm Hope Lancaster. That's my husband, Mark, over there playing water tag with those kids, and that's Jennifer, our daughter, in the yellow swimsuit." She patted her abdomen. "And this is number two. By the way, where's Theresa? I haven't seen her yet."

"Oh, she'll be down soon. She's the kind who likes to be fashionably late so everybody sees her entrance," Paul offered before turning away.

"So how far along are you?" Hope inquired.

"Eight months, but it feels like about two years right now." Connie winced as the baby kicked her in the diaphragm. "How about you?"

"I know that feeling! Almost three months. I just got over the morning sickness, and I'm starting to feel really good, but that last trimester's coming," Hope declared with a face that told Connie she was excited about being pregnant but not looking forward to the coming discomforts. "How's Theresa doing? I last spoke with her on Thursday, and she was feeling really down."

"Oh, she has her ups and downs. You know, the funeral was only two weeks ago, and these past few days have been pretty rough. But she's starting to have better days. She really wanted to have this event as a chance to spend time with friends and maybe let them cheer her up some."

Hope nodded. "I sympathize. My father died about seven months ago, and I still have some times when all I want to do is hide in a corner and cry."

"I'm sorry to hear about your father. I guess you know that Robert was on the plane that the terrorists shot down."

Hope nodded. "So was my husband. They were in the same intensive-care unit at the hospital. That's how I met your mother-in-law—in the same waiting room."

Surprise registered on Connie's face. "You're the one she's been talking about, the one who was there when she needed a friend! I'm so glad

147

I'm getting to meet you," she said. "So what line of work are you in?"

"Television news," Hope replied. "I'm a news anchor over at channel 3."

A look of concern crossed Connie's face. "With all that's going on right now, I don't think that I should be talking to you or that you should even be here," she said with a chill in her voice as she backed away.

"There's nothing to worry about, Connie," Theresa Ingersoll declared from behind Hope. She stepped up to join the pair. "Hope! I didn't know you were pregnant. How exciting!"

Theresa gave Hope a social hug and turned to her daughter-in-law. "Hope was there for me before Daddy died, when I didn't have anyone else to lean on."

Disbelief still registered in Connie's face.

"Connie, for whatever it's worth, I've asked to be taken off the RMI story. Completely off. Now, if they hand me some copy to read on the air, I'm going to read it. But I'm not reporting on it or doing any research."

Connie appeared to relax a little.

"I'm sorry I wasn't here for the funeral," Hope apologized to Theresa.

"Oh, I understand. Mark was still in the hospital, wasn't he?"

Hope nodded. "But I still wish I could've been here for you. It must have been difficult for you."

Theresa nodded and looked down. "Nobody knows how difficult it is until you go through it. I don't think I would have survived if it hadn't been for close family and friends." She looked up at Hope and smiled weakly.

"I'm glad you had them here to support you," Hope replied.

Theresa suddenly became animated. "You wouldn't believe what the church looked like. I mean, the whole front of the church was a solid wall of flowers, and the place was absolutely packed. And Pastor Marchini preached this really wonderful sermon about Robert's being in heaven with Jesus and enjoying Paradise and not wanting us to be sad." Her smile grew as she spoke.

"Girls, today we're going to have fun swimming and socializing, so let's talk about happier things, OK?" Theresa prompted.

Hope noticed the scent of burgers cooking on the grill and the squeals and splashes of kids having fun. Theresa turned away to attend to something.

"So how long have you and Paul been married?" Hope asked Connie.

"Two years next week," she answered, still somewhat guarded. "How about you?"

Out of the corner of her eye Hope caught a glimpse of Mark and Jennifer talking to one of the uniformed servants. "We just celebrated our tenth anniversary the end of May in New York City, of all places."

"Have you thought of any names yet for the baby?" Connie wanted to know.

Hope blushed. "We haven't even started discussing it yet. I mean, we didn't even come up with Jennifer's name until about two weeks before she was born! What about you?"

Connie smiled. "If it's a boy, it will be Robert Merrill Ingersoll, in honor of Dad. If it's a girl, it'll be Theresa Meredith, in Mom's honor."

"So I'm hoping it's a girl!" Theresa declared from several paces away before turning to chase a cluster of dripping children into the pool.

Hope splashed in the pool for some time before realizing that Mark and Jennifer were nowhere to be found. She dripped a path across the concrete to the pool house to see if they were playing a video game in front of the large-screen TV. They weren't. A moment later she found their wet swimsuits and those of several other kids hanging on a drying rack in a dressing room. Their dry clothes were gone.

Knowing they were not in the pool prevented her from panic. Still, concern rose in her throat as she urgently scanned the pool deck and the dining area. Spotting the servant she had seen them talking to earlier, she made a beeline for the man. "Have you seen an 8-year-old girl in a floral sundress with her father?" Hope urgently inquired.

"Are you talking about the ones who wanted to go horseback riding?" he answered with a smile.

"Horseback riding!" Hope snapped. "Which way did they go?"

The servant stood up from what he was doing and suddenly looked very fit in his crisp white polo shirt and matching Bermuda shorts. "Ma'am, they left about 15 minutes ago and headed out to the riding stable. I assure you that they will be quite all right. We have some very gentle riding horses." He raised an arm and pointed toward a gate and graveled path leading through a grove of trees. "The stable's about a 10-minute walk down that gravel road if you want to go watch or ride with them."

Hope shook her head. "No, I don't want to go riding, thank you. I just want them back here," she said urgently.

"I don't think they'll be very long," the servant declared.

The puzzled look on her face spoke as loudly as words.

He chuckled. "In this heat? It's just too hot to be riding a horse."

Theresa Ingersoll approached, drawn by the animated exchange. "Is everything OK, Martin?" she inquired of the servant. "Hope?"

"She was just looking for her husband and daughter, who went horse-back riding without her knowledge," the servant answered.

Theresa smiled and looked at Hope comfortingly. "Oh, I assure you that they're quite safe and very welcome to go riding as long as they want. I hope they have a good time."

"But I told her not even to ask!" Hope protested angrily.

"Dear, dear," Theresa soothed her. "I'm happy to let them. Would you like to join them? We have some great riding horses. We even have a few retired racehorses if you want a fast ride."

Hope took a moment to regain her composure. "No, thank you," she said as she rubbed a hand across her abdomen. "Maybe a year from now."

Theresa smiled. "I'm getting hungry. Let's go see what Manuel is cooking over on the grill, shall we?"

The scents and sizzling from the grill made Hope's stomach flip. Or was it the baby turning over? She couldn't tell, but she definitely was getting hungry.

"Burger? Or a steak, maybe?" Manuel offered. "How do you want it done?"

"I think I'll go for a steak. Well done," she told the cook, who picked up a cooking fork, speared a large steak, dropped it onto a plate, and handed it to her.

"I'll take that smaller one." Theresa pointed toward a corner of the grill.

To their steaks they added pasta salad, dill pickles, and baked beans. Hope snared a canned soda from an ice-packed cooler as she followed Theresa toward the engraved glass doors along one side of the patio and inside to the home's formal dining room. Hope looked around and immediately wished she had changed out of her swimsuit before entering, but Theresa's plate was already on the carved mahogany table and she was pulling a chair back from the table. Under the glass top was a carved scene of vineyards and winemaking. Carvings in the backs of the 20 or so chairs around the table were smaller snapshots from the larger scene. Large oil paintings of pastoral scenes were spaced around the mahogany-paneled walls. A chandelier that must have had at least 100 flame-shaped bulbs and thousands of crystals hung overhead.

"Can I get you something a little stronger to drink?" Theresa offered.

"No, thank you. I'm fine," Hope responded.

Theresa disappeared into the kitchen. She returned a moment later with a glass filled with an amber-colored liquid poured over a trio of ice cubes.

"It's too hot to eat out there. Plus, I wanted some quiet time just to visit with you. You know, you're one of my few friends outside of the company."

Theresa bowed her head to offer a silent prayer over her food, then crossed herself just before lifting her head and opening her eyes.

"I didn't know you were Catholic," Hope caught herself saying in surprise.

Theresa nodded as she took her first bite of steak. "A lot of people don't know it. The only reason I attended over at Second Avenue Baptist was that Robert wanted me to be there with him. For looks, you know. Said it was good for business."

Hope stirred a puddle of hot sauce into her baked beans and scooped up a spoonful. "Then why was the funeral held at the church?"

"Because Robert was a member there. Father O'Malley, my priest over at St. Steven's, came to the house afterward and held a private memorial Mass for us."

Hope pondered the revelation as she chewed and swallowed. "Then maybe you could explain something for me. I mean, if you don't mind."

Theresa nodded.

"Something I've never understood. What is the purpose of a memorial Mass? Why is it important for a Catholic?"

A smile crossed Theresa's face, the biggest one Hope had seen yet today. "Well, strictly speaking, as a non-Catholic Robert couldn't be granted admission into heaven. So in the Mass the priest grants the deceased absolution for his unbelief and opens the way for him to be admitted to Paradise. That was important to me because I don't want to have to spend eternity without him, and that was the only way I could be assured he would be there."

The pair ate in silence for a few moments.

"It's good to see that Mark has recovered so well," Theresa offered.

Hope couldn't help smiling. "Oh, I know! We're so thankful. From what I've heard, he almost died at the airport before they even got him to the hospital."

Theresa reached over, put a hand on top of Hope's, and looked her in the eye. "I'm happy for you."

"Thank you," Hope found herself saying automatically. "I'm really sorry about Robert."

Tears welled up in Theresa's eyes. She made no effort to stop them as she took a ragged breath and nodded. "Thank you," she said shakily as the first tear began tracing her cheek. "I know he's gone, and there's nothing

I can do to bring him back. I'm just not sure how to go on living without him. I mean, I know I've got to keep going. I just don't know how."

"How long were you married?" Hope asked softly.

Theresa looked up at the chandelier and calculated the time. "Twenty-four years and five months." She paused while considering her thoughts. "Strange how it seems like such a short time and yet so long ago."

Theresa's gaze came back from the ceiling. "I'm just taking one day at a time. I guess that's all I can do. One day at a time."

The pair continued eating in silence for a time.

"I trust the legal affairs are working out OK?" Hope inquired.

Theresa nodded. "Kevin Williams has already taken over as acting CEO until the board of directors' meeting next month. I think he'll do a good job."

"I meant such things as his estate."

"Oh, that. Everything will work out. The lawyers have been sitting on his will to give me a few days to pull myself together. Tuesday we're having a meeting to begin all that legal stuff relating to his will. I'm just going to let the lawyers take care of everything."

Hope let Jennifer have it as soon as they were in their vehicle and headed home. "Jennifer! I told you not even to ask about riding the horses, and you went ahead and did it anyway. You're in trouble for disobeying me, and when we get home—"

"Hope!" Mark interrupted.

"—there's going to be a penalty. I haven't decided what it's going to be yet, but I'll figure out something," Hope continued angrily.

"But Mom!" Jennifer protested.

"Don't 'but' me, or I'll make it worse." Hope's anger was rising. Jennifer turned toward the window and began crying. "And as for you, Mark, I'll figure out an appropriate punishment for you, too."

"Hope, there's some—"

"I don't want to hear it, Mark!" she cut him off. "I think you set a bad example for our daughter—"

"Now, you stop right there!" Mark commanded. She stopped mid-word with her mouth hanging open. "It didn't happen the way you're thinking. Jennifer didn't suggest going horseback riding. She didn't even ask. She's innocent."

"OK, then what was your role in this?" Hope asked suspiciously.

"Nothing. One of the other fathers suggested it. We'd just gotten out of the pool to get something to drink when he suggested it. He said we'd better do it if we were going to do it at all, because it was getting really hot," Mark defended. "We were just following his lead."

"And you expect me to believe that story, do you? Just who was this other father?" Hope queried suspiciously.

"Robert Ingersoll, Jr."

"You're saying it was Robert Ing . . ." Hope began, then swallowed her words. Silence reigned in the SUV for the next mile.

"I'm sorry, Mark." Hope finally broke the silence. "Jennifer, I'm sorry I got angry with you. I guess I'm the one who's in the doghouse when we get home."

Jennifer smiled as she gazed out the window. "That's OK, Mom."

A mile down the road Mark turned on a rock 'n' roll oldies station to fill the lack of conversation. Another mile along he glanced at the back seat to see why Jennifer was so quiet, only to discover that she was sound asleep.

"I'm going to have to buy some maternity clothes pretty soon," Hope said quietly, almost as if no one was listening.

"What did you say?" Mark questioned gently.

"I need some maternity clothes," Hope said a little louder. "More like a whole wardrobe. I gave away all my maternity things a couple years ago, remember? I don't have anything to wear these next few months. Not a single thing."

Mark rolled his eyes. "You know what I remember about those maternity clothes?"

"What?" she asked.

"The prices. They were outrageous. I couldn't believe they were getting away with charging that much for something you were going to wear for *maybe* six months and then never again."

"I remember a few of them. Like that one top with the arrow pointing down that said 'Under Construction.' Then there was another one that said 'Future Tax Deduction,' or something like that."

Mark smiled at the memories.

Hope laughed. "The big thing I remember, besides being so unbelievably big, was how long it took us to pay off the charge card when we bought everything. It took us, what . . ."

"Fourteen months," Mark finished her sentence. "She was eight months old when we finally paid off the clothes you weren't wearing anymore."

"'Bout time we did it again, don't you think?" Hope's words were as much a statement as a question.

"Well, the mall's still open for a couple of hours this afternoon. You want to go shopping?" Mark suggested.

"You mean you're going to turn me loose with a charge card at the mall?" Hope smiled teasingly.

Mark watched traffic for a moment and changed lanes. "Do I have a choice?"

Chapter Eighteen

Mark and Jennifer were searching the kitchen cupboards and deciding what to fix for supper when they heard the garage door opener begin to hum and rattle as the door slid up. A moment later they heard Hope's SUV pull into the garage and stop, followed by her struggle to get through the kitchen door with arms loaded down by overstuffed shopping bags. They rushed to relieve her load. Hope immediately turned around to retrieve still more bags of different sizes from the vehicle.

"You weren't kidding when you said you were going shopping!" Jennifer exclaimed. "What'd you do? Buy the whole store?"

Mark surveyed the bags where they lay across the couch and on the floor in front of it. "I feel my wallet shrinking," he observed with alarm. "How much did you spend?"

"Not as much as you're thinking," she said as she laid the last armload on the couch.

"Well, considering how much I was thinking and how much I'm seeing here, not as much as I was thinking is still a small fortune!"

Hope eyed him nose to nose and gave him a kiss. "Before you panic, let me tell you what happened."

"This better be good. I see all those Saks Fifth Avenue bags, and I know that's one store we can't afford to shop in," Mark argued.

"Well, yes. But . . ."

"I've a feeling this is gonna be the biggest 'but' I've ever heard," Mark interrupted.

"Saks is one of channel 3's sponsors. You know how at the end of each

155

newscast there's a slide saying that so-and-so's wardrobe is provided by Saks Fifth Avenue?"

Mark nodded. "So?"

"Well, when I was shopping, the clerk recognized me and called the store manager. Tomorrow he's going to call the advertising department and have the slide changed to say that Hope Lancaster's maternity wardrobe is provided by Saks. How do you like that?"

Mark thought for a second. "What does that mean? For us? For all these things?"

"What it means is that I didn't have to pay for any of the outerwear items. All I had to pay for was the underwear. You know, the panties and nursing bras, nightgowns, that sort of thing." Hope smiled broadly. "Now, how do you like that?"

His eyes wandered over the bags one more time. "I guess it sounds good. Exactly how much did you spend, and how much did you save us on this little shopping trip?"

Hope reached into her purse, extracted a foot-long sales receipt, and studied the inadequately inked print. "Well, for the personal items . . . I spent . . . $314.28."

Mark's face showed a combination of shock and relief.

Hope reached for the first bag and began extracting items. They could determine how much she had saved if they added up all the price tags. Mark retrieved a pocket calculator, and Jennifer set about helping her mother spread her new wardrobe out for display. The total was just under $1,600.

"There are fringe benefits to being in the news business," Hope observed with satisfaction as she loaded an arm and started for the stairs. "I just hope I have room in the closet. Maybe I'll have to move some of your things to make room," she teased.

"Oh, no, you don't," he protested as he ran up the stairs to catch up with her. "You know, I wonder if this was what your mother had in mind when she called the other day and told you to shop at Saks."

Their eyes met with a gaze communicating words they did not want their daughter to hear.

～

Walking back into the nearly empty Featherweight Software offices after his absence was almost as shocking as walking in the first time after the layoff. The emptiness weighed heavily, even depressingly, on him. He swiped his ID card in the security reader and opened the door after he heard the buzzing. Then he walked down the empty hallway toward his work area. Basically this morning would have been like any other Thursday except for the knowledge that Art Whitfield would not be there.

"Hey, Mark! Welcome back!" Tony Wilson called out as soon as Mark opened the door to the team's room. Tony rose from the chair in his cubicle to give Mark a warm handshake and a pat on the shoulder. "I'm glad to see you up and around. We weren't expecting you till next week!"

"Hey! Good morning!" Mark returned the greeting with a big smile. "I'm feeling much better. I just hope guilt over disobeying my doctor doesn't make me feel so bad that I have to go home."

His coworker smiled. "It's good to have you back. You know Gene Mitchell's coming in today to meet with us, don't you? He's taking us out to lunch at noon."

Mark held up his personal-sized cooler with his lunch inside. "I heard he was coming, but I didn't know about the lunch part. Well, I guess I can eat this for supper."

The two just looked at each other for a moment.

"Well, what are we doing?" Mark asked. "How's the project going? What should I get started doing?"

Wilson shook his head. "Nothing for now. Last word from Gene was for us all to just sit tight and wait for the meeting."

Mark looked around for a moment. "You know, I'm going to miss Art."

A look of sadness crossed Tony's face. "We all are," he said.

"Any idea who Gene's going to appoint to take Art's place?"

Tony shook his head. "Not a word. Maybe he'll tell us today."

"So, what to do until Gene arrives? Guess I can at least scan my e-mail," Mark said as he turned toward his cubicle.

∼

Hope was buried in work the moment she walked through the newsroom door. The combination of a full storyboard on the wall and two critical people being out sick turned everyone's day into a scramble.

"Where exactly is it that we're going?" the camera operator asked as Hope closed the passenger door of a Ford Taurus boldly bearing the channel 3 logo on both sides.

"We're headed downtown to the state highway department to interview some bureaucrat about how they don't have any money to repair a lane on I-55 that's gotten so bad that it's causing wrecks and people are suing the state."

Marty Chang eased the car out of the station parking lot and into traffic. He turned up the fan on the air-conditioner to remove the green-house-like heat and surveyed the cloudless sky. "Looks like it's going to be another scorcher today. Any chance we could go out and do the stand-up on the highway first before it gets too hot?"

Hope shook her head. "Sorry. I've gotta get the details before I can talk about them, and this whoever-he-is is somebody the state's PR folks lined us up with. I've not actually spoken with him yet."

"So what's his name and where's his office? Do I turn left or right?" Marty asked as they slowed behind a line of cars stopping for a traffic light.

Hope looked around and realized she'd left the assignment sheet on her desk. "Uh, Marty?"

"Something's wrong. I can tell by the tone of your voice. You forgot something, right?"

"Uh-huh. The assignment sheet."

"Well, that's a first!" Marty exclaimed and began looking for a place to reverse course.

Hope eyed the fax machine located on the center of the front seat. "This is a fax machine, isn't it? Let's call the office and have someone fax it to us," Hope suggested as she pulled out her cell phone and started dialing the unlisted newsroom number.

Marty grunted a negative. "I have enough trouble managing all the new digital gizmos on my camera that I told 'em not to give me one of those machines in my car. Besides that, I always pick up my assignment sheets."

"I'll bet you've never forgotten an assignment sheet, have you?" Hope teased back.

"Never."

"Really?" she pressed.

"Well, maybe once or twice when I first started. But it's been a long, long time, I assure you," Marty defended himself.

"And how long have you been working at channel 3?" Hope pressed.

Marty hesitated until he found a break in traffic and turned the car back into the employee entrance at the station's parking lot. "One year next month."

"Oh, that's such a long time," Hope teased as she got out of the car. She dashed into the newsroom, snatched the assignment sheet off her desk, and was back in the car in under a minute. She fastened her seat belt and glanced at her watch. "We'll make it in plenty of time."

~

The scorching heat of a late-August day in the South was in full fury as Marty and Hope pulled onto the roadside.

"Man, if the heat doesn't kill you, it sure looks like that road will!" Marty exclaimed as he eased the car around the orange traffic cones keeping motorists out of the right-hand lane. He shifted into park and left the motor running so the interior of the car would remain cool. In a moment he was handing Hope a cordless microphone and shoulder-ing his camera. She scribbled notes on her narrow reporter notepad while he photographed potholes and breaks in the pavement. One hole on a bridge was so deep that a shopping cart—who knows how it got onto the interstate highway—stood half hidden in the depth of the pavement break.

Hope decided to start her stand-up a few paces away from the shop-ping cart. "It may be a year or more before motorists can use this lane on Interstate 55 again, and with good reason," she began as she walked toward the hole, then knelt beside it to bring the cart into view. "The highway department has blocked off this one lane with traffic cones while they try to find a way to turn loose the money needed to repair this two-mile-long stretch of highway."

The noise of passing traffic required Hope to shout and shoot the se-quence three times. By the end of the third take the wind from passing trucks had ruined a once-perfect hairstyle and the heat had utterly ruined her makeup, so the waiting coolness of the car interior was most welcome.

"Let's find someplace to stop and get something cold to drink," she urged as they pulled into traffic. She grabbed the loose hem of her mater-nity top and used it to fan her face.

Hope looked at her cell phone and found that she had missed three calls while doing the stand-up, two of them from Mark and one from her mother. The wind off a passing 18-wheeler shook the car as she pressed the keys. She heard a warbling sound as the line rang the first time, then a second time and a third. Then a recorded voice answered, "Hello. You've reached the voice mail of Mark Lancaster, project leader for Featherweight Software in Memphis. I'm sorry I can't take your . . ." She pressed the "end call" button.

"Rats!" she exclaimed in frustration over not being able to talk with him, then realized she had not paid attention to his voice mail message. *Project leader,* she thought. *That means he got the promotion!*

≈

Hope waited until she was back at the station and could slip into the privacy of an editing booth before returning her mother's call. Susan Morris was not home, but answered her cell phone on the second ring. The background sounds made it obvious that she was in a public place. They exchanged pleasantries and talked about how Mark's health was improving.

Hope began sharing the story of her shopping trip to Saks.

"Oh, that's wonderful!" Susan cooed. "That's exactly what I expected would happen."

"Uh, Mom? Did Daddy have something to do with this? I mean, did he give you a message for me about going to Saks?"

"Why, yes, dear. He did. Didn't Mark give you the message the other day? Daddy was emphatic that you should go, and if the manager didn't find you, then you should find the manager. Oh, darling! That's so wonderful! I mean, think of all the money you saved," Susan continued excitedly.

A wave of sadness swept over Hope as she thought of her father.

"Is something wrong, dear?" Susan asked after a moment of silence.

Hope struggled to keep from crying. "You know, Mom, I miss Daddy so much. I'd give anything, anything if I could have him back or if I could just talk to him again. Life just isn't the same without him."

Silence filled the connection for a moment.

"You know, dear, he's really not gone. He's with us all the time, because he's up in heaven watching us and looking out for us," Susan said softly.

Hope swallowed hard. "I know that, Mom. It's just that, well, this whole thing with his appearing to you—it's so different. So unusual. I'm just not sure I can believe it. I mean, if he appears to you, then why doesn't he appear to me, too? And if he appears to you, why doesn't everybody else's deceased father appear to them, too? It seems as though something odd is happening, something that shouldn't be happening at all."

"Oh, but honey! We're so blessed! We're getting messages straight from God!" Susan exclaimed.

"But how do we know it's really Daddy?" Hope blurted out, then fell silent in surprise after hearing the question come out of her mouth.

Susan's tone turned instantly from relaxed friend to a parent correcting an errant child. "Hope! How can you disbelieve? You believe that you go to heaven when you die, so you know your father is there. Plus, *your own husband* saw him there just a few weeks ago. So you know it's your father! I know it's your father!"

"But Mom—"

"This isn't a time for doubt, dear," Susan cut her off. Her voice rose as she spoke, and it took on an angry tone. "This is a time for believing. A time for trusting. A time for faith."

"But Mom, I'm just not so sure about it."

Susan took a deep breath and calmed down. "OK, Hope. What is making you doubt?"

"It's something I was reading in my Bible the other day. Remember when Jesus was resurrected—when Mary came to the tomb on Sunday morning and realized that the man she was talking to was Jesus, that He was alive?"

"I remember," Susan answered.

"Do you remember what happened? What Jesus said to her?"

"Refresh me. It's been awhile since I read it."

"Mary grabbed Him. She was so happy that she started hugging Him," Hope said. "And Jesus told her to let go of Him, because He hadn't yet gone to His Father in heaven."

"So?" Susan countered. "What's so significant about that?"

"What's so significant is that if Jesus had just been raised from the dead and hadn't yet gone to His Father in heaven, then how could anyone who has died be in heaven? How could Daddy be in heaven?"

Susan's anger returned. "Hope! How could you doubt what you've been taught to believe your whole life? How could you? What's gotten into you?"

"I just want an answer, Mom. The truth. You say Daddy is visiting you, but the Bible says Jesus didn't go to heaven when He was dead." She paused to catch her breath. "Tell you what, Mom. Why don't you ask Daddy to explain it the next time you see him?"

"That sounds fair. I think I'll do that, dear," Susan offered.

Chapter Nineteen

Susan Morris sat down on the sofa in her living room and pulled her feet up onto the cushion beside her. She picked up a remote control from the end table to her left and switched off the TV. With the same remote she tuned the radio to an easy listening station, then settled in to enjoy the latest issue of a travel magazine for mature adults.

Evening. Her favorite time of the day. The time when she shut out the world and filled her mind and heart with whatever she desired. It was also the time when her late husband most often visited. Would he come tonight?

Susan looked across the coffee table to the rocking chair where he had sat so many evenings during the years they were married. She smiled at the memory of the wonderful man God had given her. Yes, being married to a preacher had had its challenges. It had also had its rewards. There had been the lean years when his ministry first started and the paycheck was small because the church was just beginning. Still, patience had paid off, and the growth of the church was soon reflected by changes in their lifestyle. They had moved from a modest three-bedroom fixer-upper on a small lot to this five-bedroom ranch with a two-car garage on a half-acre lot in a restricted neighborhood. Just two years ago they'd bought her a top-of-the-line BMW sedan with just about every comfort available—and they'd paid for it with cash!

What a difference the years had made! All her children had gone away to school, married, and established their own homes. So the house was empty except for big family gatherings such as dinner on the first Sunday of each month or when distant relatives came to visit. Should she sell it and move to someplace smaller? That would make life simpler.

Thumbing through the pages of her magazine, Susan settled on an article about scuba diving in Mexico, chosen more for the pictures than the text. The colors of the fish were so vibrant that she wanted to make reservations. Yes, she was a pretty good swimmer. No, she'd never worn an air tank on her back or a mask and fins. But considering all the new things she'd tried as part of her single seniors group these past months, she had the confidence to attempt anything. She'd even tried parasailing, an experience that took her from terrified to thrilled in barely a minute.

"That looks like fun," a familiar voice called to her from the rocking chair.

Susan looked up and smiled. "It's good to see you again, my love," she said. "What news do you bring?"

He shook his head. "No news. I just wanted to see you again. I'm looking forward to when we can be together again—only in heaven."

The thought broadened her smile. "What a wonderful thought. How long will that be?"

Her husband shook his head. "You have something more immediate to be concerned with. Hope is beginning to have doubts about what we taught her to believe. She must be persuaded to change her ways."

"I know. We've had some talks about it, and you know what? She's started asking me some really hard questions," Susan declared.

"Such as?"

"Well, such as the scene right after Jesus' resurrection. You know the scene in which Mary grabs Jesus and He tells her to let go because He hasn't yet gone to His Father?"

He nodded. "I was a preacher, remember? I know the passage well."

Susan swung her feet to the floor and sat up straight. "She wanted me to ask you to explain something: If Jesus had been dead and hadn't gone to see His Father yet, then He was saying that He hadn't been to heaven, right? And if Jesus didn't go to heaven when He died, then how can anyone go to heaven when they die? How could you be in heaven?"

His face flushed red with anger, and he leaned forward. "I see the problem. Tell me, dear. Do you believe what you see?"

"What do you mean?" Susan wondered.

"Am I your husband?"

Susan nodded and smiled. "Yes."

"Did I die last January?"

Another nod.

"Am I sitting here talking to you?"

"Yes, you are," Susan affirmed.

"Do you believe what you see?" he quizzed.

Susan nodded and thought for a moment. "Maybe you could talk to her."

He shook his head. "What greater proof does she need? Do you remember the parable of the rich man and Lazarus in Luke 16?"

Susan had to think for a moment before replying. "I remember."

"Do you remember the lesson Jesus drew out of the parable?"

She puzzled for a moment. "It's been awhile since I read it."

"They have the law and the prophets. If they won't believe them, they will not believe, though one were raised from the dead," he summarized.

"Hope knows what she has been taught from earliest childhood. It's just as in the parable: If she won't believe what she's been taught, then she won't believe even if I appear to her," he finished.

For a long moment only the background music and the ticking of the nearby grandfather clock could be heard.

"My love, I must leave you. Please, be faithful so we can be together for eternity," he said tenderly.

"Oh, I wish that I could touch you and hold you," Susan declared as she came to her feet and took steps toward the rocking chair. She reached out to take him in her arms and give him a loving kiss just as he vanished.

Susan's forward motion carried her into the rocking chair as it rolled forward in his absence, then rolled back and smacked her in the face. She recoiled in pain and fled to the bathroom, where she wrung out a washcloth in cold water and pressed it against her left eye. In moments it was obvious that she would soon have a large bruise around her left eye. The growing pain made her grimace. *I haven't had a black eye since I was a kid! How am I going to explain this?*

❧

Two weeks passed. A wave of cool weather broke the summer's heat and began making people think about autumn. However, the heat was back this morning, though without the sticky humidity of August. How many more days would she be wearing her summer maternity outfits? Hope wondered.

Hope had barely sat down at her desk in the newsroom before the phone rang. "Hope Lancaster," she answered with barely a glance away from her computer screen.

It was Peter Leventhal. With the advance of her pregnancy she wanted more and more to stay at home. But his calls usually meant a trip somewhere and perhaps a night or two away from home. She was actually looking forward to maternity leave when she could use her prepacked travel bag for a trip to the hospital instead of another city.

"What can you tell me about Anna-Marie Cassarelli?"

Hope thought for a moment. "The name doesn't ring a bell. Let me check my notes." She typed the name into her computer terminal and did a name search through the stories she had covered. "Sorry, Peter. Nothing on record."

"OK. Here's the story. The *National Informer* is running a story in their edition that hits the grocery store magazine racks tomorrow about her and Robert Ingersoll allegedly having an extramarital affair. She's claiming Ingersoll was the father of her child. Further, she's claiming that he wrote both her and the child into his will and that the company's lawyers are trying to prevent them from claiming their portion of his estate. I want a report ready to air by noon."

Hope felt her stomach twisting into a knot. "Uh, Peter, I'm not sure what I can do for you on that story. I asked to be taken off it, remember?"

"Well, you're my reporter in Memphis and you've been on the story in the past, so I need you to work on it," he ordered. He paused to let his words sink in, then resumed as Hope was opening her mouth to reply. "You're close with Theresa Ingersoll. Maybe you can get a comment from her."

"I can't do that, Peter. I just can't do it," Hope protested.

"Can you at least get an official response from the company spokesperson? I've got a feeling this story is going to get big."

The knot in Hope's stomach grew. She knew Peter's sense about stories. When he said it was going to get big, he was usually right.

"Listen. I'm faxing a copy of the *Informer's* press release down to you so you'll know what's in the story," Peter said.

"I'll see what I can do," she answered weakly before hanging up the phone.

What a dilemma! On the one hand, Hope enjoyed Theresa's friendship. Just last week they'd had lunch together and had spent the time talking about pregnancies and babies. Their friendship was growing closer by the week, and Hope had promised to protect it. She'd even written Peter a letter telling him that she could not continue covering the RMI story because of that friendship. She just could not be objective about it, and pressing for answers would violate the trust she felt growing between her and Theresa. On the other hand, she was MBS's local network correspondent. That usually meant taking the work product from a team of producers, adding an on-camera stand-up or voice-over to finish the package, and shooting it over a satellite to New York for broadcast later in the day.

But this was different. She wanted to protect her friendship. Still, if she did, and if Peter wanted to make an issue of it, she could lose her job.

Just then a messenger dropped the fax on her desk. She felt a tremor in her hand as she reached for it, then hesitated before picking it up. *Do I really want to touch it?* Her hand hovered there for a few breaths. *At least I need to know what Theresa's going to be facing.*

Apparently Anna-Marie Cassarelli was a secretary in the administrative offices of RMI's Cincinnati branch. She claimed to have been Robert Ingersoll's lover for almost a decade and to have borne him a son, now 3 years old. Her biggest claim was that Robert Ingersoll had written them into his will.

In a photo Cassarelli held aloft a copy of what she claimed was the will. She said that Robert Ingersoll had owned 40 percent of the company's stock, that half was assigned to her and her son, and that the other half was to be divided among Ingersoll's other children.

Hope sat back in her chair. *I wonder if Theresa knows about this. Wait! She has to know about it, because she's been meeting with the attorneys to settle the estate issues.*

She considered her situation for a moment. *I can at least research it and e-mail Peter with a summary,* she thought.

If Robert Ingersoll owned 40 percent of RMI, who owns the rest of the stock? Hope turned to the Internet and accessed the Web site of the Securities and Exchange Commission. Once there she opened the company's latest quarterly report and scanned it until coming to the section titled "Company Ownership." Indeed, Robert Ingersoll owned 40 percent. Theresa was the second-largest shareholder, with 11 percent. Other family members owned smaller increments, thus putting 76 percent of the stock and firm control of the company in the hands of family members.

Hope charted the ownership on a legal pad. If all of Robert Ingersoll's stock was willed to family members other than Theresa, his oldest son would become the largest shareholder. However, if Anna-Marie Cassarelli really was being willed 20 percent, none of the others would end up owning more than 12 percent, and she would be the largest shareholder. In other words, she could take over control of the company!

Hope leaned back in her chair and stared at the ceiling to ponder the situation. She could picture the headline in that afternoon's newspaper: "Mistress Taking Over at RMI." *I wonder if that's ever happened before in the business world.*

"Whatcha staring at?" The news director stood in front of Hope's desk. "I've got a story for you," Bob said as he dropped an assignment sheet on her desk.

She shook her head and handed it back to him. "Sorry, Bob. I've got a network story to do."

"How long is it going to take you, and who do you need?" he wanted to know as he retrieved the story sheet.

"Peter wants something on the satellite before noon, and it'll be solo work. After that, I don't know."

Bob looked at his watch. "Guess you better get cracking. That's less than an hour away New York time." He dropped the story sheet back on her desk. "When you get done with the network piece."

Hope turned again to the Internet and went to the RMI Web site to get the phone number for the company's public affairs office. She dialed, identified herself, and asked to speak with the company spokesperson. No, that person was not available, she was told. What was her question? A reply would be faxed to her as soon as possible.

Now all she could do was wait. Or was it?

Hope dialed Theresa Ingersoll's cell phone. She answered on the second ring from somewhere on the road.

"How are you?" Hope inquired.

"Not real good right now. Have you heard about what's happening?" The stress was obvious in Theresa's voice.

"They just dropped a fax on me from tomorrow's *National Informer.* Sounds like a real bomb."

"That's the understatement of the year! I'm still in shock. I mean, I can't believe what this gold digger's done and that she's gonna get away with it."

"I'll be praying for you and asking a few close friends to be praying for you too," Hope offered.

Theresa began crying. "Thanks. I need all the support I can get right now. I mean, I heard about it yesterday afternoon, and I spent most of last night praying to my saints . . . but it's as if they're not listening. It's as if I'm alone."

Hope took a deep breath. "You want to do lunch?" It was an offer from her heart, one that she had no idea if she could fulfill, because she had no idea how her day was going to line up.

"Maybe tomorrow," she answered. "I'm on my way to meet with the lawyers to discuss what we can do about it . . ." Her voice trailed off into tears.

"Tomorrow it is. Where do you want to meet?"

Theresa took a moment to answer. "How about the Germantown Country Club? Noon OK for you?"

~

The fax from RMI Holdings was short and to the point. The issue of what was or was not in Robert Ingersoll's will was in the hands of the lawyers, so the company would have no comment about Anna-Marie Cassarelli's claims.

"Lot of help they are," Hope grumbled as she dropped the three-sentence fax onto her desk and again turned to the RMI Web site, where she located the number for the company's legal department. *At least I can say that company officials would not comment on the matter.*

~

Hope sent Peter an e-mail summarizing the matter in hopes that it would satisfy his need. Minutes later he was on the phone insisting that she do an on-camera report. She felt her stomach tying into a fresh knot.

"I'm not asking you to betray anything personal. Listen, I've reported controversial things about members of the United States Congress—representatives and senators—and then played golf with them the next day as if nothing had happened," Peter declared. "It's just the way the game is played. You know that. You protect what is shared in private but report what is stated in public."

That did little to relieve Hope's tension.

"You're OK. Just do it," Peter ordered.

Hope turned back to her computer. It took three tries before instinct took over and she began the mechanics of putting together a report that she could read on camera. Midway through she phoned the broadcast control room to tell the production manager that she would need to tape a report in the studio. Could they be ready to tape in five minutes and then feed it over the satellite in 30? She would need the green screen with a series of photos inserted beside her for illustration.

After writing her on-camera copy, Hope sent it to the teleprompter so she could read it off the slanted mirror in front of the camera lens. Next she checked and adjusted her hair and makeup before turning toward the studio door. After wiring her cordless microphone, she stood on a tape X on the floor, the same starting spot used by whoever did the weather reports during the evening news and where the satellite maps were seen behind them.

On cue Hope began her report. "If a Cincinnati woman's claims are true, then control of a multibillion-dollar-a-year industrial empire could soon pass from the deceased CEO to his mistress." A glance at the on-air monitor showed the tabloid's photo appearing beside her. "In tomorrow's issue of the *National Informer* Anna-Marie Cassarelli, a secretary in the Cincinnati office of RMI Holdings, claims that CEO Robert Ingersoll, who died following the July Diamond Airways crash in Los Angeles, fathered her 3-year-old son."

The on-air photos now included a stock picture of Robert Ingersoll.

"Cassarelli claims that Ingersoll's will gives her half of his 40 percent share of company ownership. If true, that would make her the largest shareholder and put her in a position to take over control of the $3-billion-a-year industrial group," Hope continued. "Officials at RMI Holdings declined to comment on Miss Cassarelli's claims and referred questions to the company's legal department, which also declined comment. Hope Lancaster, MBS News, Memphis."

Hope kept her eyes on the camera for a three-count before turning away. "Did that look good?" she asked the control room.

A disembodied voice came from a speaker somewhere up above the studio lights. "That's good. Want us to put it on the satellite for you?"

Hope nodded as she unclipped her microphone. "Go ahead."

"Where'd your enthusiasm go to?" the voice wondered.

"Wherever it is right now, I'd sure like to get it back," she grumbled as she headed for the studio door.

CHAPTER TWENTY

Mark awoke early the next morning to the realization that he was alone in bed. The bathroom light was off and Hope's rocking chair was empty, but there was a faint glow of light in the hallway that indicated that a light was on downstairs. He sat up, swung his feet over the side of the bed and stepped into his shower clogs. Downstairs he found Hope at the dining room table with her Bible and concordance open and a legal pad with a half page of notes.

"Up this early and with notes like those? I'd almost think you were an overworked lawyer," he quipped.

She jumped. "You startled me! I didn't hear you coming."

Mark put a filter in the coffeemaker, poured in a scoop of coffee grounds, and went to the sink to get water. "What's got you so deep into the Bible?"

Hope sat back in her chair. "Oh, a bunch of things, and they're all jumbled together." She pulled back the chair next to her and beckoned for Mark to sit down. "You're a programmer. You're trained to think logically. Maybe you can help me figure this out."

Mark opened a cupboard and pulled out two coffee mugs. "Want a cup?"

She looked up from the pages just long enough to nod. He poured the steaming liquid into each, then stirred in the favorite amounts of cream and sugar before making his way to the table. "OK, what are we trying to figure out? Does it have anything to do with what's going on with your mother?"

"Does it ever! I'm so confused!" Hope almost moaned. "She said she asked Daddy my question about how anyone could go to heaven when they died if Jesus didn't go when He died. You know what he said?"

Mark sipped his coffee and shook his head. "No. What?"

"That I should believe what I've been taught since I was a child. And then he referred her over here to Luke 16 and this parable about the rich man and Lazarus. That's where I'm having a hard time."

Mark shook his head. "I don't think I'm going to be much help to you there, hon. I'm not much good when it comes to interpreting parables. I mean, your father was the family expert in that area."

Hope had been twirling a cheap ballpoint pen in her right hand. Now she slammed it against the table in frustration. "That's exactly the problem. I get the feeling that I'm getting one answer from the Bible and a different one from Daddy. What's frustrating is that he was a minister, so I guess I was expecting that what he said would be consistent with the Bible. Only it isn't!"

Mark pulled the Bible in front of him and scanned the passage. "OK, we've got this rich man who dies and ends up burning in hell. Then there's this poor beggar named Lazarus who used to beg outside the rich man's home. He dies and ends up in Paradise. The rich man asks for someone to go to his brothers and warn them about what fate awaits them. Lazarus tells the rich man that they have the law and the prophets and that if they won't believe them, they won't believe even if someone comes back from the dead and warns them. Right?"

Hope nodded. "Right."

Mark paused to survey the text again and think. "Well, the first thing that strikes me is the warning to believe the law and the prophets. So I guess the message from your father is right, that we need to be studying the Bible."

"That makes sense. OK, what else?" Hope answered.

"There's something about this story that looks odd, but I just can't put my finger on it," Mark observed. Then he snapped his fingers and jumped from his chair. "Remember those books your mother gave you from your father's library? I think there was a set of Bible commentaries in there. I'm going to go look."

In a moment Mark was out the door and in the garage. Hope heard the sounds of boxes being moved and grunts from the person moving them. After a couple minutes he reappeared bearing a large hard-bound volume held high, as if it were a just-won prize.

"Luke, right?" Mark asked.

Hope nodded. "Chapter 16."

Mark thumbed the pages to find the matching section in the commentary and began scanning the discussion. After a number of paragraphs he let out a whistle. "Listen to this, hon. It says the Jews had a concept that you could measure a person's closeness to God by the volume of their temporal blessings. Thus a rich person was considered to be living a life much closer to God than a person in poverty, such as a beggar. But in this parable Jesus reverses the outcomes as a way of directing people away from measuring their spirituality by their wealth and back to the Scriptures."

"You don't think Jesus was saying that people go directly to heaven or hell when they die?" Hope asked.

"It sure doesn't sound as though that's what Jesus is teaching here at all. It sounds as though Jesus is warning people to get back to the Scriptures, that the Bible's where we'll find out the truth about God," Mark declared.

"Thanks. You know, you're not a half-bad theologian. Maybe you missed your calling and should be a preacher instead of a programmer," Hope said as she pulled her husband close for an affectionate kiss.

"Yeah, right. I'm interviewing at the church over in Podunk next week," he answered with a sarcastic grin, then scanned her note sheets. "Boy, you've got a lot of notes here! What else is bothering you?"

Hope took a ragged breath. "OK, let's go back to this thing about Daddy appearing to Mom. That's what's bothering me."

"Why's that bothering you? I mean, he's in heaven."

"Is he? That's what I thought until I read this about Saul when he went to visit the witch of En-dor." She turned pages in her Bible until finding the twenty-eighth chapter of 1 Samuel. "It says that Saul drove out all the witches and mediums. Then he turned around and went looking for one of them. Why would he drive them out in the first place?"

It was Mark's turn to be stumped. "Guess it's time for another trip to the garage," he muttered as he headed for the door. For a time he could be heard moving and opening boxes before returning with another Bible commentary volume. He plopped it onto the table, thumbed to the related pages, and began reading.

"It says here that God told Saul to drive out the witches and mediums because they were servants of Satan who would corrupt God's people if allowed to remain in the land."

Hope considered the answer for a moment. "So if God had told Saul that they were evil, why would he go to one of them?"

Mark pulled the Bible in front of him and began reading chapter 28.

"Aha!" he exclaimed. "Verses 4 through . . . 7. The Philistines had invaded. Saul was terrified and God wasn't answering him, so he was looking for guidance."

Hope pulled the Bible in front of her and kept reading. "You know what strikes me? This wasn't a witch he went to see; it was a medium who called up the spirits of the dead. And you know what else? She didn't call Samuel down from heaven; she called him up, as up from the grave."

"What's significant about that?" Mark questioned.

"Direction. We think of heaven as being 'up' and hell and the grave as being 'down.' If this spirit medium called Samuel 'up,' then either he wasn't in heaven or it wasn't Samuel."

"So?" Mark sat back and crossed his arms.

"So it means that the spirit wasn't from God . . . and it means that whoever's been visiting Mom isn't from heaven . . . and isn't Daddy." Silence filled the room for a moment as Hope considered her realization. "It isn't Daddy who's visiting Mom. It's an evil spirit from Satan."

"But your father is in heaven! I saw him there!" Mark argued. "I know what I saw!"

Hope put her hand on top of her husband's and looked him in the eye. "I know you believe that is what you saw, but I can't believe it anymore."

Disbelief covered his face. "You . . . what?"

Hope shook her head. "You weren't dead. I mean, you weren't dead-in-the-grave-for-four-days-dead like Lazarus. You may have been considered clinically dead because you didn't have a heartbeat and weren't breathing for a time, but the paramedics revived you, so you weren't really dead-dead as in take-you-out-and-bury-you dead."

Mark shook his head. "I wasn't *that* kind of dead, but I know what I saw, Hope. I know what I experienced!"

"OK, tell me this. If Lazarus went to heaven after he died, then when Jesus raised him back to life, why didn't he come out of the grave talking about being in heaven? Why wasn't he complaining about being brought back from Paradise? I mean, doing that seems pretty unfair to me. Maybe even cruel."

"So what do you mean? What are you getting at?" Mark half argued.

"It means Lazarus wasn't in heaven. And if Lazarus wasn't in heaven—and you remember my question the other day about Jesus saying He hadn't gone to heaven—then Daddy can't be in heaven, and it can't be Daddy who's visiting Mom. It has to be an evil spirit—a demon—visiting Mom."

Mark's face twisted in confusion. "Let me see if I'm getting this straight. You're telling me that—in spite of what we've been taught all our lives—we really don't go to heaven when we die? So there's no way your father could be in heaven right now?"

"I guess that's what I'm saying," Hope confessed. "You know, when you were in the hospital, God showed me this text in Psalms." She flipped pages until she found Psalm 146, verses 3 and 4. "Listen to this. 'Do not put your trust in princes, in mortal men, who cannot save. When their spirit departs, they return to the ground; on that very day their plans come to nothing.' That sounds pretty plain to me."

Mark began shaking his head. "I'm just having a hard time accepting it. How could it be true if we've been taught something else all our lives? I know what I saw. I saw your father and Jesus, and I saw them in heaven!"

The faint sounds of music from their clock radio wafted down the stairway.

"Good morning, dear." Hope leaned over and kissed her husband. "It's time to get up."

"I'm already awake, thank you," he grumbled, "and I don't like what I'm hearing."

"Why's that?" Hope countered.

"OK. If, like you say, Jesus and Lazarus and Samuel weren't in heaven, then what happened to me? Where was I?"

Hope shook her head. "I can't answer that right now. But I do know it's time to get our daughter up and get started on our day. We both need time to pray and think about all of this. We can talk later."

◞

"I'm going to lunch in a little bit, and after that I'll be doing some re-search on the RMI story," Hope announced to the news director on one of his sweeps through the newsroom. He grunted acknowledgment and continued on his patrol.

At 11:28 Hope went to the newsroom status board and moved the colored block beside her name so that it was under the "out to lunch" heading. A minute later she was in the car and heading toward the Germantown Country Club. At five minutes before noon she turned her SUV into the entrance, was admitted by the guard, and found a parking space. The maître d' directed her to the table where Theresa awaited.

"It's such a relief to see a friendly face!" Theresa exclaimed as she rose to greet Hope with a hug.

"How are you?"

Theresa shook her head as she sat back down. A waiter placed a glass of water and a menu in front of Hope and announced politely that he would be back soon to take their order.

"Right now I feel as though my whole world's been turned upside down," Theresa said without even a trace of a smile. She lifted the short, square-bottomed liquor glass beside her plate and downed what remained of the liquid. Theresa signaled the waiter and pointed to her glass.

"Had a rough morning?" Hope guessed.

"What would you like to drink? Maybe a daiquiri? We can order you a virgin one. You know, everything but the alcohol."

"It's been a long time since I had a strawberry daiquiri. Sure, a virgin daiquiri sounds good," Hope smiled.

The waiter picked up Theresa's empty glass, took the order, and excused himself.

Theresa placed the back of her hand against the corner of her forehead. "Hope, you don't know how rough it's been—and it's only the beginning." She paused for a moment. "I still can't believe it."

"Believe what?" Hope asked.

"I still can't believe what Robert did to me." The anger rose in her voice as she spoke. "All those years I trusted him. I bore him a child. We built a home together!" She was beginning to hiss and getting louder by the word. "Then he goes and has an affair and gives half his estate to that bimbo in Cincinnati! That *slut!* I mean, have you seen the pictures of her? I may be in my 50s, but I'm a whole lot sexier and a far sight prettier than she is!"

People at surrounding tables began looking around to see who was talking so loudly.

"How much do you know about her?" Hope asked. She made a downward motion with her hand, signaling Theresa to try to lower her volume.

The waiter returned with their drinks. "One scotch on the rocks and one virgin strawberry daiquiri," he announced as he placed the drinks in front of them. "Are you ready to order?"

Hope took another scan down the menu. "The Mexican chicken salad looks good. I'll go for that."

The waiter turned to Theresa.

"I'll have whatever she's having," she said with just a hint of a slur. "And keep these coming." She pointed to her glass.

"Uh, ma'am, two is your limit unless you can show me that someone else is driving you home."

"You bet I've got someone driving me home. My driver's eating his lunch right over there, and we've got the limo today," she boasted.

"Very well, ma'am." The waiter nodded, took their menus, and departed.

The pair sat in silence for several moments while a couple in golfing attire walked past and settled in at a table looking out on the golf course. For a long moment Theresa looked as though she was composing a thought. "I can't believe he did that to me," she mumbled. Her words were almost inaudible over the background music.

"Have you seen the *National Informer* story?" Hope wondered.

Theresa nodded. "Oh, yeah! I've seen it!" She leaned forward in her chair, planted her elbows on the table on either side of her place setting, and looked Hope in the eye. "You know, all these years I've been going through the grocery store checkout line seing all the covers about what celebrity's dating who and whatnot, and I never believed a word of it." She waved her hands in a crossing motion for emphasis. "Not a word of it. Now they're writin' about my beloved Robert, an' it's true. Prob'ly the first true words they ever printed, and it has to be about how my beloved Robert's been goin' to bed with a secretary in another city an' how he's givin' half his fortune to her instead of me."

"Can you fight it?" Hope wondered. "Is it legal? I mean, is there anything you can do?"

Theresa sat back and shook her head, then leaned forward again, her hands becoming more animated than ever. "Where do you think I was this mornin'? Getting my hair done?" The anger rose in her voice. "No! I was in my lawyer's office learnin' that my husband's been unfaithful to me and there's prob'ly nothing I can do about it 'cause it's the latest version of his will. Dated just last year. All signed and witnessed and notarized 'n all that other stuff."

"Can you fight it in court?"

Theresa let out a loud, short laugh. "That was the first question out of my mouth—after I stopped screaming." She smiled a tight, short-lived grin. Then her smile inverted, and she looked as if she would cry. "All fightin'll do is make the lawyers rich."

Theresa downed half her drink as the waiter placed loaded plates in front of them.

Hope reached across and took Theresa's hand. "Will you join me in a blessing? At least thank God for the food?"

She nodded and bowed her head while Hope prayed. When she opened her eyes, Hope saw tears streaking Theresa's makeup. They quickly disappeared with a dab from a tissue.

Hope tasted her salad. "M-m-m. This is good. Looks as though I'm going to have to get a membership here!"

Both women smiled. "I seriously doubt you could afford a membership here. But if you'd like, I can put you on the permanent guest list. That way you can at least come to the restaurant whenever you want, even if I'm not here."

"That would be great. I'd really like to bring Mark here sometime. You know, show him how the upper half of the world does lunch."

Their conversation wandered across several topics, but kept coming back to the will. It gave Theresa the house and the land around it and Robert's personal effects. It had no effect on her ownership of the 12 percent of the company stock already in her name.

"I told you before and I'll tell you again—my driver's waitin' fer me with the limo," Theresa protested to the waiter as she demanded a fourth drink, which had been consumed by the time they discussed ordering dessert.

"I think I'll pass on the dessert. Uh, can you point me to the rest-room?" The baby was sitting on Hope's bladder.

The waiter gave her directions.

The maître d' and Theresa were discussing something when Hope returned. She was already reaching for her purse to leave.

"I've gotta get out of here—quick! They just told me there's reporters out there an' they're looking for me—an it's all 'cause of that bimbo," she fairly hissed.

Hope looked at her in surprise, then jerked her head toward the front door, where she expected to see a pack of reporters with cameras, microphones, and notepads pushing their direction. Only restaurant patrons were visible.

Was Theresa becoming the center of a media frenzy? At once Hope wanted to shift back into reporter mode and be part of the crush holding out microphones, pointing cameras, and yelling questions. On the other hand, this was her friend. Theresa was normally a private person unaccustomed to being the focus of a hostile, prying press. She needed protecting. Most of all, she needed a place to sober up, because the worst thing she could do right now was get caught drunk on camera.

They needed a plan. The waiter called over the maître d' for a conference. The country club's security guards were keeping the press off the grounds. But unless she wanted to drive across manicured lawns and through lush flower beds to reach the club's service roads, there was no alternate route of escape. What could they do?

"Are the windows on your limo tinted? How dark?" the maître d' asked.

"Pretty dark. I mean, you can't see who's inside," Theresa answered.

"Good. That'll work," he observed.

"Yeah, but what if they recognize her limo? Or if they see her getting into it?" the waiter countered.

"Good point. Is there someone else who can drive you home?" the maître d' asked.

"If we let the limo leave without her, maybe they'll follow it, and then I can take her home," Hope offered.

"Das shweet of you," Theresa smiled as she reached across the table and patted the back of Hope's hand.

It was then that Hope got a good look at the ring on Theresa's left hand. An oblong diamond that must have been at least two carats was surrounded by two arcs of alternating rubies and emeralds. The price tag must have been a multiple of Hope's annual earnings. Her eyes grew wide at the sight before jerking herself back to the moment.

"Are your windows tinted?" the maître d' asked Hope.

Hope shook her head. Then she remembered a feature Mark had insisted that she get when ordering her Mercedes M-class SUV: windows that could be made nearly opaque simply by flipping a switch. She and Jennifer had once played a game of hide-and-seek with Jennifer inside flipping the switch on and off.

The maître d' devised a plan. The limo would be pulled around to the side entrance, and the country club's security people would make sure that no nonmembers were on the grounds, so no press spies would be able to see that no one got into the limo. It would depart normally and drive straight home, entering through the main gate. Hopefully the press mob would think Theresa was inside and follow.

"So how am I supposed to get home? I mean, if they're camping outside her gate, then somebody'll figure out it's me driving in, and they'll start wondering what I'm doing there," Hope argued.

"There's a couple of dirt roads. You know, all grown up with grasses and weeds. We only ride horshes on them," Theresa offered. Her speech was becoming more and more slurred.

"I've got four-wheel drive if we need it," Hope volunteered. "I've never used it, but I'm up for an adventure."

The women sat and looked at each other in silence while the maître d' put his plan into action. After several minutes he returned with a report that the limo had departed with most of the press in pursuit. There were still a few stragglers left, but it looked as though they were packing up to leave too.

"Sorry, but I have to use the restroom again," Hope said as she stood up. "We can leave as soon as I'm done."

Theresa tried to order a final drink, but the waiter refused, saying she'd consumed her limit even if someone else was driving. He watched as she swayed a bit before gaining her feet.

Theresa waited for Hope before the two of them left the restaurant, surveyed the perimeter of the parking area, and walked to Hope's SUV.

Two camera operators were still there, but seemed to be packing up. One car displayed a channel 3 logo. *Don't tell me we're in on it too. This wasn't on the storyboard when I left. I wonder who got sent to cover this?*

The last camera operator was closing his trunk as the women passed. Hope thought she saw a look of recognition on his face, and her eyes darted to the window switch. It was still in the "dark" position. Was the system working? In seconds it did not matter, because they were in traffic. Hope circled a block twice and watched her rearview mirror to see if anyone was following. No tail was apparent.

Theresa's initial fear of the press faded into curiosity about how many reporters were still outside her gate. She wanted to at least drive past and go around the north side of the estate on her way to the back entrance, but Hope vetoed it. No sense flirting with the chance of getting spotted, she argued.

Ten minutes later Hope was helping her intoxicated friend into the house and into the care of a servant. She departed the way she had come, but her curiosity about the press pack was growing. With her windows still darkened she turned onto the road leading around the north side of the estate, then south past the main entrance. Outside the gate was a traffic jam with a half-dozen press vehicles pulled onto the shoulder. Reporters and photographers milled about. Two men were setting up a satellite truck from a station in Nashville. A technician from one of the Memphis stations was aiming the tall microwave tower on the back of his van for a live video feed.

Only a single traffic lane remained open. *They at least need the sheriff's department out here for traffic control.* Hope reached for her cell phone to make a call, then pulled her hand back. *It's their problem. Officially I'm not here and have no idea what's happening.*

∾

Hope walked in the newsroom door at 1:45 p.m. and almost immediately was confronted by the news director. "Where've you been?" he demanded.

She smiled while her mind raced to answer without revealing anything. "As I told you, I was doing some background work on the RMI story."

"Well, I hope it was good, because this story's exploding," he answered.

"Oh, what's new?"

"Well, just after you left we got a fax from RMI Holdings about a re-quired filing they'd just sent to the Securities and Exchange Commission reporting a change in ownership. They've confirmed that Anna-Marie Cassa—whatever her name is—is the new largest shareholder with 20 per-cent of the company's stock," he said. "New York wants us to keep a cam-era and reporter staked out on her 24/7 for the next few days. They want to know everything she does. You're working the RMI story for the net-work, so I want you on it."

Hope swallowed hard, and the smile vanished from her face. This was turning into something even bigger than she'd imagined!

"Something wrong?" he asked.

"Uh, no. I guess not," she fibbed. *How am I ever going to be a reporter and Theresa's friend?*

Hope turned back to Bob. "Why do I get the feeling there's more to this than what you just told me?" she wanted to know.

"Well, we're doing the usual. The network wants footage. Plus, we're offering our footage for sale to whoever wants to buy it. We're just seiz-ing the opportunity to make a little money."

Thoughts careened inside Hope's cranium as she tried to act normal. Fortunately, she had a reason to escape when her bladder demanded that it be emptied.

CHAPTER TWENTY-ONE

Hope quickly wished she'd called in sick the next morning.

"I can't believe you're doing this to me!" Hope protested to the news director as she shook the story assignment sheet in his face. "In case you've forgotten, I've asked Peter Leventhal to take me off the story because of a conflict of interest. I can't be objective." She dropped the sheet on his desk.

"Do I look like Peter Leventhal? And what's this about a conflict of interest? You didn't tell me about it," the news director shot back. "Listen. I don't have anybody else I can put on the story today. The network's all over me for any tidbit they can report. And if you recall, that show *Tell-All TV* is produced by MBS, so New York's double-breathing down my neck wanting a scoop nobody else can give 'em. Plus, because of your pregnancy I can't send you on any strenuous assignments like . . . climbing Mount Everest. So the way I figure it, sitting in an air-conditioned car or in a chair under an umbrella on the side of the road is about as 'limited' a duty as I have available to give you." He sat down behind his desk and waited for her to open her mouth.

She started to say something, then closed her mouth. She could tell by the look on his face that there was nothing to be gained by arguing.

"Look, Hope, it's about the best I can do for you today, OK?" he said in a more agreeable tone. "Look at it this way. I just had to send a team down to Shreveport to work the serial killer story for a couple of days just because the network asked for it, and you didn't have to go because you've got an appointment with your doctor tomorrow."

A knot began to form in Hope's stomach. She turned and left the office without saying a word. *If I have to do it, then I guess I'll just have to do it. But I've got to figure out some way to protect Theresa. She's really hurting right now and needs a friend.*

A glance at the morning sun told Hope that it was going to be an SPF-45 kind of day. She made a mental note to stop someplace and buy a bottle of sunscreen on the way out to the Ingersolls' gate.

Marty Chang readily agreed to a stop at Wal-Mart, where they also loaded up on six-packs of sodas and bottled water, a Styrofoam picnic cooler, and ice to fill it.

"You're being awfully quiet today," Marty observed as they finally set course for the Ingersoll estate.

"Oh, I've just got some things on my mind" was all she admitted.

Music from the radio filled the car as they drove. The knot in her stomach grew with each mile.

The sheriff's department had set up barricades allowing the reporters and their vehicles to occupy one lane while steering passing cars into the remaining lane. One crew from a competing network's scandal show had an air-conditioned RV parked on the shoulder and a lookout posted so the reporter could jump out and arrive on-camera looking fresh and ready to shout questions on short notice. Fortunately, they were parked downwind, and the breeze carried the muffled sound of their generator away from the scene.

Marty opened the trunk and pulled out a pop-up sun shelter big enough for the two of them to sit under with the cooler between them. Folding canvas chairs followed. Within minutes they were swapping tales with some of the other reporters, who crowded into their shade. Someone produced a deck of cards. Two more chairs appeared from somewhere, and a game of penny-ante poker developed using the cooler top as a table.

Hope's mind wasn't in the game, and she began losing money. Then the baby moved, and she decided it was time for an urgent break at the convenience store two miles down the road.

"Uh, Marty, can I have the car keys?" Hope held out her hands.

"Sure. What's up?" he asked.

She patted her abdomen. "Gotta run down to the corner store."

"You know they deliver, don't you? Well, not that kind of delivery," one of the other reporters joked.

"I'll be back in a few. Let me know if I miss anything," she said as she turned toward the car. She arrived at the store just in the nick of time.

Back in the car an idea struck her. She hit the speed dial on her cell phone and a moment later heard a groggy "Hello" on the other end.

Theresa had a hangover and felt as though the army was marching around inside her head. Her mouth felt as though it was full of dry cotton balls, and her—well, she wouldn't talk about the other thing.

"Can you do me a personal favor? Can you stay inside today? I mean, don't go near the front gate. If you have to go out, can you use the back road, as we did yesterday?"

Theresa mumbled something about it being no problem. "Why are you asking?"

"Because my boss sent me out here to be part of this pack of wolves camped outside your gate, and I thought I'd warn you so you could stay out of sight. That way I don't have to be one of the people shouting questions at you."

Theresa groaned. She just wanted someplace with no lights and no sound so she could sleep off the hangover.

Lunchtime came and went. So did 2:00 p.m. The card game ended with the camera operator from the Nashville station pocketing his winnings.

Hope felt beads of sweat forming on her forehead and looked around. Waves of heat were rising in every direction, and there were two mirages shimmering from the roadway in either direction.

"Let's get out of here," Hope said.

Marty looked around. Everyone was about to wilt in the heat, and there was a look in Hope's eyes that told him to not argue. He folded the canopy and chairs and put them back in the trunk while Hope started the engine and aimed three air-conditioning vents in her direction. Next was his camera gear. Last was the cooler, from which he extracted fresh drinks for the two of them.

Hope took a look at herself in the vanity mirror mounted on the back of the sun visor. There was no way she was ready to go on-camera for the evening news looking like this! She punched the speed dial on her cell phone to tell the news director three things: First, they had no story. Second, she had to go home, shower, and change clothes before she could anchor the evening news. Third, if this was his idea of a limited-duty-while-you're-pregnant assignment, well, she didn't like it.

"Oh, guess where I'm going next Monday," Mark announced as he and Hope settled onto the couch to talk and read after putting Jennifer to bed.

There was something in the way he said it that put her on guard. She just looked at him and waited for what he would say next. After being married to him this long, she knew he'd spill the beans rather quickly. He just couldn't keep a secret very long.

"Los Angeles."

Hope felt a stab of fear, and her eyes grew wide.

Mark nodded. "Yep. The customer wants us back there on Monday. Looks as though we'll be home Friday afternoon." He reached out, took Hope's hand, and squeezed it. "It'll be OK. Listen, I've checked the weather, and you know what I found? On the other trip the winds were coming off the desert. That happens only for a few weeks each summer. All the rest of the time they're coming off the ocean. That means the planes all come in toward the airport over land, not the water, so there's no danger."

Fear still filled her eyes.

"Look. Everything's going to be OK. The FBI said the other day that they'd wrapped up their investigation. Plus, I've heard reports about security being increased around the airports to keep attacks like that from being repeated. There's no danger, hon," he tried to comfort her.

It helped only a little. Silence filled the room for several long moments as they studied each other's face.

"It'll be OK, dear," he offered. "We just have to trust that it'll be OK."

Hope took a deep breath. "I guess you're right. It's just . . . well . . . after what we went through just a few weeks ago . . . I guess I'm not ready for you to go away. Not yet, and especially not there."

"Well, I wanted to let you know as soon as I heard."

"Thanks," she muttered and turned back to her book. Several minutes passed. "You know what else that means?"

Mark looked her way without answering.

"I don't know who's going to watch Jennifer between when you usually pick her up at Mom's and when I get home. I'm sure Mom won't mind changing her schedule for a day or two, but not much more."

"What about the child-care center? Don't they have extended after-school hours?" Mark wondered.

"Yeah, it'll just cost us more," Hope declared. "But at least it's only for a few days."

~

For Hope, arising and preparing for church on Sunday morning was as routine and as automatic as breathing. As far back as she could remember, it was just something her family always did. She enjoyed the routine. Church gave her a chance to be with friends, and when she was a kid she got to participate in a lot of fun activities, including summer camp and mission trips.

Of course, having Daddy in the pulpit had meant that Hope had to pay attention to his sermons, because Sunday dinner was quiz time to see how well the kids had paid attention. The inability to answer his questions correctly could mean going without dessert. Correct answers could mean a scoop of ice cream with a slice of cake or pie. So she had learned his sermons well. Though he had tried to write new ones all the time, Aubrey Morris had occasionally dusted off all or part of an old one. It had happened just often enough that sometimes Hope could close her eyes and deliver his next lines from memory.

Hope was proud of her father. Most of the time she had felt he really was a good father and a good preacher. But there were sermons that she had not liked, the ones about facing judgment before God's throne in heaven and when he talked about the wicked being tormented in the flames of hell and suffering through eternity while never dying. Thinking about the possibility of being lost and eternally punished by an angry God in the flames of hell had given her nightmares more than once.

It was at the end of one of her father's hellfire sermons that Hope had responded to his altar call and went forward to accept salvation. It was not out of any new love for God, but out of fear of being lost and suffering eternally in hell. The smile on her father's face as he baptized her the next Sunday morning had told her that at 10 years of age she'd made a grown-up decision. Now as she scurried about the kitchen and up and down the stairs getting her family ready to go to church, she wondered what the new pastor's sermon would be about.

Jennifer came dashing into the kitchen, a CD player in hand and headphones on her ears. "Have you seen my shoes, Mom? You know, my sandals?" She danced to the beat of a tune Hope could only partly hear.

The sight warmed Hope's heart and made her smile. Any other day of the week Jennifer was all child. But this morning she had transformed herself into a pretty girl who'd obviously raided her mother's makeup bag. The eye shadow and blush were a little too heavy, but with practice she would do better.

Should I tell her to go take it off and turn off the music? Hope glanced at the clock and decided she didn't have time to squabble over either. *After all, she is taking after me. And those colors do match her dress.*

"Uh, I think I saw them under your bed," Hope answered. "Near the head of the bed."

"Where did you say, Mom?"

Hope leaned forward, spotted the pause button on the CD player, and stabbed at it, making just enough contact on the moving target to be effective.

"I said, look under your bed."

"But Mom! I've looked there, and I can't find 'em," Jennifer protested. "Come help me, please!"

"I'm kind of busy here. Go look again," Hope instructed.

"But Mom!"

"Go look again," she repeated, and Jennifer turned away.

Mark was still in his bathrobe and settled into his recliner to read the Sunday newspaper. He had not shaved, and breakfast was about to be on the table.

"You need to get a move on if you're going to be ready on time," Hope admonished her tardy mate.

"I think I'll stay home today," he replied from behind the sports section.

Hope marched from the kitchen to the den and pushed the page aside. "Now just a minute!" She waved a spatula she'd just used to flip a pancake. "We attend church as a family, and it's time for you to go get ready," she ordered. "Get moving."

He shook his head and repositioned the paper.

Hope swatted the sports section aside with the spatula and made eye contact. "What's going on?" Her tone was demanding but something less than a direct order.

"I just don't feel like it today," he answered.

"Why don't you feel like it?"

"I just don't."

Hope thought for a second. "This isn't like you, Mark," she said in a softer tone. "Is something wrong?"

"No." He shook his head and turned back to the page.

"Well, something's changed your thinking, because this isn't like you. Normally you're ready before me."

Mark finished a paragraph before answering. "I just don't feel as though I need to go to church anymore."

Hope's puzzled gaze told him he had some explaining to do.

"I'm saved. My salvation is secure. I mean, I've been to heaven and back, so I feel as though there's nothing I can do to change my fate. It's sealed. I'm going to heaven when I die, so why do I need to go to church and hear some preacher telling me that I need to repent and avoid hellfire?"

"What's that got to do with not going to church?" Hope wanted to know.

"Everything. If I'm sure of my salvation, then I don't need to go to church. So I'm not going. It's that simple," he declared with calm assurance.

"Well, can you at least come and join us for breakfast?" Hope asked.

The paper came down, and the trio gathered around the table. Hope offered a blessing because Mark did not seem eager to do it. Before bowing her head, she shot him an accusing gaze just long enough for their eyes to meet before he looked away.

~

Monday morning something awoke Hope while the world was still dark. A glance at the clock showed that two hours remained before she had to awaken Jennifer and get her ready for school. Next she would take Mark to the airport for his trip to Los Angeles. For a few minutes she stared at the ceiling and tried snuggling up to Mark in hopes that sleep would again overtake her. Then her baby-pressed bladder called an alarm, and there was no choice but to get up.

Moments later Hope's slippers pressed the carpet as she crossed the hallway to look in on Jennifer. *She looks like an angel,* Hope thought as she studied her daughter's face in the glow of the night-light.

Hope settled onto the couch in the living room and tucked her feet up under the expanse of her long nightgown. In the lowest setting of a three-way lamp she opened her Bible and concordance and began a word search. A twinge of fear struck her as she turned the pages of the concordance to find the letter *d* and then the letter *e*, until she finally found the word "dead." *If my mother's talking to her dead husband and if my husband died and went to heaven and got sent back, then I want to know what the Bible says happens when a person dies.*

After several minutes she put the books aside long enough to get up and find a legal pad and pen. After making a page of notes from texts using the word "dead," she began looking up related words. The passing of an hour found her working on "death" as the first rays of dawn poked through the windows. She was working on "grave" when she heard the clock radio in their bedroom come to life.

Mark came padding down the stairs about 20 minutes later looking freshly shaved and showered. "Morning, hon. Whatcha studying?" he asked as he headed toward the coffeemaker and began preparing a brew.

"I'm trying to find out what the Bible says about what happens to us when we die," she said matter-of-factly, barely looking up from where she was adding a line to her notes.

"I can answer that one," Mark said as he finished pouring water into the machine. "In fact, you already know the answer. If you're saved when you die, your soul goes to heaven and lives in Paradise with God. If you're lost, your soul goes to hell and burns forever. It's that simple."

She shook her head.

"I'm telling you, it's that simple," he argued before she could get a word out of her mouth. "I'm saying that because of what I've experienced. I know what I saw and what I felt that day when I went to heaven. So I'm telling you what I know is true."

"Then we have a problem," Hope said as she got up and set about preparing breakfast.

"Really? What kind of problem?" Mark asked as he watched brownish liquid begin flowing through the hole below the coffee filter.

Hope stepped in front of her husband and gave him a warm kiss. "First, let me say good morning." She opened a cupboard and began extracting plates and glasses. "Now, the problem is that the Bible seems to be telling a different story than you are."

"Oh?" he questioned.

Hope set a stack of three plates on the table and picked up her notes. "I'm finding all sorts of interesting things. Like this one in Ecclesiastes, chapter 9, verse 5, where it says that the dead know nothing. Oh, and Jesus' friend Lazarus. Jesus told His disciples that Lazarus was asleep, and they thought it was good, that he would get well. But they misunderstood, so He had to tell them that Lazarus actually was dead. So Jesus was comparing death to sleep."

"Now I suppose you're going to tell me that we're dead when we're asleep," Mark argued playfully. "I think it's time I got Jennifer up."

"As deep as she sleeps, sometimes waking her is like waking the dead," Hope joked as she set her notes aside and set the table.

CHAPTER TWENTY-TWO

Diamond Airways Flight 940 turned westward on a direct course toward Los Angeles International Airport. It was the same route that had once been numbered 886, only the airline had retired the other flight number after the crash.

Mark's gaze moved from the magazine he was reading to the window beside him. The view was limited because of the smog toward which the plane descended. Only what was straight down or a little out to each side was visible through the haze. Beyond that the smog became so thick that it became a gray-brown blanket covering the entire Los Angeles basin, trapped between the mountains to the north or south.

Mark's stress level rose as quickly as the plane descended. The giant wing just ahead of his window began reshaping itself as the plane slowed. First the giant trailing-edge flaps slid outward and downward from the back of the wing. Later other panels on the leading edge of the wing slid forward and downward. At slower airspeed it gave the effect of a much larger wing.

The plane was in the smog now, and the ground was rushing by more quickly. Houses and trucks that once looked like toys now began revealing more of their details as the plane drew closer to the earth.

"You OK?" the passenger next to him inquired.

For an instant Mark pulled his eyes away from the window. "Yeah. Yeah. I'm OK," he nodded.

"You look pretty scared to me," the man observed. "Your face is white, and you've got a death grip on your seat."

Mark glanced down and realized that his seatmate was right. He peeled his hands off the armrests and flexed his fingers to get some color back into them. Then he grinned sheepishly at the other passenger and continued gazing at the window. Soon his hands went back to their colorless grip.

The plane was down to a few thousand feet now. "What's got you so scared?" the seatmate inquired.

"You remember that Diamond Airways flight that got shot down back in July?"

The seatmate nodded.

"I was on it."

The seatmate looked sharply over the reading glasses set halfway down his nose. He started to say something, but was interrupted by the lead flight attendant's announcement that they were about three minutes from touchdown. "Would everyone please make sure your seat is in the full upright position, your seat belt is securely fastened, and the tray table in front of you is stowed?"

Mark did a quick check to make sure he was in compliance before locking his eyes on the outside again.

"What was it like? I mean, what happened?" the seatmate wanted to know.

"Well, I was sitting over there." Mark pointed to the left side of the plane. "The missile hit that engine." He pointed out the window to his right.

"Sounds pretty dramatic," the seatmate offered.

Mark nodded. "The worst was after we were on the ground. We were all trying to get out through the emergency exits, and there was a lot of smoke. I mean, just imagine all these people on this plane trying to get to the emergency exits all at once."

Their conversation was interrupted by a hydraulic whining that was followed by a series of thumps and the steady rushing of wind over the once-sleek airframe made rough by extending the landing gear.

"I guess I really can't imagine what it was like," the seatmate offered.

Mark turned back to the window. The ground was moving faster. What was their altitude? Not more than a few hundred feet. Then the runway slid beneath them, and everyone waited for that pregnant pause until the wheels thumped against the pavement. The plane slowed to taxi speed and turned off the runway. Mark sank back in his seat and released his death grip on the armrests.

The seatmate reached inside his jacket, extracted a colorful brochure, and handed it to Mark. "I've a strong feeling you will appreciate this."

Mark eyed the brochure and read the title: "God's Power to Face Your Fears."

"Thanks," he said as he took it. "I'll read it. But you know what I really need to do?"

The seatmate shook his head. "What?"

"I need to get into the terminal so I can use my cell phone and tell my wife that I got here safely. I think her knuckles have been whiter than mine for a lot longer."

⁓

Lower humidity made the waning days of September much more tolerable than the earlier days. With the relief came an invitation to a pool party celebrating Theresa Ingersoll's birthday on the last Saturday of the month.

The TV scandal shows had long since aimed their cameras at other people, so no one was parked outside the gate as the guests arrived. Hope accepted Mark's hand as they followed the signs guiding guests through the garden beside the house on their way to the pool.

Jennifer halted and stared at something in the flower garden. "I don't believe it! Look, Mommy! Daddy! Look!" She pointed at a sculpted shrub. "It's a bunny rabbit! It looks like a giant bunny rabbit!"

Sure enough, a four-foot-high shrub was indeed shaped to look like a bunny in midhop.

"And look over there! What's that?" Jennifer squealed excitedly.

The parents looked and began guessing. A pony? They couldn't quite decide. They looked around more and discovered that the large garden was populated with a number of shrubs shaped in whimsical ways. In one direction stood a trio of deer. In another was a dog. A number of shrubs were being shaped, but their final form was not yet identifiable.

"How good to see you!" Theresa Ingersoll hailed them from the gate. "I see you've found our newest project."

"That's a bunny rabbit, isn't it?" Jennifer asked excitedly.

"Sure is. We call this our *Alice in Wonderland* garden. A few months ago some of my grandkids watched the movie, and we got the idea it might be fun to have a garden with shrubs shaped like the creatures in the story. The gardeners are having a real challenge with some of them." She pointed at the incomplete creatures. "I'm not sure what they're going to be or when they'll look like whatever they're supposed to be."

"It looks like fun," Jennifer declared cheerily.

Hope leaned forward and embraced Theresa. "It's good to see you again. Thanks for inviting us. Happy birthday."

"Oh, thank you. I'm glad you could join us," Theresa cooed as she led them through the gate and onto the pool patio.

Jennifer spotted a number of kids in and around the pool. She fairly snatched the gym bag away from her mother and made tracks for the pool house to change into her swimsuit.

"Guess we know where she's going," Theresa laughed as she turned to Hope. "You want to go swimming?" Then before Hope could answer, Thersa added, "Or, hey! How about going for a ride with me first?"

Hope looked at Mark for permission.

"Go ahead. You'll be back in a while, won't you?" he said.

"I promise I won't keep her very long. I guarantee that you I'll have her back by dinnertime," Theresa nodded.

"You don't mind?" Hope asked Mark.

"Go ahead. That pool looks really inviting right now." He waved her on. "You go ahead. Go on."

Hope gave her husband a kiss. "Thanks. See you, well, whenever."

"Where are we going?" Hope inquired.

"Oh, I wanted to show you something. Bounce an idea off you, if that's OK with you." Theresa eyed Hope's expanding belly. "I thought about riding around the place on the four-wheelers, but looking at you, would you rather ride in my Suburban?"

Hope's hands moved tenderly across her abdomen. "The four-wheeler sounds like a lot of fun, but I think the Suburban would be better," she answered.

Moments later they were motoring at a modest pace down a gravel road with a pasture bordered by a whiteboard fence on one side and a hardwood forest on the other. Theresa took the turn leading toward an expansive horse stable.

"You seem to be doing well," Hope observed.

Theresa smiled. "I guess I am. You know, as much as it hurts losing Robert, I guess I'm learning to live without him."

"I sympathize. It's been eight months since Daddy died, and I still find myself doing such things as starting to dial the phone to call him. But I can't even imagine what it'd be like if I lost Mark," Hope said. They turned into the area in front of the stable and pulled to a stop.

Theresa pulled her door latch. "I don't wish the experience on anyone. I guess it's one of those things in life that you don't look forward to, but somehow you get through it and keep going."

She closed her door and walked around the front of the vehicle. "You know what's surprised me about it? How many really nice people there are. How many people really care about you when you're hurting the deepest hurt of your entire life."

"I trust you're not talking about those reporters that were camped outside your gate!" Hope joked.

Theresa laughed as she walked to the fence. She set one foot on the bottom rail and waved her hands for emphasis. "Definitely not them. No, I'm talking about the people who were courageous enough to call or write and come see me in spite of those reporters who camped out there. Hey, now here's the idea I want to share with you."

Hope found a spot a few feet away where someone had nailed a board flat across the top of the fence boards. She stepped up on the lower rails, eased her bottom onto the flat board, and waited for Theresa to continue.

"I've been thinking about making some changes around here," Theresa stated, her eyes on something in the distance.

"What's set you to thinking this way?" Hope inquired.

Theresa turned to her friend and smiled. "You know how to ask questions, don't you?"

"That's what I'm paid to do. But I'm not charging you."

"Sounds like a bargain to me!" Theresa grinned. "What's happened? Well, before Robert died we were living on his paychecks. We set aside money, so I'm set for retirement, but it'll be nearly 10 years before I can touch the money. The whole place is paid for. Between now and then I have a monthly life insurance check, but it goes only so far. It's only about half of what he was bringing home. The other day I looked at my savings and checking balances and realized that I had a whole lot more money going out than coming in. So I've been thinking and trying to come up with some ways of reducing expenses and generating income."

"So . . . what's your idea?" Hope inquired.

"First I've gotta tell you a little story. It was really strange. The other day I got this phone call. I don't know how they got my number. Anyway, it was a producer for this TV show *Great Beyond* or something like that."

Hope shook her head. "Can't say I've heard of it. It sounds like one of those shows that's all about the host giving you messages from the dead."

Theresa nodded. "They said it comes on in prime time on some cable network. Anyway, I've never seen it. The producer said they wanted me to come on the show because the host had a message for me from Robert."

"Did you believe him?" Hope asked with increased curiosity.

"I wanted to believe him. I believe that your soul goes to either heaven or hell. I want to believe that he's in heaven. So yeah, if Robert has a message for me, I guess I want to hear it. Wouldn't you?"

Hope thought about it for a long moment. "I'm not sure about that . . . but I can see where you're coming from."

"Well, the producer puts me on hold, and a minute later I'm talking to the host of the show—Greg somebody or other. He say's the message was three words: 'Develop the property.' Then he invites me to come on the show and hear more details."

Hope looked at Theresa and waited for her to continue. She remained silent.

"Well, are you?" Hope prompted.

Theresa shook her head and looked Hope in the eye. "You want to know what kept me from doing it?"

Hope shook her head. "What?"

"Thinking about those reporters who were camped outside my gate. If they were waiting for me then, I can just imagine how they'd swarm around me if I went on a TV show during which you get messages from the dead," Theresa shrilled. She waved her hands back and forth for emphasis. "No way. I'm not doing it."

Hope adjusted her posture. "So what are you going to do? What's your plan?"

"Oh, that. I almost forgot. I came up here to ride the next morning and realized that, of the 60 stalls we have, only about 20 are being used. That leaves about 40 open. So I've decided to start boarding people's horses, and in a couple weeks we're opening a riding academy. Do you think Jennifer would like riding lessons?"

Hope grinned. "I think she'd love it. Doesn't she have to own a horse?"

Theresa shook her head. "Not a problem. She'll need a little personal gear, but we've got plenty of good riding horses. Gentle ones. Come over here."

Theresa pointed to the other side of the driveway and helped Hope down from where she was perched. She pointed off into the distance toward a field standing tall with corn almost ready to harvest. "We've got about 30 acres over there that we lease out to Danny Milburn, our neighbor who runs the farm across the street. I'm thinking about taking a corner of that field over toward Burgreen Road over there"—she pointed into the distance—"and turning it into a maize maze next year."

"A what?" Hope puzzled.

"A maize maze. You know, a cornfield that's planted so there's a maze in it and people pay for the fun of getting lost in it."

"Sounds like fun. I know Jennifer would love that. We all would, now that I think about it," Hope answered.

Theresa smiled. "That's the idea. Family fun. I've already talked to Danny about it. He said he can program the maze pattern on his computer and feed it into the GPS unit on his tractor that runs the planter, so there won't be any seeds where the paths will be. He and I will split the admission price, so we'll both make money off it."

"Sounds like a deal. But that won't be any income until next year," Hope countered.

"Hey, I'll get by until then. I just won't travel as much or buy a new designer wardrobe in the spring, that sort of thing. I'm thinking about some other things, including one you've got to promise not to tell anybody, OK?"

Hope nodded. "Promise."

Theresa pointed off into the northwest distance. "I'm thinking of taking the 20 or so acres over on that corner of the place and selling it for residential development. I'm also thinking about leasing out the airstrip. I mean, the Lord knows I don't need it."

"You don't like to fly?" Hope wondered.

"Oh, Robert was the only one who ever flew out of here. There's a wooded area between the house and the airstrip, and there's an old farm road from the other side that we can improve so it'll still be private here."

The pair took in the sights and sounds around them for an extended time.

"Sounds like a plan," Hope broke the silence.

A question weighed on Hope's mind, but she was unsure whether she should ask it, or when. After another minute or two filled with the sounds of nature, she decided to take a chance. "How are things working out with what's her name? Cassarelli, was it?"

Theresa looked as though she'd just been seized by a stomach cramp and took a deep breath before answering. "Believe it or not, things are working out."

"Really?" Hope wondered, amazed.

Theresa nodded and looked her in the eye. "It's really been my kids and the company board of directors that have handled things. You know, RMI Industries is a publicly traded company, but the majority of the owners are family members, so we've taken some actions to keep her from ever getting a seat on the board or making much from the stock."

"But she's the largest single stockholder," Hope countered. "I mean,

20 percent of the company is a lot of shares. Doesn't that automatically give her a seat on the board?"

Theresa smiled and shook her head. "Well, yes and no. We fixed that."

The puzzlement on Hope's faced spoke louder than words.

"Look. Miss Cassarelli"—she spat out the name as though she was clearing a sour taste from her mouth—"may be the largest shareholder, but she doesn't run the company. The board of directors runs the company, and at the shareholders' meeting . . . Oh!" Theresa grinned widely as she relished a thought. "I couldn't believe what they did to her! It was poetic justice!"

"What did they do?" Hope asked eagerly.

"Well, for starters, they voted to issue a new category of stock—common stock—that does not get paid any kind of dividend or have a vote to elect board members. Then they voted to convert all her shares to this new kind of stock. They wanted to do more to dilute her shares, but the lawyers got into the act and told them they couldn't do it. Anyway, it means she still has a pretty valuable chunk of stock—but the only way she can make any money off it is to sell it."

"Any idea how much it's worth?" Hope asked.

"Well, taking my husband to bed has made her a millionaire. Oh, she's worth somewhere around $16 million, give or take a mil or two. But that's only a paper fortune, because she can't sell it for at least one year." Theresa walked into the stable and began going down a row of stalls. She stopped in front of one and fingered the bridle hanging on a peg outside the door.

"How much would she have gotten if they hadn't converted her shares and taken away the dividend?" Hope wanted to know.

"Oh, she would've earned an annual dividend of something above $200,000—all of it for seducing my husband," Theresa spat out the words.

"You're still pretty angry, aren't you?" Hope observed.

Theresa whirled to face her with fire in her eyes. "I trusted Robert. I trusted him completely. But for five years he went to Cincinnati at least twice a month and was there for two or three days at a time. I trusted that he was there on genuine business. I had no clue that he was having an affair with that . . . *tramp!* If you'd been deceived and the way you found out about it was by reading it in a supermarket tabloid, how do you think you'd feel? Happy?" She was roaring.

Hope just stared at her friend. "I'm sorry."

Theresa led them back into the sunlight. "I appreciate you listening to me when I need to rant and rave." She stopped out in the pasture and watched as a foal nuzzled up to its mother and began nursing. "You remember that day you called me and told me to stay home? That day the reporters were camped outside my gate?"

Hope nodded.

"I'll always be grateful for you calling me when you did, because I was drunk and getting ready to go out there and give the world a piece of my mind. Miranda, one of my household staff, was telling me the same thing, but I wasn't listening to her. You . . . you kept me from doing something really, really stupid. Something that would've just made my pain a whole lot worse."

Hope struggled for words. "I had no idea."

"There was no way you could have known. But you reached out to me when I was hurting and when I needed it, and you kept me from doing something really stupid, and I appreciate that. I really do."

Theresa turned toward the Suburban. "You feel like getting wet?"

"I've got a brand-new swimsuit waiting for me, so why not?" Hope grinned.

Theresa started the engine and shifted into reverse. "I know I keep discussing this, but do you think Robert's in heaven or hell?"

"Well, from what I've been studying in my Bible lately, I don't think he's in either place."

Theresa hit the brake, shifted into drive, and twirled the steering wheel. "Explain."

"Do you read your Bible?"

"Some," Theresa answered.

"Do you remember when Jesus first came out of the tomb? When Mary found Him and grabbed Him? Do you remember what Jesus said?" Hope questioned.

"No."

"He told her to let go of Him because He hadn't yet gone to His Father. Now, if Jesus had just been in the grave and He hadn't gone to see His Father, where was He?"

"I don't know. In the grave?"

"That's the only answer I can find that makes sense. He wasn't in heaven, and He wasn't in hell," Hope said. "So the grave has to be where we are until Jesus calls us out at the resurrection."

"But what about heaven and hell? I've always believed a person went to heaven or hell when they died. Or their soul went there. And you hear these hellfire preachers talking about how the wicked are burning in hell right now. What about that?"

197

"Mind if I get back to you on that one? I've not studied up on it," Hope deferred.

"Shall we meet for lunch one day this week?" Theresa offered. "The country club again?"

"Sounds like a plan to me."

For a long moment neither spoke.

"If you could see Robert again, I mean, if you really could, what do you think you would do? How do you think you would feel toward him?" Hope asked cautiously.

Theresa thought for only a second. "First . . . I'd give him a great big hug and a kiss and tell him how much I've been missing him. Second . . . I'd strangle him. I'd literally put my hand on his neck and try to strangle him for what he did to me. And if that didn't work, I'd ask Father O'Malley to say a special Mass to make sure he went straight to hell—or at least suffered in purgatory for a very long time after I'm in heaven."

CHAPTER TWENTY-THREE

How many memories Hope had of things that had happened in these hallways! All she had to do was close her eyes, and she was a 13-year-old smelling the fresh paint on the way to her Sunday school class in the church's brand-new wing. Only now she was escorting her daughter along these same halls.

A couple doing the same thing greeted her. "Is Mark with you? I need to talk to him," the husband inquired.

An odd pain, a loneliness, tugged at Hope's heart as she shook her head. "He decided to stay home this morning." To the others it was an excuse. To her it was a recognition of what he didn't put into words: "I don't *need or want* to go to church *anymore.*"

She held the pain in her heart while delivering Jennifer to her class and reversing course as far as the stairway to the second floor and her class. She arrived as the teacher was reviewing everyone's progress on their plan to read through the Bible in one year.

Hope confessed that she'd fallen far enough behind that she was just now reading through Revelation, the book she should have finished nine months before. "At this rate I'll catch up to you about a year from December," she wisecracked.

"Or you'll have a big head start on us come January," the teacher responded.

The day's lesson was about God's power and how it was demonstrated in the creation of the world. Though her mind was miles away, Hope opened her Bible to the first chapter of Genesis and followed along halfheartedly. *"In the beginning God created the heavens and the earth. Now the earth was formless and empty,"* she read.

Her eyes scanned through the first chapter and into the second. Verse 7 seemed to jump out at her: *"The Lord God formed the man from the dust of the ground and breathed into his nostrils the breath of life, and the man became a living being."*

How does that read in the King James? She searched the empty seats beside her on the back row. Two chairs down she found a hardbound King James Bible, reached for it, and thumbed to the verse. *"And man became a living soul."*

She read the verse again and again. It was as if God had a message for her here, only she wasn't seeing it. *Just read it and let the verse say what it has to say.* Then it became obvious: it was like a mathematical equation. *One plus one equals two. A plus B equals C.* God formed man from the dust. That was the A. He breathed into man the breath of life. That was the B. Then man *became* a soul. That was C. Take away either A or B, and C no longer existed.

God did not give Adam a soul. Adam became a soul. To have a soul, you must have both a body and breath. Take away the breath, and you no longer have a living being, so the soul ceases to exist, she realized. *So there's no way the soul can be eternal.*

Whoa! Hope stared at the page for a moment and pondered her latest discovery.

"Uh, Mrs. Lancaster. Would you like to share with us what's on your mind?" the teacher cut through her isolation.

"Oh, I was just thinking about something I read," Hope tried to pass off the inquiry. *I hope she goes on with whatever it was she was doing.*

The teacher leaned forward and rested her arms on the lectern in front of her. As she did, her long hair flowed forward over her shoulders and onto the top of the lectern. "Well, you know, in Bible times in the synagogues it was common to ask if anyone had any news or thoughts they wanted to share. That was how the apostle Paul was able to stand up and share about Jesus. So how about sharing what's on your mind? Maybe you've found something that will be meaningful to the rest of us."

Hope hesitated. "Well, I was just reading here in the second chapter of Genesis, uh, verse 7."

The sound of turning pages filled the room as the dozen other class members all found the text.

Hope read it aloud from the New International Version. Two others read aloud from other translations.

200

"What about this verse caught your attention?" the teacher prompted.

"Well, I guess it's more of a question than anything," Hope struggled for a proper answer. "I guess it goes to the heart of a question I've been dealing with since my father died. You know what we believe happens when a person dies, right?"

Heads around the room nodded.

"Your father was a godly man, so his soul's in heaven with Jesus," one class member offered.

"Well, I'm not sure the Bible supports that. I mean, look again at that verse we just read. It doesn't say God gave Adam a soul. It says God formed the man, breathed the breath of life into him, and he *became* a soul. Adam was a soul. He wasn't *given* a soul that continued to exist after he died. There's a big difference," Hope countered.

Questioning faces looked at her. "I don't follow. What do you mean?" one inquired.

"This verse gives us a formula: A plus B equals C. God forms Adam's body from the dust of the ground. That's A. Then God breathes into him the breath of life. That's B. The result is that Adam begins to live. That's C. The King James Version says that Adam 'became a living soul.'"

Heads around the room nodded. "So what's the question?" some-one asked.

"The question is If you take away A or B, what do you have? Do you still have C? Do you still have a soul?" Hope asked.

"Well, we believe that when we die, our soul goes to God," the teacher answered. "So I guess that if you take away A or B, then you have a soul going to be with God."

"That's what I've always believed too," Hope replied. "But according to this verse, in order for you to have a soul you've got to have a body with breath in it. Take away the breath, and the soul no longer exists. Like that mathematical equation—if you take away A or B, then you can't have C."

Murmurs of disagreement spread through the room.

"Hold on," the teacher countered. "Mrs. Lancaster's raising a valid issue. I know what we believe. Now, let's prove it *from the Bible*. It's one thing to know what you believe. It's another thing to be able to prove it from Scripture." She nodded at Hope for her to continue.

Hope thought for a moment. "You know, we've all been taught to believe that God gave us a soul. But that's not what this is saying. The verse says that God formed Adam and gave him breath and he *became* a soul. Judging by this, the soul isn't something God *puts in us* when we're born or conceived; it's something *that we are* and something that *ceases to exist* when we die. It isn't something that can go to heaven when we die."

"Whoa! What are you telling us?" a young woman on the front row turned around and asked. "Are you saying our soul doesn't go to heaven when we die? 'Cause if that's what you're saying, that's heresy!"

Hope started to answer but was interrupted by the teacher. "Hold on!" she commanded. "We're getting a bit oppositional here. We've had a serious question raised from the Bible, so I think we should be fair and answer it *from the Bible*. Hope, the question is back to you. How do you answer it?"

"It's not what I'm saying. It's what I'm trying to figure out because I've been confronted with this puzzle. OK?"

The others generally agreed.

"Let's expand the puzzle," Hope continued. She detailed the scene outside Jesus' tomb where He told Mary that He had not been to see His Father. Then there was the passage in Ecclesiastes 9, verses 5 and 6, saying that the dead know nothing and no longer have a part in anything that happens among the living. She added the warning in Psalm 146, verses 3 and 4, about the thoughts of those who die ceasing.

There was silence in the room for a long moment.

"Well, I know what I believe, and I ain't changin'!" someone declared.

The teacher held up her hand to restore quiet. "Let me ask you a question. Is the Bible the supreme authority for what you believe?"

Murmurs of "the Bible" came from most mouths.

"OK," the teacher continued. "If the Bible is our authority, shouldn't we be willing to accept what the Bible teaches as fact"—heads around the room began nodding—"even if it means we have to change our beliefs?" Several nodding heads stopped in midswing.

"But I know that what I believe is right, so why are you asking the question?" someone accused. Several heads nodded in agreement.

"How do we know that we're right unless we read what the Bible says on the topic?" the teacher defended. "Hope, you look as though you have something to say."

"Uh, yes. Another aspect of the puzzle. If we go to heaven when we die, why does Jesus promise to come back and take us there? You read what the apostle Paul says in 1 Corinthians 15 about the resurrection and all of us being changed and putting on immortality. So why do we need to wait and put on immortality after the resurrection if we already have it? It just doesn't make sense."

"What is there *not* to make sense?" someone retorted from across the room.

The teacher opened her mouth to speak, but Hope interrupted. "Everything we believe about going to heaven when we die, that's what!" She was surprised at the force of her response and paused for a moment. "Everything," she continued more softly. "The Bible says Adam became a soul, so when he died his soul ceased to exist. Jesus said He hadn't gone to heaven—and if He hadn't gone there after He died, how can we go there after we die? And if we don't get our new bodies and immortality until after the resurrection, how can we be anywhere but unconscious and in the grave until Jesus comes?"

Murmurs of disagreement ran through the room.

∽

Monday started out with its typical pattern. Hope got Jennifer out the door to school and Mark out to work. Then she had two hours to herself for such things as reading, doing housework, getting dressed, and doing her makeup so she would look her best on camera later in the day. A whole lot of thinking and praying got combined with those activities.

Hope sat in front of her makeup mirror and reached to pick up a brush. She looked down at her expanding belly. *I've got to go to New York in two weeks for the Murrow Awards banquet, and I don't have a thing to wear!*

Halfway through applying her eyeliner, she wondered if Theresa knew anyone who could help. She went to the phone and called.

"There's a dressmaker that I've used for years, but I'm buying everything off the rack this year. The budget, you know." Theresa gave her the number. "But I've got to warn you that she's expensive, and she's usually got a backlog. I mean, a month, maybe six weeks."

"Doesn't sound as though she'll be much help," Hope said disappointedly. "Thanks anyway." What was she to do? She returned to her makeup.

A quiet movement of air in the room brushed her arms and made the hair on the back of her neck stand up. It was as if someone had just walked behind her. She could sense it. Yet there was no sound. She whirled around in surprise, yet saw nothing. Cautiously she returned to the mirror and began unscrewing the mascara brush from the tube.

What should I do? Scour the better department stores at the mall? Start calling bridal and formal-wear shops? she wondered.

"Look in your closet," a voice commanded from behind her.

Hope whirled around. No one was visible. And that voice? It sounded so familiar. It was her father's voice!

"Daddy? Are you here, Daddy?" Hope pleaded.

"Look in your closet." The voice was as clear as if he had been standing close to her, yet no one was visible.

Maybe he is standing here, only I can't see him.

For several moments she surveyed the room. "Daddy?" she spoke quietly, then returned slowly to her chair. *Look in my closet?*

She hesitated. *Wait! Daddy's dead. He's not in heaven. He's in the grave awaiting the resurrection when Jesus comes. So* who *was that?* Her eyes swept the room again, and every nerve ending was on full alert as she waited for a motion, a breeze, anything that might be a clue about what was happening. There was nothing.

Whoever that was told me to look in my closet. She turned, opened the door, and flipped on the light. Mark's clothes hung to the right. Her clothes were to the left and on the back wall. Being the newest and most often worn, her maternity clothes were first. Next came her summer clothes and then her winter things. In the far corner were the items worn rarely or kept for sentimental reasons, such as her wedding dress and the pageant gown worn the night she had met Mark and again on their anniversary.

Among them was something she did not remember seeing before. It fairly danced before her eyes with electric shades of orange, red, yellow, green, and white. As she touched the hanger, it felt as if an electric shock ran through her. Was it excitement? Was it fear? She wasn't sure. She pulled her hand back. *What's going on here? What is this, and how did it get here?*

What she pulled from the rack was absolutely the most beautiful ball gown she had ever seen. It was a strapless satin dress with a gathered skirt that had extra gathering in front to accommodate her expanding belly. With it were a matching chiffon wrap and a bouffant half-slip to spread the skirt wide. The streaks of bold colors looked like hand-applied brushstrokes.

An involuntary *"Wow!"* escaped her lips, and in seconds she was back in the bedroom trying it on. She laid the garments on the bed and let her bathrobe fall to the floor. She stepped into the slip and fastened it around her waist. It fit perfectly. She slid the dress over her head, found the zipper on the side, and pulled it up under her right arm. Last, she checked the skirt to make sure it was down all around and stepped in front of the full-length dressing mirror.

This is the most beautiful dress I've ever worn! For a long moment she just stared at herself. *This is unbelievable. I know it wasn't there earlier—and now I'm wearing it!*

Hope's eyes stayed on her image in the mirror through the second ring of the phone. Only then was she able to tear herself away and answer the ringing phone.

"Have you found it yet?" were her mother's first words.

"Found what?"

"The dress in your closet. The one your daddy wanted you to wear to the Murrow Awards," Susan Morris declared excitedly.

"But how . . ."

"He told me last night that he was going to do it. How does it fit? What does it look like?" Susan sounded as excited as a teenager asking her best friend about her prom dress.

"It's the most beautiful thing I've ever worn. It fits perfectly, and it looks like it was hand-painted. It's got this swirl pattern of just about every color you can imagine all over. I can hardly believe it," Hope gushed.

"Daddy really wanted you to have it," Mom said.

But what if somebody asks me where I got it? Nobody's going to believe me if I tell them what really happened.

Their conversation was short. Hope used the excuse of having to finish getting ready for work to cut off chitchat. Almost reluctantly she took off the dress and slip and hung them together back in the closet.

But Daddy's not in heaven. He's in the grave waiting for the resurrection. So whose voice did I hear, and who put this dress in my closet?

Hope stood looking at the side of the dress between the other hanging things as the realization struck her: *It wasn't Daddy and it wasn't God, so it could only be from the devil!* In a flash she ripped the dress and slip off the hanger and ran downstairs and out the back door to the garbage can, where she stuffed them inside as quickly as she could and slammed the lid down. Back in the house she paused long enough to wash her hands at the kitchen sink and realize that she was trembling from head to toe. Her knees sagged as she walked up the stairs and sat down to finish her makeup. Fortunately, she was almost finished getting ready.

Did I just run out there in my underwear? I hope none of the neighbors were watching! A glance at the clock told her she'd better hurry or she'd be late to work. *What am I going to wear today?* Back in the closet she made a bee-line for the maternity things. Instead of her usual deliberate pace making such a decision, she more or less grabbed whatever her hand landed on and yanked it off the hanger.

As she turned, her eyes caught a splash of color in the far corner. Electric shades of red, orange, yellow, green, and white flashed out at her. She dropped what she was holding and stepped to look closer. It was the dress!

"How can this be?" Hope asked the room. "I just threw it away. How did it get back here?" For a second she just looked at it. *It wasn't here before and it's back, so it can only be from one source. And if it's from Satan, then I don't want it in my house!* For a moment she debated what to do. Obviously, whatever power had put it there was determined that she should have it. If she left it, did that mean her home was possessed? But she'd already thrown it into the trash once. What would happen if she did it again?

Hope debated the matter as she got dressed. Taking the dress from the hanger, she held it as if it were contaminated by some repulsive thing as she made her way to the garbage can. This time she lifted out two bags from previous days and placed them on top of the dress, even going so far as to rip one open and let foul-smelling juices saturate the fabric. She pressed the lid down to make sure the can was closed. *That should do it,* she thought.

For a moment she was tempted to lift the lid and double-check, but time was getting short. She walked back into the house to finish preparing for work while feeling terribly unsure about whether she would see the dress again.

Replacing the slippers on her feet with regular shoes required another trip to the closet. Hope opened the closet door, turned on the light, and began surveying the shoe rack below her hanging things. *Definitely something low and comfortable in case my feet start swelling. Aha! Flats!*

The shoes were in her hands, and she was standing up when a wave of fear came over her; her eyes moved slowly to her right until they encountered a blaze of colors. There was no scent of what she had drained onto the dress just minutes before.

Hope sprang from the room, propelled by alarm, her breathing fast and her hands trembling. How would she ever get that dress out of her closet? For several moments she leaned against the hallway wall and shook. *I'll get rid of it if I have to cut it into a thousand pieces!*

That was it! Cut it up! She ran downstairs and retrieved a pair of scissors from the junk drawer in the kitchen. She grabbed the hem of the skirt and cut upward to the waist, then repeated the action several times in different places. Pulling it from the hanger, she began cutting random angles from the top down. After several minutes she was again en route to the garbage can, where she didn't care how the contents were arranged so long as the dress was out of sight and the lid securely closed.

She would have checked the closet again, except that she was now late for work.

"Something wrong? You look as if you've seen a ghost," a coworker observed as Hope tried to make it to her desk without being seen by the news director.

She tried to shrug off the question and begin focusing on her work as she surveyed the story assignment sheet in her in basket. Doing either was next to impossible.

～

Hope phoned Mark before he left work to advise him and Jennifer that she would be late getting home from work. As quickly as she could get away after the 6:00 p.m. news, she was heading for the mall, where she made the rounds of the formal-wear sections in the larger department stores. She found a lot of beautiful dresses that would fit if she were not pregnant.

She prayed as she watched the hands of the clock swing toward 9:00 and closing. There was one more department store to go to, and she made a beeline for the finer dresses. Again, nothing looked as though it would fit.

What was it Mom taught me? If no solution is obvious, improvise! One alternative was to match separate pieces. One rack held a variety of beaded tops that could be matched with an array of pants and long skirts on the next rack. In moments she had found a combination of a glittery, short-sleeve top and a loose-fitting iridescent black skirt that reached the floor. So what if her belly pushed the skirt outward? She was pregnant, after all. And it was the kind of outfit she could probably use again in the future when she wasn't pregnant, such as for one of those 24-hour fund-raising telethons that came around every year.

Hope's energy sagged as she drove homeward. However, she felt good about finding her own solution to the challenge and demonstrating rejection of what had been given her that morning. Mark greeted her at the door. His warm affections comforted her and helped her feel as though everything would be OK, even though it was with rising apprehension that she ascended the stairs.

He had even done a load of laundry that now was folded and sorted across their bed. Should she put the hanging things in the closet? No! She did not even want to open the door for fear of what she might find.

As was his habit, Mark entered the closet to select what he would wear to work the next day. Why did it seem he was taking forever in there? Hope held her breath for fear that he might make a certain observation and comment about it. Finally he came out and hung his selections on the hook on the outside of the closet door. If he had seen something unusual, he gave no indication.

Together they put the sorted laundry into various drawers and a pile on the foot of Jennifer's bed for her to put away when she awoke.

Retiring to bed, Mark curled up with a magazine that soon was slipping from his fingers onto his chest. Hope took the magazine and nudged him enough to turn out his bedside lamp.

Then she turned out her lamp and tried to go to sleep. She kept trying to shove the dress episode to the back of her mind. But was it gone? The only way to know was to look.

Quietly, fearfully, Hope arose from the bed and tiptoed through the thick carpeting to the closet door. She moved inside and closed the door before turning on the light so she would not disturb Mark's slumber. Her eyes adjusted to the brightness and went straight to the spot where the dress had hung before.

It was back!

Hope's heart rocketed into her throat, and she stifled a scream. Her hand swept downward across the light switch, and she bolted from the closet. She flew out of the bedroom and took the stairs two at a time before finally halting in the den. For a time she leaned on the end of the couch as she hyperventilated and felt her racing heart pounding in her ears.

Calm down. It's only a dress. It's not like it's the devil himself in there, she tried comforting herself. *But it's from the devil!* She began praying urgently for God to overrule Satan.

The clock showed that it was a few minutes after 1:00 a.m. *I've got to get some sleep.* It seemed as if an eternity passed before her breathing and heart rate slowed to normal and tiredness overtook her body. She prayed silently as she crept back up the stairs and slid back into bed. She kept praying as her wide-open eyes studied the soft patterns of shadow and light playing across the ceiling. Sleep still evaded her as she listened to Mark's steady breathing.

CHAPTER TWENTY-FOUR

The morning's alarm reached through Hope's slumber, and she struggled to move her weary bones. When had she finally fallen asleep? Sometime well after 2:00 a.m.? It took all her energy to sit up and put her feet on the floor.

"Good morning, hon!" Mark greeted her cheerfully from the bathroom door. Then he looked closer. "Rough night?"

She grunted something unintelligible.

"Something make it hard to sleep?" he asked as he headed for the door.

She mumbled something else he couldn't understand.

All too quickly Mark and Jennifer were out the door and the house was quiet. The one thing Hope wanted most was to crawl back into bed. A glance in the mirror told her there was no way makeup could overcome how she looked and make her presentable enough to go on camera later in the day. So she called in to work claiming she was sick. *How do I tell them it's a spiritual battle, not a physical illness, that I'm fighting?*

Ah! The covers felt so good as she slid back into bed. Hope had just fallen back asleep when the phone rang. She wished it would quit, but the phone was on her side of the bed, and each ring reached deeper into her sleep. *Why did we set the answering machine to pick up on the fourth ring?* Then she heard the machine pick up and begin playing her recorded answer. Then her mother started talking. The machine was downstairs in the living room. That was far enough away that she couldn't understand what her mother was saying, but close enough to know the voice.

Hope reached for the receiver, pulled it to her ear, and croaked a sleepy "Hello."

"I can't believe you would try to get rid of such a beautiful gift from your father!" Susan sounded somewhere between angry and hurt.

Hope tried to recover some clarity of thought from the depths of her sleepiness. "Uh, what are you talking about, Mom?"

"You know what I'm talking about! Your father told me you put the dress in the trash. Why would you do such a thing?"

"But Mom . . ."

"Don't you go giving me that 'but Mom' line. You know better than that!" Susan snapped. "You haven't talked to me that way since you were a teenager!"

What could she do but pause for a moment and consider her words? Yes, she was this woman's daughter. She would always be her mother's daughter. But she was a grown woman with a family of her own.

"Mom, I'm sorry if I've hurt you. But there's something you've got to understand," Hope said as kindly as possible.

"I'm listening."

Susan's tone of voice reminded Hope of times as a child when she got in trouble and her mother would stand in front of her with her arms crossed and an angry look on her face that would not change no matter what she said. Still, she would let Hope say her piece before inflicting punishment appropriate to the offense.

"Mom, I've been studying my Bible a lot lately, and from what I've been reading, I don't believe that dress was from Daddy."

The way Susan inhaled told Hope that she'd struck a nerve and that her mother didn't know quite how to react.

"If it wasn't, then why has your *father* been visiting me?" Susan's tone was that of a mother telling her child that she'd better believe what she was being told because it came from her mother and her mother didn't lie.

"That isn't Daddy. It's a demon that just looks and sounds like him."

"A demon? How dare you—"

"Stop! Mom! Listen to me!" Hope cut her off. "I'm telling you! It's not Daddy! Daddy is dead. He's in the grave awaiting the resurrection that'll happen when Jesus comes."

"How could that be?" Susan accused. "He's been visiting me! He's told me things that only someone who is in heaven with God could know!"

Hope offered a silent prayer for wisdom, then began reminding her of what Jesus had said in His encounter with Mary outside the tomb and of verses she had learned saying that the dead are unconscious. "Mom, Satan is lying to you. He's the father of lies, and he's deceiving you. That isn't Daddy who's been visiting you. It's a demon sent to deceive you so you'll lose your salvation."

"I don't believe you."

"It's what the Bible says. You believe the Bible, don't you?" Hope pleaded.

"Of course. But I also believe what I see, and your father is standing here right now, right in front of me," Susan argued.

"Then we've got to pray and ask God to make the demon go away!" Hope was getting desperate. "Heavenly Father! I call on You in the name of Jesus. Please protect my family—Mark, Jennifer, Mom, and me—from Satan's attack. I ask you in the name of Jesus: make this demon go away and leave us alone! Drive him out of my house, Lord. Drive him out of my mother's house! Please, God. Drive the evil one away!"

Silence filled the connection for a long moment.

"Mom? Are you there?"

"I'm here." Susan's voice was barely audible.

"Is something wrong?" Hope inquired.

Another long moment of silence. "He's gone. He opened his mouth to say something . . . and then he . . . he just . . . disappeared." Susan began to cry.

"Praise the Lord! Thank You, Jesus!" Hope exclaimed.

"I don't see how you can be so happy. You just made my husband go away!" Susan wailed.

"That wasn't Daddy. That was a demon," Hope said softly. "Daddy's dead. You've got to accept it, Mom. He's dead, and he's not in heaven."

"I've got to go. I'll talk to you later," Susan said quietly before hanging up.

Hope slid her feet over the side of the bed and guided her toes into a pair of fluffy slippers. She rose and walked to the bathroom, where she slid her arms into a satin robe and tied it around her waist. The front showed just a peek of her nightgown over her expanding belly.

Curiosity began drawing Hope toward the closet. Strangely, she felt no fear as she had the night before. Her heart actually felt light as she opened the door, turned on the light, and began scanning down the row of her hanging things.

The colorful dress was gone.

～

Being project leader did have its perks. While the rest of the team's cubicles were clustered around a central conference room, Mark had a corner office, one with real walls, a door, and windows along one side where he could see out into the mostly empty parking lot. On the opposite wall he had an eight-foot whiteboard that was filled with scribbles. He preferred outlining the team's efforts on the large board instead of keeping track of details on sheets of paper that got shuffled, misplaced, or even lost.

Mark and his coworker Shane Roth were outlining something on the whiteboard. "So how's it going this week, Mr. Mom?" Terri Pelosi queried with a smile as she joined them.

"Oh, pretty well. I can nuke a frozen dinner with the best of 'em," Mark answered with a smile. "And my daughter knows how to separate the whites from the darks when she does the laundry."

"*She* does the laundry?" Terri's eyebrows went up.

"How else do you think I manage to keep the clothes looking so good?" Mark shot back.

"That, or your wife's left you a lot of clean clothes to wear. I mean, after all, it's only Tuesday."

"So where's Hope off to now?" Shane wondered.

"New York. She's cohosting the *Sunrise Show* on MBS this week. Jennifer and I are flying up Friday afternoon," Mark answered. "I guess I should be thankful it's a studio assignment in New York and she's not trekking off to who-knows-where at all hours."

The ringing of Mark's desk phone interrupted further banter. Shane and Terri tried politely not to listen at a distance, yet they understood clearly what news had been delivered.

"Sorry. I've gotta go pick up Jennifer. She's got a fever, so she can't stay at school and she can't go to the day-care center after school—and I don't know if I can get her in to see the doctor today or not."

"Not a problem. I sure hope it's just a minor bug," Shane sympathized.

Mark halted for a second as he remembered how sick Jennifer had been a year before with leukemia. "Yeah, I hope that's all it is. Something minor," he answered distractedly as he double-checked to see if he'd picked up everything he needed to take home. He started for the door, then thought about taking his notebook computer. He unplugged it from the network and the wall and dropped it into his carrying bag. At least he could do a little work at home tonight. Well, maybe he could.

"Hey, uh, ya'll keep working on this challenge. I'll check in with you later and let you know how things are going on my end. Terri, you take the lead while I'm out, OK?"

Terri nodded her assent. "I hope she gets to feeling better soon," she said to Mark's back as he disappeared out the door.

Mark looked at his watch. Eleven-thirty. That'd be 12:30 in New York, where Hope was this week. Would she be where he could call her? Yes, she was anchoring the morning show. That meant she had to get up at the terrible hour of 3:00 a.m. Eastern time or 2:00 a.m. Central time to go on the air at 6:00 a.m. But starting that early meant she got off early. It also meant he couldn't call her after 6:00 p.m. because she had to be in bed early.

Mark punched the speed dial on his cell phone after pulling out into traffic.

Hope answered on the second ring. No, she couldn't talk long. She was in a very important meeting. Dr. Peter Chapman was Jennifer's regular pediatrician at the clinic, but he might have to take whatever doctor was available, she instructed. Oh, and if he really, really had to go back to work, Emily Lombardi, two doors down the street, would be willing to take care of Jennifer until he got off work. "But call and double-check with her first," Hope instructed.

I wonder what she's in the middle of that she can't talk, Mark wondered.

Almost two hours later Mark looked at his watch and wondered when the doctor would arrive. The clinic had said to bring Jennifer on in, that they would work her into the schedule. After arriving, they had waited a half hour before being escorted to an exam room. Then another hour had passed, and there still was no sign of a doctor.

They must be operating on medical time instead of real time, Mark thought.

Dr. Chapman arrived and apologized for making them wait so long. After a quick exam he announced that Jennifer had what looked like a mild viral respiratory infection. "Just give her an over-the-counter painkiller to bring down her fever, make sure she drinks plenty of fluids, push the vitamin C, and wait it out," the physician advised.

"Will she be well enough to fly to New York on Friday afternoon?" Mark asked.

"Hopefully," the doctor replied with a smile. "What's taking you to New York?"

"To be with Mommy," Jennifer replied weakly. "I miss her when she goes away."

"Well, I sure hope you're feeling well enough to go." Dr. Chapman patted Jennifer on the head and shook Mark's hand before leaving.

Mark glanced at his watch. It was late enough that it wasn't worth going back to the office. He'd just take Jennifer home and hope Emily Lombardi would be willing to care for her the next day.

~

Jennifer answered the phone.

"How's my baby doing?" Hope inquired immediately.

"I'm doing better. Mrs. Lombardi says she thinks I'll be back to school tomorrow."

"Oh! I'm so happy to hear that. I'm sorry I can't be there to take care of you." Hope almost cried at the thought of being separated from her daughter while she was sick. "You're going to be well enough to fly on Friday, won't you?"

"Hey, Mom!"

"What is it, honey?"

"You know the Lombardis' dog, Raffles?"

Hope had to think for a moment before remembering the dog, a spaniel something-or-other breed that always seemed overly pampered. "Yes."

"She's going to have puppies, and she might have them tonight! That's what Mrs. Lombardi says. She could have them any day. I asked her if I could have one, and she said to ask you 'cause they're worth a whole lot of money."

"Well, Jennifer . . ."

"Can I have one? Please! Please!" Jennifer pleaded.

"Jennifer! Hold on! As I recall, Raffles is a purebred show dog. That's why the puppies are going to be so expensive. I think your father and I need to talk about this first."

A disappointed Jennifer handed the phone over to Mark.

"So how's it going?" he wanted to know.

"Easier than for you, I'll guarantee it. You know, it's only two days until you'll be here, but I can't wait to see the two of you!" Hope gushed.

"Well, we're excited about seeing you, too," Mark cooed.

"Are the two of you ready for Friday night?"

"Sure are. I pick up my tuxedo at the cleaners tomorrow afternoon. Jennifer's decided to wear that same blue dress she wore when we were there the end of May," Mark replied.

"Better have her try it on. You know, make sure it still fits," Hope counseled.

"Yeah, she is on a growing streak."

"On a more serious note . . ."

Mark felt his guard going up. What news did she have?

"We've got a big decision to make. How would you like to move here? To New York?" Hope asked.

"Uh, I don't know. What's happening? I mean, is somebody making you an offer?"

"Oh, yeah!" Hope said with some excitement. "For the first time in my life I've had to hire an agent to handle negotiations. You're not going to believe this, but every day since I got here—Monday, Tuesday, and Wednesday—I've had lunch or dinner with executives from a different network. Each one of them has made me an offer for either an anchoring or hosting position here in New York. I mean, I've got so many offers on the table; that's why I hired the agent. And I've got another dinner appointment tomorrow night."

"Tell me about them," Mark answered guardedly.

"Well, the first offer was from MBS. They want me to come aboard as regular cohost of the morning show I'm doing this week. NBC wants me to do the same for the *Today Show*. Fox wants me as a regular evening news anchor. Tomorrow night's meeting is with CBS, and ABC wants to talk with me on Saturday about hosting a news magazine show, but I told them I was going to be busy," Hope detailed.

"What sort of numbers are they putting on the table? I mean, what sort of salary and perks are they offering?" Ever the analyst, Mark was already hoping the salary offers and other factors would make it worth staying where they were.

"Are you sitting down?"

"No. Should I be?" Mark's suspicions were rising.

"You better be sitting down. I mean, when I heard these numbers, I was glad I was sitting down. The first one made me choke on my juice."

Mark found the couch and sat down. "I'm ready."

"OK. MBS is offering me $450,000 a year to start on a three-year contract with at least 20 percent more each year and perks like having a limo pick me up and return me home so I won't have to drive myself in city traffic."

"What? Did I just hear you say $450,000?" Mark fairly spat out the words. "That's . . . that's 12 times what you're making now."

"Isn't that exciting? I never dreamed I could make that much money! Oh, honey! Wait till you hear the rest!" Hope could barely contain her excitement.

"NBC is offering an even half million a year for four years with annual renegotiation. FOX is making the same basic offer. CBS hasn't made an offer yet, but I guess I'll find out when I meet with them tomorrow night," Hope squealed.

"What about ABC?" Mark wondered.

"No offer. No details. They've asked to meet with me. What do you think?" Hope squealed again.

Suddenly Mark was glad he had sat down, because he was getting weak all over and almost dropped the phone. He struggled for words. "This would mean moving to New York, wouldn't it?" he finally asked.

"Yes! Yes! Oh, honey! It would be so great!" Hope was fairly dancing with excitement. "Honey, I'm at the top of my career game. I've broken into the big leagues, and the sky is the limit from here on out! Oh, we can have anything we want. We can live wherever we want, do what we want. We can take vacations to exotic places. Jennifer can attend the best private schools. You can work wherever you want. Isn't it great? What do you think?"

Hope continued before he could answer. "I know it would be an adjustment, and I know I turned down offers back in June in favor of the MBS anchor position in Memphis, but these offers are just too incredible to pass up. An opportunity like this isn't going to come up again. So what are you thinking?"

"I don't know what to think. It's going to take some time to sink in," he finally offered. "I mean, we're talking about uprooting our family from where we were raised and going off to a big city. I'm gonna have to think about this for a while."

~

Hope took one long, last look across the Manhattan skyline as darkness encroached and transformed the city of skyscrapers into a dazzle of light. She pulled the blackout curtains across the window and trod across the carpet to the bed. *I'm not used to this. This is the time when I used to put Jennifer to bed when she was a baby!*

The pressure to go to sleep only made it harder to sleep. Still, somehow she managed to relax and let the tiredness in her bones talk her brain into slumbering.

Somewhere in the darkness of her night the dream came. In it she was transported to a garden, a beautiful place where the air was scented with a thousand flowers that bloomed everywhere she looked. The grass was trimmed to perfection along a pathway that seemed to be glowing. Shrubs that she had never seen before formed a wall some distance to either side. The cloudless sky was amazingly bright, yet she did not wish for sunglasses.

"Go forward," a voice instructed her, and she began walking along the path. At the top of a small rise she halted to take in the sight of people, all dressed in white, moving about as they visited with each other, played games, and enjoyed a picnic that seemed to stretch into infinity.

"It would be wonderful if you could join us," a voice said. Hope turned to her left to see her father, dressed in a flowing, white robe, walking toward her.

"Daddy!" she exclaimed and rushed to embrace him. But the look of sadness on his face made her stop just short of him with her arms still wide apart.

His arms still hung at his sides, and a tear began tracing one cheek. "It would be so nice if you could join us. But you are turning your back on what you've been taught all your life, and you have refused a gift that Jesus Himself sent to you. So you cannot hope to be here with us unless you repent."

For a long moment father and daughter just stared into each other's eyes. Then suddenly she was falling through blackness. From below she could hear the screams of people in agony, crying out for an end to their torment as an acrid, revolting smell filled her nostrils. She began feeling intense waves of heat move over her body as she continued falling.

"Repent! Repent!" she heard her father cry out from far above. "Repent, or this is how you will spend eternity!"

Then it was over. Hope awoke in a cold sweat. Her eyes focused on the faint light that filtered through the blackout curtains and fell on the ceiling as muffled traffic noises came up from far below.

It's only a dream. It's only a dream, she tried to comfort herself. But it had been so vivid, *so real.* Was she on the wrong path? Had she misinterpreted Scripture? She could not answer that right now. She had to get up in a few hours and go to work; she had to sleep.

While it took her only a few minutes to fall asleep, the time passed so slowly that it seemed to take forever.

CHAPTER TWENTY-FIVE

Before she knew it, the phone was ringing with her 3:00 a.m. wake-up call. Forty minutes later she had managed to pull herself awake and get dressed in a casual pantsuit. She walked through the hotel lobby carrying both a gym bag and a hanging bag.

"Good morning, ma'am," the doorman greeted her. He looked less than fully awake. His long, heavy coat looked very appealing in the morning coolness.

"Thank you," Hope answered as she passed and disappeared through the open door of the waiting limousine. The warm interior was most welcome as the driver quickly pulled out into traffic. Once again she was amazed that there could be so many vehicles on the street at such an early hour. Ten minutes later they stopped outside the building housing the MBS broadcast center on Fifth Avenue just south of Thirty-second Street. Hope flashed her ID badge at the droopy-eyed security guard and made her way to the elevator that took her to the tenth floor. There she waved her badge at another security guard in front of the morning show's sunrise logo, and he buzzed her through a security door.

The door opened onto a scene of controlled chaos. Various production personnel dashed this way and that to confer with each other. Phones rang. The man in one office yelled to catch the attention of a senior producer walking past. Hope found her office, dropped her purse on the desk and the gym bag in the corner, and walked down the hallway to where she handed her hanging bag to the wardrobe person. Returning to her office long enough to pick up a legal pad and pen, she hurried to the conference room for the 4:00 a.m. preshow production briefing.

A large whiteboard at one end of the conference room was divided into boxes with segment headings matching horizontally with the names of the on-air personality who would introduce that segment or conduct that interview. Senior producer Anne Givens was busy filling in blanks.

At the other end of the conference room was a hot breakfast buffet with just about anything a person could want to eat this early. There were coffees and juices, pancakes and pastries, scrambled eggs and fruit. Hope dropped her legal pad on the table, picked up a plate, and began filling it. *Strange how hungry a person can be at this hour.*

The meeting began precisely at 4:00 a.m. with a review of the show outline. The group—on-air personalities, producers, assistant producers, the floor director, and a few others—ate while they went over the show outline. Occasionally an interview or segment was switched from one person to another. By 4:45 a.m. everyone knew what would happen during the two hours they were on the air. Or at least they had a good idea, because things could change very quickly if a major story broke.

One of Hope's assignments was to do a satellite interview with a forestry official about follow-up work after a large forest fire in the Bitterroot Mountains of central Idaho. A summer drought had created the conditions leading to the fire, and more than 20,000 acres of timber had been consumed in only a few days. Hundreds of firefighters were laboring valiantly to bring it under control. The story today was about the efforts to replant wild grasses across the burned area before approaching fall rains could wash away thousands of acres of topsoil.

Everyone seemed to evaporate the instant the meeting was over. Hope, her coanchor, and the weather guy all headed for the gym for a 30-minute workout. She jogged on a treadmill with her copy resting on the control panel, occasionally letting go of the handgrips long enough to swap sheets. Next came a fast shower followed by more copy review while sitting in the styling chair as her hair and makeup were done. Twice a producer came in with updates on particular segments.

At precisely 5:55 a.m. Eastern Standard Time she walked onto the set. The weather forecaster was already at his desk twiddling with his computer and updating his maps and radar images about a hurricane brewing in the Atlantic. She sat in her appointed chair behind the custom-designed desk and waited for the sound technician to attach and check her two cordless microphones, one a backup in case the first failed. An earplug went in her

left ear so she could hear instructions from the control room. She straightened herself in the seat and did a test read from the teleprompter so the unseen people in the sound booth could set the level on her microphones.
Her coanchor, an arm's length away, was doing the same.

Then the stage lights came on, and everybody blinked as their
eyes adjusted.

"Two minutes to air!" the floor director called out. The cameras
moved to their starting positions.

"You ready for day four?" her coanchor inquired.

"Ready as I'm gonna be," she answered with a twinkling smile. "You
got any more of your bad jokes to share with the audience?"

He snorted. "Loaded." He unfolded the notebook computer in front
of him on the desk and typed in his network log-in.

"One minute to air!"

Hope reached below the desk and picked up the water bottle hidden
there. She took just a swig, enough to wet her mouth, but no more.

"Thirty seconds!"

The sound of the program's videotaped introduction could be heard
over speakers mounted somewhere above the lights. A monitor glowed in
the relative darkness somewhere behind the camera, showing clips of news
segments against the backdrop of a brilliant sunrise and the rising of the
show logo.

The floor director held up his hand, indicating for them to wait.
Though Hope had done this hundreds of times before back at channel 3
in Memphis, there still was something exciting about this moment that
made her heart beat faster.

The floor director held five fingers horizontally and began counting
down. Then it was just his index finger that he swung toward their desk.

"There's a lot happening in our world, and we'd like to tell you about
it. Good morning! I'm Carl Quintana. My regular cohost, April Sanders,
is on assignment this week, so Hope Lancaster is filling in for her."

"Thank you, Carl." Hope picked up the script on the teleprompter
as she eyed the camera with the glowing red light on top of it. "This
morning we're going to take you to the Middle East, to China, to Idaho,
and"—she turned to Carl as another camera showed both of them—
"we're going to the kitchen for a delicious recipe from celebrity chef
Robert Zeigler."

"And Earline Picker, author of the best seller *Megadoom,* is here," Carl
picked up. "We'll be talking to her in just a few minutes. Later on we've

got the stars of the hit Broadway comedy *Whimsy*. But right now let's go down to the newsroom, where Spencer Davis has our headlines."

Both anchors held their positions until they saw Spencer's image come up on a floor monitor.

Videotaped segments gave everyone a chance to relax and even banter with each other. Carl began mimicking the serious delivery of the news anchor and the White House spokesperson. Doing so raised loud laughter from behind the cameras and struggles to be quiet when the floor director began his countdown for return to the studio.

Hope's satellite interview came up in the first half of the second hour. A production team was on-site somewhere on a burned-off mountainside. The carcasses of a few charred tree trunks littered the sun-dappled gray and black landscape now lit by a battery of generator-fed stage lights.

"Joining us now from the Bitterroot Mountains is Diana Whitehorse with the Bureau of Land Management. Diana, thanks for joining us," Hope half read, half ad-libbed.

A nervous smile spread across the woman's Native American features, and she seemed to look everywhere but at the camera. "Uh, it's nice to be with you," she answered.

"Diana, just a few days ago this area where you're standing was in the heart of the fire area," Hope continued as the picture changed to an aerial view of the firestorm sweeping up the mountainside. The sight reminded Hope of her dream and sent a shiver up and down her spine. She almost lost her train of thought. "Uh, we're looking right now at how fierce and dramatic that fire was."

The camera came back to the uniformed woman. "Show us the challenge that you're facing now that the fire's over," Hope prompted.

The woman bent down, dug her hand into the dirt, and let it flow off her hand. "This is the problem. When the fire swept through here, it burned up everything. And I mean everything. This area was a meadow, an open area of probably two or three acres. It was covered by grass and low-level brush. Now, of course, with the drought the grass was all dried up and dead, so it just burned up in a flash. I mean, a few seconds, and this whole place was gone. Turned to ashes. Even the roots were burned up."

"Even the roots? I thought there would still be roots. I mean, they're below ground, aren't they?" Hope asked with surprise.

Diana shook her head. "These grasses build a root structure that's only partly below ground. Normally they could come back up from the roots. But the area was so dry that even the roots died. Even the roots that remained would have held the dirt in place and kept it from washing away, but the dirt was so dry that the fire was able to burn down into the ground. That's why we're having to reseed the area. There are no roots left to hold the soil."

Their conversation continued while the viewers saw prerecorded scenes of the seeding team at work and what the sprouting grasses looked like. Diana and others like her hoped the rains would hold off for a few more days, or at least be light, so the ground would be moist and the seeds would have time to sprout and put down roots to hold the topsoil.

~

"Hope sure looked good this morning," Terri Pelosi greeted Mark as she walked into his office, a cup of coffee in one hand and a folded newspaper in the other.

"Uh, you know, I didn't see her." Mark looked up from his computer screen. "Guess I was too busy getting things done around the house."

Terri smiled. "I don't believe this. You mean to say that your wife's on national television and you aren't watching? I don't know if you dare go to New York. Send Jennifer, maybe, but at least don't admit you weren't watching."

Mark shuffled through some papers on his desk, found what he was looking for, and began studying it.

"So when are you moving?" Terri asked.

Mark looked up, then turned toward the whiteboard. "Who said we were moving? They've just called her up for the week because she's got this big, fancy awards dinner tomorrow night," he answered.

"Apparently you haven't seen this morning's paper."

"Huh?" Mark stopped and turned to Terri as she put her coffee cup on a corner of his desk and handed him the folded paper. She pointed to an article in the entertainment section.

"Channel 3 coanchor Hope Lancaster is in New York this week, where she is anchoring MBS television's *Sunrise Show*. Informed sources say she has hired an agent to handle negotiations in a bidding war between MBS, NBC, FOX, and at least one other TV network for a three-year contract that would give Lancaster her own show and pay her upwards of $1 million a year."

"Any truth to the rumor?" Terri inquired.

Mark's eyes grew big, and he was at a loss for words. "Uh . . . well . . . I mean, she's negotiating."

"Sounds like quite a pay raise. I mean, if my spouse were gonna be earning that kind of money, I'd sure be making plans to move."

Mark tried to ignore the remark. He turned back to the whiteboard, glanced at the paper in his hand, and began writing. "You're working on the reaction control interface, aren't you?"

∼

The end of the show brought a short period of relief. On-air the pressure was to keep things flowing, read the teleprompter and ad-lib at the same time, and pay attention to an interview while listening to instructions from the director in your earpiece. It was the adrenaline rush all TV reporters lived for, and all too soon the two hours of the show were over. Still, there was visible relief the moment the floor director shouted "We're clear!" after the show had gone off the air. Anchors began unplugging and removing microphones. Jokes about certain guests and news stories began to fly.

Robert Ziegler, the celebrity chef, had whipped up a tasty dish, so everyone gravitated toward the kitchen set for a taste and friendly conversation. His publicist then produced copies of his just-released cookbook, and he autographed them until they were gone.

Leaving the studio meant picking up the pressure of preparing for tomorrow. However, as a network anchor Hope had a staff of six assistants, each of them a qualified reporter in their own right, who were doing the research and writing for her. It was only after they had done their work and the show's producer had approved the stories that Hope put her hand to them.

One of tomorrow's stories would put her back in the studio an hour later for a satellite interview with the head of a charity trying to assist both poor Jews and Palestinians in Israel. Immediately after that she would be hustled out to LaGuardia Airport and onto a company plane for a flight to Pittsfield, Massachusetts, where she would interview the owner of an electronics manufacturing plant about how he had managed to stay in business in the face of foreign competition. If all went well, she would be back in New York by 2:00 p.m., and the story would be part of the show's lineup the next morning. After that the day belonged to her.

Somewhere in the midst of that she'd catch lunch. Maybe she'd go to the company cafeteria down on the fourth floor. Or maybe she'd go out on the street and around the corner to buy a hot dog from the vendor with the Hebrew National cart. Not only were the kosher dogs a treat that she couldn't get in Memphis, but the vendor had a kind word for everybody and was himself a treat just to meet.

Leaving the set after the satellite interview, Hope felt her stomach flip, and she glanced at her watch. It was 10:00 a.m.—definitely tummy time.

"Hey, Danny!" she called to one of her assistants some distance down the hall. "I'm headed out for a bite. Back in a half hour, OK?"

Danny nodded before disappearing down the hallway. Hope headed for the elevator and the street, where she found the warm sun and fresh air making the world a friendly place. The natural refreshment breathed newness into her body as she walked the half block to the vendor's cart.

"Ah, Hope! How good to see you again!" the vendor greeted her from three paces away as their eyes met.

"Terrell, you've beaten me again! You greeted me before I got a chance to greet you. How are you?" Wide smiles painted both of their faces.

"I'm just glowing in God's love. How about you?" the vendor answered. "What'll it be today? I've got some fresh sauerkraut ready to go on your dog. Or I've got some nice chili that's just m-m-m, m-m-m!" He rolled his eyes as he said it.

Hope thought for a second. "I think I'll go for a foot-long with the chili today. That sauerkraut's just a little bit spicy for my refined Southern taste buds," she replied with a Southern drawl that brought laughter from both of them.

Adding a bag of chips and a chilled root beer brought the tab to $4.75. She handed him a $5 bill, dropped the quarter change in a pocket, picked up her items, and turned to leave.

"Wait a second, Hope! Gotta give you the thought for the day!"

Hope turned back. "OK, what's the thought for the day?"

Terrell smiled broadly. "God loves you so much that He's doing everything He possibly can to get you into heaven, not to keep you out."

"Thanks. I needed that." Hope waved her root beer in a parting salute as she turned to make her way through the crowd on the sidewalk. She made her way to a bench outside a street-level boutique, where she could sit in the sun and be out of the main flow of pedestrians. All too soon her lunch had been consumed. She started to rise, then decided to sit a few more minutes and just enjoy the warmth of the sun while it could still be felt before disappearing behind another skyscraper.

Back in the office she grabbed the briefing folder prepared by an assistant, picked up her purse, and headed to the parking garage in the basement, where a car waited to deliver her to the airport. She read the briefing papers as the driver found his way through midtown traffic to the Queens Midtown Tunnel, then onto the expressways toward LaGuardia Airport.

An hour later her plane was touching down at the airport in Pittsfield, and 30 minutes later she was tossing her first questions at the company owner.

The flight back to New York gave her some time to think. Yes, the interview had gone well. The videotape she carried would be edited down to just under two minutes for use on tomorrow morning's show. That would be done by the editors. All she had to do was write an introduction for the story. Or she could give that job to one of her assistants. No, she would do it herself, she decided. That way she was still functioning as a reporter instead of just reading copy somebody else wrote. Once she did that, her day would be done.

Hope watched the twin propellers beat the air. In the relative calm of the skies her mind went back to the dream—no, the nightmare—she'd had sometime in the night.

"Repent!" her father had appealed to her.

Repent from what? I've only accepted what the Bible says, so what is there to repent from? No, there are all these things that have been happening. The spirit visits to Mom. The dress that I couldn't throw away, which finally disappeared after I prayed. How "Daddy" disappeared from Mom's house when I was praying. It just doesn't add up. What is there to repent from?

But the dream had been so vivid! She'd smelled the smoke of burning flesh rising from those tormented in hell. She'd felt the heat of the flames. She'd been warned to repent or possibly face that same fate herself.

Where was it that the Bible talked about hellfire? Hope reached into her purse and dug around before locating the pocket-sized Bible she carried there. *What were those texts Daddy used to use in his sermons? Yes, Malachi 4.*

She thumbed the pages until she came to the passage: Malachi 4:1-3. "'Surely the day is coming; it will burn like a furnace. All the arrogant and every evildoer will be stubble, and that day that is coming will set them on fire,' says the Lord Almighty. 'Not a root or a branch will be left to them. But for you who revere my name, the sun of righteousness will rise with healing in its wings. And you will go out and leap like calves released from the stall. Then you will trample down the wicked; they will be ashes under the soles of your feet on the day when I do these things,' says the Lord Almighty."

Hope took a pen from her purse, turned over the briefing sheets, and began making notes.

"The day is coming," she wrote. *That means it isn't here yet. So if that day is coming and isn't here, then hell isn't burning right now.* For a long minute her eyes watched the ground passing below. They were passing over Long Island Sound and beginning their descent toward LaGuardia.

That's logical. If Jesus didn't go to heaven after He died, then nobody can be in heaven yet. So nobody could be in hell, either.

They "will be stubble, and that day that is coming will set them on fire." *There it is again—future tense. It's coming but isn't here yet. But what did it mean about stubble?* Hope's thoughts went back to the satellite interview she'd done during the broadcast. What was it the woman had described? The fire had burned up even the roots. There was nothing left but ashes. It was exactly what the text was describing.

"They will be ashes under the soles of your feet," she wrote. *Ashes are what remain after the fire has burned out.* "There will be a beginning and an end to hell. It is not burning now, nor will it burn forever," she noted.

It all was becoming clear. What she had been taught since childhood was incorrect. More than that, Satan was trying to keep her from believing truth! The spirit visiting her mother and the dream she'd had that morning were just part of the horrible plan by the evil one to deceive them and prevent them from believing God!

Despite her father's appeal in the dream, she had nothing to repent from! *But what about Mom? How do I help her see what I've learned?*

Hope's cell phone rang. It was Simon Goldstein, her agent. He had new numbers from two of the networks and an offer from ABC. When could she come by his office? She looked at her watch and calculated how long until she would be back at her office. She could make it in an hour, maybe an hour and a half.

"Simon, how much do you think the Murrow Awards are playing in all this?" she wondered.

"Quite a bit, actually. It means you're hot this week. We need to ink a deal this week or next, or they'll start looking at someone else," he said. "Right now the numbers just keep getting better. We need to talk about what kind of numbers you want on your paychecks."

Hope hesitated. "What sort of numbers are they offering?"

"Well, ABC's offering $600,000 the first year alone and your own evening news magazine show."

The thought almost made Hope drop the phone, and it was a moment before she could answer. "Uh, Simon, do you know any good real estate agents, 'cause I think I'd better start house hunting pretty soon."

"I've got several good names for you, depending on where you want to live," Simon answered. "I'll see you when you get here."

Chapter Twenty-six

The big house was quiet again. It was Saturday night, and Susan's few dishes from supper were in the dishwasher. The dusting was done, and the many rooms of her home were straightened and cleaned. *This house is too big for just me,* she thought. *But I don't know how Aubrey would feel about my selling it and buying someplace smaller.*

She tuned the radio to an easy listening station and set the volume down to where she could use the sound for company in the emptiness. Then she settled onto one end of the couch and scanned the end table for reading material. A light layer of dust on the Bible caught her eye. *I know I dusted this afternoon. Why is it dusty again so soon?*

Susan debated dealing with the dust, then decided it could wait. She was comfortable. Besides that, this was the time her husband most often appeared. Only he hadn't come for several days. Would he return this evening?

What was it her husband had said so many times at the pulpit? "Dust on the Bible is a sign of dust in the heart." Yes. That was it! She eyed the Bible for a moment before picking it up and puffing off the dust. *What should I read?* She thumbed pages back and forth, then stopped in the New Testament. She shifted her position on the couch, and more pages moved; suddenly her eyes fell on 1 Corinthians 15.

"I declare to you, brothers, that flesh and blood cannot inherit the kingdom of God, nor does the perishable inherit the imperishable. Listen, I tell you a mystery: We will not all sleep, but we will all be changed—in a flash, in the twinkling of an eye, at the last trumpet. For the trumpet will sound, the dead will be raised imperishable, and we will be changed. For the perishable must clothe itself with the imperishable, and the mortal with immortality. When the perishable has been clothed with the imperishable, and the mortal with immortality, then the saying that is written will come true: 'Death has been swallowed up in victory'" (verses 50-54).

For a long moment she just stared at the passage. *Is it possible that Hope is right—that Aubrey is in the grave and awaiting the resurrection? But . . . if she's right . . . then who has been visiting me?*

"Hello, my love."

Susan looked up to see Aubrey sitting in his familiar rocking chair. She let out a startled gasp. "Oh, I wasn't expecting you."

He smiled kindly. "It's good to see you again."

Susan just looked at him for a time.

"You act as if something is wrong. Is something bothering you?" he inquired soothingly.

She just looked at him, unsure of where to start or exactly what to say. "Who are you?" she inquired timidly.

"I am your husband," he answered confidently. He studied her face. "You believe me, don't you?"

"I'm not so sure anymore," Susan answered.

"You've been listening to Hope again, haven't you?"

Susan nodded, and her gaze dropped to the floor. "She believes you're a demon sent to deceive me."

"I know that," he said with frustration. "I've warned her that if she doesn't repent, she's going to spend eternity in hell."

Susan shook her head. "That's not what's bothering me."

His eyebrows went up.

"It's the way you disappeared the other day when she was praying. If you went away like that, how can I be sure you're from God?"

"You remember that old saying, don't you? 'Believe none of what you hear, half of what you read, and all that you can see and prove.' I'm here. You believe what you see, don't you?" he asked soothingly.

Susan shook her head. "I want to. I mean . . . well . . . I'm not sure. If you went away when she called on the name of Jesus to drive you away, then . . . how can I be sure that you're really my husband? that you're from heaven? that you're not a demon sent to deceive me? You know, like the spirit the witch of En-dor called up to deceive Saul."

For several moments they just looked at each other.

"Who are you? Who are you? Really?" Susan commanded. "In the name of Jesus Christ, tell me who you really are—and if you are a demon, in the name of Jesus, leave and never come back!"

Aubrey's visage flashed from peaceful to unfamiliar rage. His voice changed from the refined tones of a practiced public speaker to the deep and guttural hissing sounds of something very threatening. "You will soon see what happens to people who reject me!" he screamed as he disappeared.

A tremor seized Susan's entire body, and she began hyperventilating. "What was that?" she screamed to the empty room. It seemed an eternity before the soothing music from the radio reached her soul and she realized she was again alone. It took another few minutes before she quit shaking. For a time she sat motionless, pondering what had just happened. Then a new shaking overtook her, the sobs of a heart broken by grief as she realized that her husband really was dead and in the grave. In moments her tears were flowing freely.

∾

Come bedtime, sleep overtook Susan with ease. Though filled with grief, she was at peace knowing that she was no longer being deceived.

It seemed she had barely fallen asleep before the smoke alarm began shrilling its tooth-rattling scream, jerking her from slumber. At first she thought she was dreaming. Then the acrid smell of smoke reached her nostrils. She threw off the covers, flipped on a bedside lamp, and realized she could not see the ceiling for the layer of smoke thickening against the plaster. She drove her feet into a pair of fluffy slippers, grabbed a thick bathrobe from where it was thrown over a chair, and dashed out the doorway into the hall. The smoke there was now low enough that she had to bend over to breathe clear air.

Should she go out the back door or the front? The room was lit in shades of orange and red by the flames filling and erupting across the family room ceiling from the dining room and kitchen. As she considered escape routes, the leather-covered sofa began gushing smoke; then a line of flames raced across the top, and her view of the back door was obscured. That left only the front door and the searing heat driving her in that direction.

At that instant the windows along the back wall of the family room began blowing out, and the inrush of fresh air added venom to the flames. The growing crackling and hissing seemed to chase her out the front door and into the coolness of the night that was shocking in its contrast. The relative quiet outside seemed almost silent until she reached the curb and turned around to survey her house. Large tongues of fire curled upward from each end of the roof. The entire roof seemed to be giving off smoke, and a line of flames was spreading from each end toward the center. Somewhere a window blew out, and glass cracked and tinkled as it hit the ground. A thick column of black smoke blotted out the stars and moon as it climbed skyward.

A glance both ways along the street showed only darkened homes. Fearlessly she rushed to the house directly across the street and began banging on the door. "Fire! Fire! My house is on fire! Call 911! Call 911!" she screamed.

An upstairs light came on; then a light shone through the windows beside the door as someone on the inside unlocked the door. Susan fairly rushed inside. "Call 911! My house is on fire!" she screamed.

Marty Beckham started toward the phone on an end table in the living room. But Susan spotted it as soon as he turned, and beat him to it. She snatched it off the table, punched the numbers, and waited for the answer. "C'mon! C'mon!" she fairly screamed as the line rang once, then twice, before the emergency operator finally answered.

"My house is on fire! My house is on fire!" she yelled, then paused as the operator asked for her address. She answered several questions before hanging up.

By now the entire Beckham household was awake and in a state of alarm. A preteen daughter produced a small fire extinguisher from the kitchen, then looked out the door and realized the futility of her gesture.

Susan pulled the robe tight around her body and went back outside. By now the entire house was ablaze, and all she could do was stand in the street waiting for the fire trucks to arrive. Off in the distance she could hear the approaching wails winding up and down. How many were there? Two? Three? She couldn't tell.

A police car was the first to arrive. Then two fire engines. The first paused by a hydrant two doors down the street as a firefighter jumped out, pulled off the end of a hose, and threaded it onto the hydrant. Then the driver pulled away and stopped across the street from the Morris home. Though the firefighters worked quickly, it seemed an eternity before their hoses were charged and they were spraying water on the flames. Additional hoses from a third fire truck were turned on the neighbors' houses to protect them from the intense heat radiating from the Morris house.

An hour later the firefighters were occasionally spraying what hot spots remained in the rubble. The outside walls, some of them no longer full height, were all that remained to identify what had shortly before been a comfortable home.

Charlotte Beckham pushed a steaming mug of coffee into Susan's chilled hands, put an arm around her shivering shoulders, and guided her into the warmth of her home. "You can stay here with us," she offered. "Is there anyone you need to call?"

Susan wrapped her fingers around the warmth and nodded. "I need to call my kids." Over the next several minutes she made a half dozen calls to family and friends. Forty minutes later her son, David, arrived, confessing that he'd broken every speed limit along the way. Daughter Allison and her husband were en route from their home in Mississippi. A stream of friends from church began showing up, despite the clock's approach to 2:00 a.m.

"What about Hope and her husband?" Charlotte asked.

Susan shook her head. "She's in New York. I've left three messages on her answering system. She must have her phone turned off."

"Do you know where she's staying? Can you call her there? Or leave a message?"

Susan shook her head. "The note with the number where she's staying was beside the phone in the den."

A uniformed fire officer interrupted the group. "I'm terribly sorry for what's happened tonight," he offered. He lifted the clipboard in his left hand, pulled a pen from his pocket, and began writing on the attached incident report form. He inquired about who lived in the home, who owned it, and similar things.

"Do you have any idea how the fire started?" the officer inquired.

Susan shook her head and recounted everything that she could remember. Then her eyes followed the officer's pen onto the fire report form where he checked the block marked "unknown" under the heading "Area of Origin."

~

Hope got the message the first thing in the morning after taking her cell phone off the charger. After restraining her initial alarm, she woke Mark and Jennifer and got them packing while she ordered breakfast from room service and got on the phone to the airline. Could they get an earlier flight? They barely had time to eat breakfast before flagging down a taxi to take them to LaGuardia Airport. They were back in Memphis by midafternoon and making a beeline for the Beckham home.

It was a race from the car to embrace Susan, who stepped out onto the porch when she heard Mark's SUV pull into the driveway. Jennifer won the race by being seated on the left side and having her door open before Mark shifted into park. "Grandma! Grandma! I'm so glad you're safe!" she screamed as she flew down the sidewalk. "I was so worried!"

"Oh, Mom! I'm so glad you're all right!" Hope cried as the trio embraced Susan.

"I'm safe. It was close, but God saved me," Susan said with quiet confidence.

Everyone turned to look across the street at the burned-out ruin of the house. "Unbelievable!" Mark summed up everyone's thoughts.

They walked across the street to take a closer look, and Susan filled them in on the details of her narrow escape.

"How do you think it got started?" Hope inquired.

"I didn't know. It started on this end of the house, in the area of the kitchen, I think." Susan waved an arm toward the part of the ruin where the kitchen had once been.

Hope thought she saw the remains of several kettles. They were about the only recognizable things left.

"Sounds like you have an idea," Mark prompted. "Jennifer! Be careful!" he shouted to his daughter, who was poking with a stick at something in the area of the back patio.

Susan nodded. "It was that spirit that was coming to see me, the one that looked and acted like Aubrey."

Puzzlement painted Hope's and Mark's faces.

"Did he come to see you again?" Hope wanted to know.

"About 9:00 last night. I demanded that he tell me who he was, and he turned out to be a demon. He threatened me before he left, and it was a few hours later that the fire started."

Hope reached out and squeezed her mother's hand. "I'm so thankful you're safe! How are you feeling—I mean, now that you know it wasn't Daddy coming to see you?"

Susan looked around as she searched for words. "I miss him. Aubrey, that is. Not the demon. I know he's in the grave and waiting for the resurrection."

Mother and daughter shared a long gaze that communicated more than words. Mark took it all in, processing this new information and realizing his need to reevaluate his thoughts on the subject of death and the state of the dead.

Maybe I should ask Hope to share some of her notes with me once things settle down and we get back home, Mark thought.

After a few moments of silence Mark interrupted everyone's thoughts. "Want to go shopping?" he suggested.

Susan smiled. "That sounds like a timely thing to do."

"Get your purse, and we'll go. Jennifer! Come on. We're taking Grandma to the mall," Mark called.

Susan shook her head. "I don't have a purse. What I'm wearing, well, this is out of Charlotte's closet. All I own is what I was wearing."

The revelation made Hope and Mark stop for a moment.

"But you know what I do have?" Susan quizzed.

"What's that, Mom?" Hope asked.

"I have the peace that comes from knowing I'm not being deceived anymore. Yes, I'm sad that Aubrey is gone, but I guess that's part of life, and it's time for me to move on."